Masquerade

by

P L Crompton

Copyright: © P. L. Crompton 2014

ISBN: 978-0-9866701-3-8
EAN-13: 978-0-9866701-4-5

http://plcrompton.wix.com/cromptonfiction

For Lisa, Colton and Liz

CHAPTER ONE

Roz hadn't expected so many bruises after yesterday's action in Regent's Park when boyfriend Mike and his mates practised their rugby moves. Cold, bored, and angry, she tried a flying tackle on Mike and took him down. She didn't expect to hear from him again.

Dark hair pinned up, she stepped into the full tub and sank into the hot water with a sigh, closed her eyes, and allowed the heat to ease her sore muscles.

Perhaps she shouldn't have tried to do so much today, but she accomplished what she set out to do. She'd lugged her belongings across London on Sunday buses, hauled them up two flights of stairs, and put everything away. It was important to finish the move into her new flat so she could concentrate on work the next day. Her first job since leaving design school, she didn't want to lose it.

For the next production, the male lead's costumes were going well. Even the female lead's gowns caused fewer problems because Empire-line gowns were loose fitting below the bust line. It also meant fewer adjustments to make them fit Angela Duke's understudy. Angela's weight kept fluctuating and the actress often missed fittings, but Roz dared not complain because Angela was the theatre owner's light of love.

The plays the Nostalgie put on were mostly farces interspersed with comedies or raucous pantomimes that compared with West End theatre offerings. The wardrobe mistress' job was just demanding but unlike theatres that were more prestigious, Roz had only Agatha to help sew the costumes she designed, drafted and cut.

For the next play, she had visited every museum in London for authentic examples. A chance remark by a curator at the Victoria-and-Albert led her to the Scarborough and a display of clothing from the early eighteen hundreds. Even luckier, she saw a *For Rent* sign in a house adjoining the museum. The theatre was just four streets away.

From the main room came a thump and crash, followed by a series of creaks from the floorboards, then a door opened and closed.

"Hello?" Roz sat up in alarm. "Is anyone there?" When no one answered, she stepped out of the water, wrapped herself in a bath towel, and crept to the door.

Although gloomy, enough daylight allowed her to see around the flat. Everything looked normal as far as she could remember.

It was an old house and she should expect odd creaks and groans. The rental agent told her six others lived in the house, and a young family occupied the basement. She might have heard one of them.

Unperturbed, Roz pulled the plug to let the water out and emerged into the main room. The clock showed it was only nine, so she had time to finish sewing the hem on Angela's costume. She crossed to the window to close the curtains and looked out. It was raining.

A movement on the road caught her attention. A dark figure shied away from a patch of street lighting and peered over his shoulder as if to check if anyone followed. She caught only a glimpse of the man before he scuttled around the corner.

Huddled over something he carried everything about him screamed furtive, and something else. . . . Was he dressed in an odd way or was it a trick of the light? When he didn't reappear, Roz closed the curtains and switched on the overhead light.

An L-shaped room furnished with mismatched pieces that looked comfortable together, the only incongruity in the shabby-chic shamble was the floor-to-ceiling mirror. It jarred the senses as if the cosy group was in constant disagreement with its elegant companion. The mirror stood defiant, like an arrogant lady surrounded by a huddle of charwomen.

Earlier, Roz decided the mirror would be less obtrusive behind the door. She knew it would be heavy to move but felt sure she could walk it across the floor. She had taken a firm grip on the frame and tugged. Nothing happened. With her hands in different places, she'd tugged again. It still wouldn't budge. She should have expected them to fasten a mirror of that size to the wall. No screws marred the frame but somebody had secured it in place. She would never move it without damaging the wall.

With no bookshelf, Roz had stacked her hoard of novels on the floor before the mirror. Now they were scattered. She went to straighten them.

Barbara Cartland, Jean Plaidy, Georgette Heyer, Norah Lofts, and Mary Stewart, romantic fiction and historical romances, all of uniform size but for one. A self-help tome was larger—*Where to Find Romance in the Modern World*. It hadn't helped her in her quest.

She had followed the book's guidelines and frequented the places where it said she would meet eligible men. It led to a string of disappointments. Those she met had one thing in common—they grew bad tempered when they couldn't get her into bed on the first date. Roz wanted more than one-night-stands and leg overs. Perhaps, because her rounded cheeks made her look sixteen instead of twenty-four, some men thought they could flatter or cajole her. The book proved a useless guide and she tossed it towards the pile destined for the rubbish bin, but she hadn't had much success going it alone, either.

She may be old-fashioned but Roz looked for a man strong enough not to feel emasculated by romantic gestures, one to bring her flowers or hold her hand. Such a man existed somewhere. She hoped they would meet before they were both too decrepit to care.

Barefoot, she walked to the kitchen area, filled a kettle and plugged it in.

While the kettle boiled, Roz put on a camisole, a pair of lacy underpants, and a dressing gown. From a drawer she took a tablecloth she had embroidered herself during evenings spent alone. With every stitch into the gowns the women wore, she'd woven dreams of what it would have been like to live in those days. Ladies were ladies, and men—gallant, chivalrous, elegant. How different from the men she met now.

Her bits and pieces of china were mismatched oddments bought when something took her eye. Her favourite was a sugar bowl with a woman in a flowing gown depicted on the side. Circa 1805, she decided, the same period as the costumes she was making, when fashion entered the Romantic Movement and Napoleon won the heart of an emperor's daughter.

Tea made, she carried her cup to the table, sat, and switched the radio to a music program before taking Angela's costume from the bag. She sipped and sewed while listening to a piano recital and allowed her thoughts to dwell on what life would have been like for the woman on the sugar bowl.

As she put the last stitch into the hem, the radio announcer gave the time as nine thirty and the name of the next pianist to play a medley of English folk songs. The first song was Scarborough Fair.

Humming along with the radio, Roz held up the gown and studied it. She'd have to try it on to make sure the hem was level. She took her dressing gown off, slipped the gown on over her underwear, drew the lavender ribbon tight under her bust and tied it in a bow. Angela was a couple of inches taller so Roz needed something to stand on to see if the hem hung level.

The tower of romance novels caught her eye. Roz moved them away from the mirror, stepped onto them and studied herself. The front and sides of the gown looked fine. To see the back, she eased around on her precarious perch.

The books toppled and Roz lost her balance. She yelled and put out a hand to brace her fall as she slid sideways. Her hand sank into a liquid the consistency of quicksilver. Unable to stop herself, Roz fell through the mirror.

**

CHAPTER TWO

Disoriented, wincing at the pain where she'd hit her head and grazed her elbow, Roz scrambled to her feet. She was in an opulent bedroom. Had she fallen into the Scarborough Museum next door? Afraid to move, she expected a guard to rush in to investigate the crash. She had to get out of there fast.

A canopy-bed draped in white lace stood against one wall. A flimsy lavender-coloured gown lay across the coverlet, its hem brushing the silk rugs on the polished wood floor. Pots and ribbons strewn around a carved jewellery box littered a graceful dressing table. Half hidden under a snippet of lace, silver-backed brushes gleamed in the flickering candlelight.

Nothing resembled her flat except for a mirror like the one she had fallen through. It appeared older than the one in her flat and offered a wavering reflection in places; but there was no sign of breakage and no glass crunched underfoot. The mirror was intact but, as she fell against the one in her flat, she had the distinct impression it had been . . . what? Fluid? But that was impossible.

Roz touched the mirror. It was solid. Had it swivelled? Were there two mirrors, one on either side of a door, and she triggered the mechanism that revolved them? She felt all around the frame, pressing her fingers into likely places, seeking hidden springs or latches, but the mirror stayed firmly in place. As Roz continued to check the mirror, the door behind her opened.

"There you are, Cousin Rozzie." A girl of about twenty stood in the doorway. Elegant and beautiful enough to be a model, she had light brown hair and a creamy complexion; her skin glowed in the candlelight. The girl called over her shoulder, "She is here, Mama."

Roz gaped at her. She wore a gown like the one Roz was making for Angela.

"Rosamund? Where have you been?" An older woman wearing a floor-length gown with a short train pushed into the room. She pointed to the costume Roz wore. "What is that you are wearing? Take it off at once!" She stepped to one side and motioned to a girl in a black dress and white apron to move forward. "Help Miss Rosamund, and do not dawdle, Jenny."

"Yes, Lady Imogen." Eyes wide and surprised, the maid curtsied.

Imogen turned to Roz. "Do not gawp, girl. Lord and Lady Erdington have arrived, and you were not in the receiving line. You make sure Jenny hurries, Adele. Be quick now." With that, she swept out.

"Come on, Jenny." Adele advanced upon Roz. "What is this you are wearing? Have you been play-acting again?"

Roz stood confused while Jenny loosened the ribbon and slid Angela's costume from her shoulders. She felt dizzy, and with every second, her bewilderment increased. What was happening? How did these people know her? At any moment, she expected the police to arrive and charge her with trespass or worse.

"Let me tell you—" she began.

"We do not have time for explanations. If we did, I would ask where you found the underwear you have on." Adele waved a hand towards Roz and then turned to the mirror to fiddle with her elaborate coiffure. "While Jenny arranges your hair, I will choose the jewellery you should wear with the lavender." Adele opened a carved box on the dressing table.

"But—"

"Sit down to let Jenny work her magic."

Roz sat. "I have to tell—"

"Hush, now. Uncle Stephen and Mama were angry because you are not in the receiving line with us." Adele rooted through the jewellery box. "Cousin, dear, where is the amethyst pin Mama gave you last Christmas? Did you give it to the poor? It will not do. Uncle Ruffy says they are accustomed to being poor. We must not spoil them with gifts that will be stolen or sold and the money used to buy gin."

In the mirror, Roz saw Jenny redden. She looked up from brushing Roz's hair and their eyes met. Roz tried to smile but her cheeks wouldn't respond. She felt wooden. Like a doll. A marionette manipulated by people who thought they knew her while she had no idea who they were. It had to be a dream. One of those dreams where one couldn't run or scream. A dream where one discerned something was wrong but couldn't do anything about it.

"You don't understand—" Roz tried to explain but Adele cut her off.

"I understand perfectly. You do not wish to join the adults. Nevertheless, you must. You cannot stay in the nursery all your life." Adele untangled strings of beads. "You will wear your nice new gown and behave like a lady."

Evidently, they intended her to wear the lavender gown draped on the bed.

Was she dreaming? Had she fallen from the books, hit her head, and even now laying on the faded rug in her flat? Could one feel the soreness of a scraped elbow in a dream, or pain each time the brush touched the lump on one's head?

A sound of wheels rumbling on gravel came from outside and Adele rushed to the window. The noise stopped as she reached it. "It is only Uncle Ruffy. He will not expect us to greet him, but do hurry. I want to be there when Lord Mindon arrives." She moved away from the window and wandered about the room touching this and that. "Hurry up, Jenny," she admonished. "You are such a lazy besom."

9

Roz had read the term in a novel and learned it was not a compliment. The maid looked near to tears. "Don't talk to her like that."

"Why not? She is a servant."

"She's a person. You have no cause to speak to her that way."

Adele tossed her head. "And you should not talk to me like this with a servant present. Who do you think you are, pray tell?"

"If you'll listen for a minute, I'll tell—"

"Yes, yes. You do not want to go to the party. What the matter is with you, Rozzie? When I was your age, I could not wait to wear fancy clothes."

That was it, a fancy-dress party. One of the charity evenings she'd seen advertised on her visit to the museum, when guests dressed up in old-fashioned clothes. They were mistaking her for one of the actresses.

Jenny's reflection smiled at Roz as she wove a length of lavender ribbon through the curls. Around her finger, she twined a tress to rest on Roz's shoulder.

"You have never met Lord Mindon," Adele went on "but I dare say you will agree with me he is the handsomest gentleman to make my acquaintance."

Jenny stepped back, took the lavender gown from the bed, and motioned Roz to stand.

Instinctively, like a child being dressed, Roz raised her arms to slide them into the puffed sleeves as Jenny dropped the silky length over her head. She stood still while the maid arranged the folds over her hips and the hem dropped to the floor with a whisper.

She had to tell them she wasn't the right actress. "You must let me explain—"

"I have no need to know where you were. You are always tucking yourself away in improbable corners and making us search for you."

Jenny opened the wardrobe and produced a pair of satin slippers in the same hue as the gown.

This is where the charade would end. No two women ever had the same size and shape of feet. Roz slid her feet into the slippers and they felt made for her. Now she was more confused than ever. She looked up and found Jenny watching. Something in the maid's eyes made Roz wonder if Jenny realised she wasn't the right actress.

"You know I'm not—" Roz started to tell Jenny.

"You are not used to wearing such finery. We know. Let me see you." Adele studied Roz then took her by the shoulders and turned her around. "I think you will pass muster."

"*Good grief!*" Roz was growing angry at the way Adele cut short her explanations or dismissed them.

"Good grief?" Adele's eyes were sharp. "Can any grief be good? Your choice of words may have been acceptable in the nursery but they will not do now, Cousin Rozzie." Adele led Roz to the mirror. "Look how pretty you are."

Roz stared at her reflection. She looked different. The same mole marked her right cheek, the same pinprick throbbed on her finger, her elbow stung, and her head hurt, but she didn't appear to be Roz any more.

The neckline of the dress hung lower than any she'd worn. She tugged at it to lift it higher and Adele slapped her hands away.

"Your first grown-up gown." Adele stood behind Roz as Jenny fastened the silk cord of a fan about her wrist.

The first. . . .

Roz studied herself again. She had always looked young for her age, even so her eyes held an innocence that hadn't been there for years. It had to be a trick of the light, a distortion of the mirror. She touched her fingers to her reflection. The surface was cold and hard.

"You are much too sallow." Adele reached from behind and pinched Roz's cheeks, ignoring the way Roz shrank from her hands. "That is better. Now, we must go or Mama will fall into a swoon." She caught Roz by the hand and led her from the room.

Although it was odd they would act out their parts in private, Roz relaxed. If caught, all they could accuse her of was impersonating the girl chosen to play Rosamund.

Now she had an explanation, Roz decided it might be fun to pretend to live in an earlier century, after all, she watched actors pretend every day. Nevertheless, she wondered how long it would take the real actress to turn up to expose her.

*

Candelabras sat on every surface and a chandelier lit the main hall. Roz remembered the curving stairway from her visit to the museum. Bare oak then, it now sported a red carpet. She followed Adele down and studied the people in the hall. The actress playing Lady Imogen stood next to a tall man dressed in a soldier's uniform complete with gold braid. Too young to be Imogen's husband, he might be the Uncle Stephen Adele mentioned.

They reached the hall and Imogen scrutinised Roz from head to toe, as if searching for something wrong. Evidently satisfied, she nodded and turned to the door when the butler opened it to announce guests.

"It is just as well we made haste," Adele whispered. "We should have been in Mama's bad books if we had not been here to greet Lord and Lady Harburt." She dipped a curtsy when the elegant couple paused before her. He also wore a soldier's uniform.

"So this is Rosamund." Lady Harburt raised an eyebrow in Roz's direction.

Roz bobbed a curtsy, not sure if she should reply but obviously not. Lady Harburt raised an imperious hand to greet someone across the room and walked away.

"Lord Alexander Mindon," the uniformed servant at the door announced.

"Here he comes!" Adele whispered. "Here he comes! Is he not the finest figure?"

Roz glanced at Adele; her pink cheeks owed nothing to being pinched. She leaned forward to peek at the object of Adele's admiration. He was tall, dark and if you liked the saturnine type, handsome. She could not fault his clothes. Over white trousers, a fashion Beau Brummell started, he wore a dark-blue-velvet frockcoat. Roz decided his necktie, snowy white and intricately tied, must have taken him hours to get to sit properly.

"Alexander, my dear, so good of you to come," Imogen gushed and held out her hands.

Lord Mindon clasped her hands, bowed over them and murmured: "How gracious of you to invite me, Lady Imogen."

He left the older woman simpering and stepped towards the younger women.

"Lord Mindon," Adele breathed when he paused before her.

"Miss Adele." He bent over her hand.

Adele nudged Roz with a sharp elbow, and her voice-betrayed nervousness. "L-lord Mindon, m-may I present Rosamund, my cousin. Rosamund, this is Lord Mindon."

Roz nodded and gave a small smile. He looked puzzled when he looked at her but he recovered quickly and bowed over her hand.

"Alexander Mindon. It is your début into society, I believe."

Roz nodded, wondering why he was studying her so closely.

He gripped her hand tighter. "Such innocence, it is to be hoped society will not divest you of that charm."

Aware of the tension in the woman beside her, Roz pulled her hand from his. "I shall make certain of that, Alex."

The dark eyes took on a mocking gleam as though she had confirmed something he suspected. He bowed and turned away.

"You were rude." Adele hissed. "You must never call a Lord by his first name, and you should never shorten the name."

"Then it will give you a reason to talk to him to apologise on my behalf."

For a moment, Adele's eyes showed her confusion, and then she smiled. "Thank you, Rozzie."

A dowager passed before them followed by two giggling girls dressed in identical pink. Roz followed Adele's example and nodded to them. There then came a portly man, his wife and a moon-faced daughter; a gaunt man with brooding eyes; and a plump-bosomed woman, who sallied by like a ship under full sail.

Another woman passed and, unbidden, Roz's training caught up with her. The woman did not belong. Her dress, more suited to a younger and slimmer woman, suggested she might be an actress or one of an even older profession. Roz reminded herself they were all actors; dressed up for the evening, but. . . .

She glanced down at the ruched neckline barely covering her breasts. Hand stitched and beautifully done, the stitches were as even as if machined. It was hard to believe anyone would go that far to be authentic. Perhaps they borrowed the gown from one of the glass cases.

Roz looked up to find Alex Mindon had seen her scrutiny of the gown. Perhaps he thought she was studying the swell of breasts above the low neckline. Embarrassed, Roz blushed and looked away.

When there was a momentary lull in the arrival of guests, music carried to them from the salon. Mozart, but she forgot the name of the piece. Studying her slippers, she was trying to remember when the door opened and another guest arrived. She looked up and caught her breath. Here was a man she considered handsome. He was tall, his hair a sandy colour, a blond neither ash nor yellow, in contrast to darker brows and lashes. Tanned skin clung to high cheekbones and a firm chin, and his lips were sensual and kissable. He too was elegantly dressed; his frockcoat a deep mulberry colour over cream trousers, his cravat impeccable. A man she would like to meet.

Roz checked as he bowed over Imogen's hand. No ring on his wedding finger, but a heavy gold band graced his right hand. Imogen spent little time greeting him and Adele was cool when she introduced Roz.

"Rosamund—David Ridley."

Disconcerted by the rude introduction, Roz smiled to counteract the impression Adele must have made. "Mr Ridley. It is a pleasure to meet you."

"Miss Rosamund." He bowed but did not take her hand.

Roz extended hers, forcing him to take it as she dropped a curtsy, and was rewarded with a warmer look in his eyes. Blue as a summer sky, they bathed her with a tenderness that caressed and aroused. He was drop-dead gorgeous.

"Perhaps you will do me the honour of allowing me to accompany you to supper." His voice was deep and smooth;.

"I should be delighted, Mr Ridley."

He smiled and raised her hand to his lips before bowing and turning away.

"How dare you!" Adele hissed. "You were much too forward."

"I think he's a handsome man." Roz admired David Ridley's rear view as he walked away. Broad shouldered with a narrow waist, the flare of the frock coat hid his butt, but she imagined how it would look in tight jeans. Then she noted Alex Mindon, half-hidden behind a palm, still watched her. What was his problem?

"Perhaps so but—he is penniless, Rozzie. A second son; he will never inherit."

Roz glared at Adele. "I think you are taking this playacting thing a bit too far. And, anyway, is that how the people of this period judged men—by their wealth?"

A confused look crossed Adele's face before she answered. "Of course. Mama will give you a trouncing over this."

Trouncing? Roz managed to still the chuckle that threatened. "It will be worth it just to talk to him over supper."

"Rosamund!" Adele was aghast. "You are no longer a child. You are behaving like a hoyden."

"No more hoyden than you when Lord Mindon arrived." Roz retorted.

"Oh! You— You—"

"Girls!" Imogen stood before them. "We shall have no nursery squabbles here. We have guests in the house and you shall conduct yourselves in an appropriate manner."

"Yes, Mama," Adele said quietly.

The older woman looked at Roz. "Rosamund?"

"Yes, Imogen," Roz mumbled and a wide-eyed, tight-mouthed expression settled on the woman's face. "Aunt."

Just how well rehearsed was this play? It was an elaborate affair, no expense spared, nevertheless, they hadn't even asked if she was the right actress or if she knew her part. She felt as awkward and inadequate as Angela's understudy professed to be. She had to get out, make an excuse, go outside, and walk around the corner where one of the other tenants could let her into the house. As she turned towards the door, the man playing Uncle Ruffy took a firm grip on her elbow and she had no choice but to accompany him into the salon.

**

CHAPTER THREE

There were many people, all acquaintances, and all but the two giggling girls in pink commented on her début into society. Overwhelmed by the blend of heavy perfumes and pomades, Roz wandered close to the French windows where a breeze billowed the lace curtains to freshen the air.

"How fortunate only family and close friends are here," said the man Adele told her was Uncle Ruffy. "You have fewer people to contend with."

He gave her a gentle smile, and she felt comfortable with him. He wasn't putting on airs like the others. No lord he, but a clergyman. What did Adele say? Uncle Ruffy said not to give money to the poor because they would spend it on gin. Hardly a charitable thought, but an aspect of the character he played. At ease in his company, Roz stayed at his elbow until Imogen dragged her away to meet the woman who intended to regale them with a song.

"Play the spinet for Madame Sauvé, Rosamund."

"The spinet?" Roz squawked.

"You play so beautifully, my dear," Imogen insisted.

"But—" Now they would know she wasn't who she pretended to be.

"A tribute to this house, I think, Lady Scarbane. Especially as the event is to take place soon, hmm?" Round-faced, Madame Sauvé pursed her prim lips, raised her brows, and looked like an inquisitive owl.

If Roz hadn't found herself in such a predicament, she might have laughed.

"How thoughtful of you, Madame," Imogen said.

Roz looked blankly at both women. "Tribute? Event?" she squeaked and cleared her throat.

"Why, Scarborough Fair, of course, a tribute to this house and to the fair to be held in a few days."

Scarborough Fair. Thank goodness. At one time, she'd had the sheet music. Although Roz knew the tune, she wondered how the notes would fit a spinet keyboard.

Imogen took an iron-like grip of Roz's elbow and guided her across the room. "Come, Rosamund, there is no need to be shy."

She'd played the piano at Aunt Lily's, but always made sure no one was around to hear. Without causing a scene, she couldn't free herself of Imogen's hold. She glanced over her shoulder and saw Madame Sauvé following. Behind her, the other guests faced the spinet, and the dowager took command of the central chair.

Imogen shoved Roz onto the stool before the spinet and leaned a heavy hand on her shoulder to hold her there. "My friends, my lords, my ladies, tonight my niece, Rosamund, who is celebrating her seventeenth birthday, will accompany our dear Madame Sauvé in a charming rendition of one of our most beloved English airs."

A faint murmur of genteel approval followed the announcement. Madame Sauvé nodded to Roz and placed herself in front of the spinet.

Roz looked at the keyboard and sighed with relief. The spinet had the same two-three layout of black keys as a piano, but she hated playing before an audience. She looked up in panic.

Alex Mindon stood beside the fireplace, one elbow resting on the mantle. Mouth twisted into a mocking smile, as if he knew she wasn't one of them, he waited for her to fall flat on her face.

A quick glance around the room brought David Ridley into focus. His smile was encouraging, his eyes filled with anticipation of a pleasant musical interlude and something else—he looked proud of her and she had done nothing yet. Feeling more confident, Roz placed her fingers on the keys and began to play the introduction.

She remembered the notes and playing well. Madame Sauvé turned to give her an approving smile as she stroked the silver pearl-and-amethyst sprig-of-heather brooch pinned to her ample bosom. Roz decided it must be a good-luck charm. Angela Duke always carried a tiny gold horseshoe pinned to her bra and refused to go on stage without it.

Then the diva was singing and Roz shot Alex Mindon a look of triumph before she allowed her gaze to rove back to David Ridley.

Aware he hadn't taken his attention from her, she smiled. The song was for him. She whispered the few words she knew: "Are you going to Scarborough Fair? Parsley, sage, rosemary, and thyme. Remember me to one who lives there; he was once a true love of mine."

Now Madame Sauvé was singing the second verse and David Ridley's lips were moving soundlessly to the words. Roz was entranced.

Tell her to make me a cambric shirt. Parsley, sage, rosemary, and thyme.

Adele moved to stand in front of David and broke the spell. The look on her face told Roz she had breached some sort of etiquette and was in for a trouncing from Imogen.

Trouncing? *Good grief!* She was beginning to think with Adele's words. However, it was hard to remember this was a charade because they all played their roles so convincingly. If she knew her part, she could fit in better.

Madame Sauvé's rendition ended. There were cries of *Brava* and a few men clapped their hands against their thighs.

"That was excellent, Rosamund." A man beamed at her as she rose from the stool. "I am very proud of you."

"Thank you." Roz had seen him standing in the receiving line next to Imogen. "You are playing my Uncle Stephen, right?"

A flash of anger darkened his eyes and his mouth tightened. "That is enough, Rosamund!" he spat under his breath. "You are not in the nursery now."

Sensing all eyes upon them, Roz crept to the chair vacated by the wife of the portly man who Rose to accompany him as he sang Drink to Me Only in a throaty tenor. When all eyes were intent upon the singer, Roz risked a glance to where David Ridley had been standing. To her disappointment, he wasn't there. A small cough drew her attention to where he sat opposite her. By his smile, she knew he had seen her looking for him. She smiled back and lowered her eyes lest Adele or Imogen were watching.

Next, the two giggling girls in pink perched before the spinet to play a duet and read the notes from sheet music they placed on the stand. Their mama took the floor to sing Blow, Blow Thou Winter Wind. As if on cue, when they began the second chorus a gust of wind surged through the lace at the window, lifted the sheet music from the spinet and whirled it into the fireplace. One glance at David Ridley showed Roz the merriment in his eyes. She opened her fan and hid behind it to give vent to her own laughter. Luckily, Imogen was too busy to notice as she comforted the singer. The accompanists ran from the room in tears just as the butler sounded a gong.

Roz got to her feet and Uncle Ruffy came to her side.

"May I escort the most charming young lady in the room to supper?" At her hesitation, he lowered his voice, "Under the circumstances, you would do well to accept my invitation."

Behind him, David Ridley waited.

"I promised another."

"Adele has acquainted me with your word to another. It would be circumspect if you would accept my invitation." He crooked his elbow and she rested her fingers on his forearm.

"Adele told you?" So much for cousins.

"She is a meddling minx, I dare say, but she has the right of it."

"I meant only to take supper with him." Roz protested and flashed a look of apology to David.

"What may seem innocent to you may not appear so to others. You are newly come to society and may not be aware that an invitation to supper is also a declaration of interest. The young man may wish to call upon you." Uncle Ruffy led her into the room she had visited when she came to study the costumes in their glass cases. Now it was a ballroom with an orchestra at one end and several small tables at the other.

"What is there against him, except he is not wealthy?"

"You must be more circumspect, young lady."

His reproof made her angry. This was a charade, for heaven's sake, and he was treating her like a child. "Please excuse me, I need air." With that, she walked out of the room. If it wrecked their play, so be it.

A footman stood beside the front door. She hurried towards him and he looked surprised as he opened the door for her to pass through.

It was dark outside with only pools of light from the windows to show the way. There had to be a power cut. Roz ran down the steps and then gravel cut into the satin slippers. Confused, she came to a halt. They must be doing road repairs. Somewhere in the darkness, there would be bollards and signs to warn pedestrians. Cautiously, she moved forward.

Even during a power cut, there would be lights in the windows of some houses because most people kept candles for such an emergency, but there were no lights. An overcast sky meant no moonlight. Against the dull grey, where there should be the square solidity of houses, trees loomed.

Where was she? Where were the houses?

She looked back. The façade of the building from which she emerged was the Scarborough but no such grounds surrounded it when she went to study the costumes. Had she taken the wrong door and emerged into the museum's garden?

"Miss Rosamund!" A voice hissed from the shadows. "It's me, Jenny. Ye must come in afore they know yer out here."

"Jenny?" Roz made towards the sound of the girl's voice. "Where am I?"

"Yer in the garden, Miss. Please to come in afore the night air does yer harm."

Gentle but firm fingers touched her arm. Relieved, Roz said, "So, this is the museum's garden."

"Don't know no museum, Miss."

"Then whose garden is this?" Her voice rose in panic. "Where am I?"

"Be quiet now, Miss. Oh, please do. And come in afore madam knows yer out here and has the vapours."

"Vapours?" Roz didn't know whether to laugh or cry. "Imogen has the vapours?"

"Something awful, Miss."

Roz laughed. "This is a dream. It's all a dream. I was sewing and my mind filled with images of the woman on the sugar bowl. I was listening to Scarborough Fair on the radio and I must have fallen asleep."

But she hadn't. She remembered falling through the mirror. She had to accept that but the thought froze her mind. Had she travelled back in time? But—such a thing was impossible, wasn't it?

"Miss?"

"Take me to my room, Jenny."

"Yes, Miss. If we goes the back way like we done afore, they's not going ta see yer."

"Good. Quickly now, Jenny." Roz pushed the actress playing the maid ahead of her.

The back stairway was dark, but before they reached it, they passed through a corner of the well-lit kitchen. Several liveried coachmen sat around a massive table and turned surprised looks in her direction.

Roz decided they must be part of the group that organised the evening because they too were dressed in nineteenth-century costume.

There would be gossip and the organisers were sure to hear of it, but why should she worry? She wasn't part of this carry on. She had done nothing wrong, but she felt sorry for the actress who was to have played Rosamund when they asked her to explain why she left early.

Back in the bedroom with the gilt mirror, she had Jenny help her out of the lavender gown. She thanked the maid and asked her to inform all and sundry that Rosamund had a headache and taken to her bed.

"Yes, Miss."

Jenny had no reason to play her part in private, so— though her mind baulked at the explanation, Roz had to accept she'd travelled back in time.

Once Jenny left, Roz gathered up Angela's costume and walked with purpose across the room. At the mirror, she paused. "You know what?" she told her reflection. "If you don't allow me back to the other side I will smash you to smithereens." It was an idle threat. She dare not damage museum property.

Voices came from the hallway and she froze. Glancing at the door, expecting it to open at any moment, she put out her hand to the mirror and her fingers encountered the liquid-silver texture of fluid glass. Quickly, she leapt through . . . and fell on the tumble of books. With the costume bundled in her arms, she couldn't break her fall in time to avoid slamming her head into the chest of drawers. She winced and stayed where she had fallen while she gathered her wits and fought the threatening darkness.

Moments later, a woman banged on the door and called out. "Miss Reid! Are you all right, Miss Reid?"

Roz struggled to her knees and pulled herself upright with the aid of the chest. One hand to her throbbing temple, Angela's gown clutched under her arm, she made her way to the door and opened it. She squinted at the sixty-plus woman standing there. "Who are you?"

"I'm Minnie Wilton. I live under you. I heard a crash, then, when I didn't hear any more noise, I wondered if you'd fallen and been hurt. I've been away for the weekend. I got back ten minutes ago so we haven't had a chance to meet yet. I go to visit my niece in Southend quite often, you see. Did you fall?"

"Yes." The barrage of words left Roz dazed. She opened the door wider to allow the woman to enter. "I fell off those books." The room wavered and she closed her eyes in an effort to steady herself.

Minnie placed an arm around her and helped her to a chair. "Why were you standing on the books?"

Roz explained, touched the sore spot on the side of her head and grimaced. "I'm going to have a lulu of a headache."

"I'll make you some tea. That will help." Minnie walked into the kitchenette, filled the kettle and plugged it in. "Do you have painkillers? I always say a cup of tea and an aspirin can cure most ills. Did you say you had some?"

"In the bathroom." Roz waved a trembling hand in that direction.

She glanced at the mirror. It must have been a dream. She fell off the stack of books, hit her head, and only dreamed she'd fallen through the mirror. It had seemed so real.

"I found your dressing gown in the bathroom." Minnie came back with Roz's fleecy robe over her arm. "It won't do for you to catch a chill after such a fall and the camisole you are wearing won't keep you warm. This house gets cold at night."

Roz stood, swayed, and slipped her arms into the robe Minnie held out.

"There, now. You settle down and I'll make the tea."

24

Minnie poured water into the teapot and rummaged around until she found the tea bags. The fridge door opened and closed.

Roz rested her head on the back of the chair and glanced at the clock. Ten-thirty. She remembered the radio program changing at nine. It was a dream, just a dream.

"Why don't you pop into bed?" Minnie produced a hot-water bottle along with the tea and aspirin. She placed them on the table and drew back the bedcovers while Roz swayed across the room, one hand to her throbbing head.

"There we are." Minnie tucked her in and gave her the tea and painkiller. "I'll borrow your key and check on you every two hours." Minnie picked up the set of keys from the table. "They say to check a person every two hours if they've had a head injury to see if they've gone into a coma."

"You really don't have to bother." Roz gave a half-hearted protest.

"Nonsense. You can return the favour if ever I feel poorly." She paused and studied Roz. "I'm being bossy, aren't I?"

Roz took a sip of tea and smiled. "Just a bit."

"Everybody tells me that and I'm trying to curb the tendency. It comes from years of bossing schoolchildren around. But I worry about you young people, so, if you don't object, I'll come up to check on you."

"Thank you."

Tucked in with a hot-water bottle and fortified with painkillers and tea, Roz fell into an exhausted sleep.

Minnie shook her awake two hours later. "I swear I heard you walking around a few minutes ago, but here you are fast asleep. Can I get you anything?"

"I don't think you could have heard me walking about."

"Maybe you were doing it in your sleep. Do you sleepwalk?"

"I don't think so. How would I know?"

"I don't suppose you would. Well, to be safe, I'd better stay up here the rest of the night. The place is strange to you

25

and you could walk out onto the landing and fall down the stairs. I'll sit over there and keep watch shall I?"

"You don't have to go to so much trouble."

"Nonsense." Minnie shook her head. "I'll take one of your books." She tidied the pile, took one and studied the cover. "Barbara Cartland. I can't say she's my favourite author but it will do. I'll sit here where I can see you if you get up. Can I get you anything?"

"No." Roz relaxed against the pillows. "Thank you."

Minnie wedged the back of a chair against the mirror and dragged another to face it. She stretched out between them, her cherry-red dressing gown a bright splash of colour in the drab room.

The woman was being very solicitous considering they met only a few hours earlier. Roz wondered why, but she pushed the question aside because Minnie's presence was comforting.

Whose footsteps did Minnie hear? Could they be the same sounds Roz heard the night before? Had someone been in the flat last night and tonight? Minnie hadn't mentioned passing anyone on the stairs. So, if Roz didn't dream the whole episode of falling into that other world, could someone follow her back through the mirror, and where was that person now?

**

CHAPTER FOUR

Roz woke to a grey dawn with rain drumming on the roof in time with the throbbing in her head. Across the room, Minnie slumbered on her makeshift bed.

Careful not to wake the other woman, Roz tiptoed close to the mirror. Had it been a vivid dream? She touched the silvered surface above Minnie's head. It was cold and hard.

Roz switched off the light and went to open the curtains. From the window, the houses across the lane stared back as the streetlights went out. Cheek pressed against the pane, she could just make out the corner where the museum stood. Wide steps led up from the pavement.

It had to be a dream after she hit her head on the chest and passed out. She'd been weaving stories about the woman on the sugar bowl and the gowns in her dream were from the same period. The one she'd worn was the same colour as Angela's costume, and she'd been listening to a piano recital, which somehow changed into the spinet.

Relieved, Roz went into the bathroom to splash cold water on her face. In the mirror, she saw a lavender ribbon threaded through her hair.

She gave a small cry and in an instant, Minnie was at the bathroom door.

"Are you all right, Miss Reid?"

"I'm fine." Roz opened the door. "And it's Roz." She swayed and gripped the doorjamb.

"I wouldn't say you were fine." Minnie caught her about the waist. "Back to bed with you, young lady."

27

"I can't. I must get to work."

"Not today. If you give me the number, I'll ring them. I'll tell them you had a fall and should rest until you can stand without swaying."

"My telephone isn't connected yet."

"I see. Well, we can do it from my flat. It's too early to ring anyone so why don't you come downstairs with me and I'll make us breakfast. Your cupboards are a bit like Mother Hubbard's."

"I must go to work. I brought home a costume they need this morning." Angela would throw a fit if it were not ready for her to try on.

"Costume?"

"I'm wardrobe mistress at the Nostalgie theatre," Roz explained.

"They can send someone to get it. Is it the costume you were working on last night when you fell?"

"Yes. The lead actress is to have a fitting today."

"Someone else can do it, or she can wait another day," Minnie said firmly. "Come on, we'll get you downstairs."

It was Roz's first real job, and the theatre owner had taken a chance hiring someone so young. She didn't want to let him down. "I don't know about this."

"I do." Minnie grabbed her arm. "Come on. We'll go easy on the stairs and then I'll make us a nice cup of tea."

Minnie's flat was larger than Roz's attic; there was a separate kitchen and bedroom. As Minnie went into the kitchen, Roz dropped into a comfortable chair before looking around. Elegant pieces furnished the room. They looked like antiques but could be reproductions for all she knew. Snowy Nottingham lace swathed the window, and heavy velvet curtains matched the deep red of the sofa and chairs. A stand held a variety of flowering plants, and to one side a cabinet held a display of delicate porcelain figurines.

"Have you lived here long?" she asked when Minnie came from the kitchen with a tea tray.

"For about five years though it doesn't seem that long. Time flies, doesn't it?"

"Yes."

Time. . . . How could she fall through a mirror and go back in time? Everything pointed to it being a vivid dream except for the lavender ribbon. However, she used lavender ribbon to trim Angela's gown. Did a length tangle in her hair somehow?

She sipped the tea Minnie handed her and wondered again—if she went back in time, did someone follow her forward? "Last night, when you heard someone walking in my flat, is there a chance someone broke in?"

Minnie frowned. "It's possible, I suppose. They would need a key because I locked your door when I left and it was still locked when I came back. I didn't hear anyone on the stairs. Why don't I ring your place of work? What's the number?"

"I'll do it." Roz made to rise.

"No, you sit there and enjoy your tea. It's better if I ring don't you think?"

Roz nodded and called out the Nostalgie's number while Minnie dialled. "Ask for Agatha, in the wardrobe department." She listened while Minnie argued with whoever answered the phone.

Minnie placed her hand over the mouthpiece. "They say Agatha won't be in until later."

That was right. Roz did the early mornings. How could she have forgotten? "Who are you talking to?"

"Somebody called Derek."

"Damn!" It would have to be Derek.

Minnie removed her hand. "Can you wait a minute?" She pressed the mouthpiece against her shoulder. "What do you want me to do?"

"Tell him to send a messenger to fetch Angela's gown. She's having a fitting today."

Minnie relayed the message and said Roz wasn't well after a fall she'd had. She gave Derek the address and hung

29

up. "You didn't want Derek to know where you lived, did you?"

"Was it obvious?"

"Is he a boyfriend?"

"No, but he'd like to be."

"So now he knows where you live."

"Agatha was the only one I told. The secretary will need to know, to update my personnel records, but I didn't want Derek to find out I lived so close. It isn't a big deal because he isn't the type to force his way in here."

"He won't get a chance." Minnie's face took on the look of a warrior—a wrinkled but feisty warrior. "He won't get past me, and I'll tell Archie and Marge not to let him in."

"Archie and Marge?"

"They live in the garden flat on the ground floor. Most people ring their bell if they forget their keys, and they often let in visitors for Major Middleton. Reggie's quite deaf."

"Major Middleton?"

"He lives on this floor; in the flat across the hall."

"I must get back upstairs and pack Angela's gown." Roz drained her cup and placed it on the table beside her chair before rising to her feet. The room shimmered as if she were seeing it through water.

In a flash, Minnie was at her side. "Hmph! And you planned to go to work today."

"I was dizzy for a second. I'm okay now." Roz straightened and turned to the door. "I'll be okay."

"Of course you will." Minnie took up her keys and held onto Roz's arm as they walked out onto the landing and made their way up the stairs.

"I'm grateful to you for looking after me." Roz said when they arrived in her flat. She gathered up the garment bag, tried to put Angela's gown into it, and found she wasn't coordinated.

"Here, let me." Minnie took over the task. "As for looking after you, isn't that what friends are for?"

"But we only met yesterday. I'm a stranger to you, yet you looked after me as well as my aunt would."

"Strangers are friends we haven't met yet." Minnie pulled the drawstring tight on the bag. "You mentioned an aunt, are your mother and father—" She didn't complete the question and seemed to want to suck back the words.

"My parents died several years ago. I lived with my aunt and uncle until I came to London." Without warning, the grief Roz suffered then returned, and she fought back the tears.

"You get yourself into bed and I'll go down and tell Archie and Marge we're expecting a visitor. They can give him the bag so you can avoid seeing him." While Roz crawled under the covers, Minnie closed the curtains on the window.

"Would you leave the curtains open, I like it to be light in here." Daylight—when anyone in the room would be visible whether they came via the door or the mirror. Stupid idea! How could anyone come through a solid mirror? She wasn't thinking straight.

Minnie opened the curtains and looked at her with something in her eyes Roz couldn't read. "Are you sure you'll be all right? Is anything bothering you?"

"I'll be fine."

"You can talk to me about anything, you know."

"I'll remember that."

Roz wondered how Minnie would react if she told her she thought she had fallen through the mirror and gone back in time. She'd undoubtedly call the nearest looney bin.

For a long moment, Minnie studied her, and then she took the garment bag and walked to the door. "If you need anything, just bang on the floor and I'll be up."

"Thank you." Roz heard Minnie cross the landing and go down the stairs. She turned onto her side and winced as the pillow contacted the sore place on her head. For comfort, though she hated doing it, she had to lie facing the wall. Barely daring to breathe, fighting down the fear someone could emerge from the mirror without her being aware; Roz lay quietly and listened to her heart thump.

A short while later Roz awoke to the sound of voices somewhere in the house. Derek's voice was unmistakable. So was Minnie's though it was no longer soft and gentle but sharp and angry. Roz propped herself up on one elbow, smiled at the tirade, and felt sorry for Derek. He would be in fear for his life if he dared climb the stairs to the attic.

When he left, Roz moved to sit on the edge of the bed. Pain lanced her brow, and she rose to fetch a painkiller and a glass of water. As she swallowed the pill, there was a knock at the door and Minnie walked in.

"I suppose the ruckus woke you." In her arms, Minnie carried a bouquet of red roses and a box of chocolates. "He brought you these."

Roz pressed her fingers to her lips in dismay.

Minnie handed her the chocolates and pushed into the kitchenette. "Do you have a vase?"

"There's one in the cupboard under the sink." Roz studied the chocolates. John Waltham gave her a box at Christmas and she declared them her favourites. Derek probably overheard.

"I assume he's the sort who will want payment in kind." Minnie filled the vase with water.

Roz placed the chocolates on the table and sat. "Most of the men I've met seem to have only one thing on their minds."

"I suppose it's been that way through the ages. Human nature; like the animals. They want to procreate and ensure the species lives on."

"Then you would say Casanova intended only to ensure human survival?"

"Of course, there would be other benefits." Minnie shot her a mischievous glance.

Roz grinned. "But at least he wooed the women he romanced. These days it's a quick drink and hey-ho into bed we go."

"Some think roses and chocolates will help their cause." Minnie placed the vase of flowers on the table.

Roz grimaced, remembering how Derek got legless at the cast party. "Nothing will help Derek's cause."

"So be it." Minnie walked to the door. "If you don't need anything, I'm going to go down to the library." She halted in the doorway. "I'm planning spaghetti for dinner. I'll bring you some so you don't need to bother with cooking."

"You really don't have to." Roz's protest sounded weak even to her ears.

"You can return the favour one night when you're better. Is there anything you need?"

Roz shook her head.

After a few minutes, when the front door banged, Roz walked to the window. Minnie was trotting down the street with a bag of books on her arm. She paused to talk to a woman pushing a pram built for twins and Roz turned to look at the room.

With Minnie out of the way, she could drag the heavy divider from behind the table and stand it in front of the mirror. Anyone coming through from the other side would knock it over.

Roz walked the divider across the room. Puffing from the exertion, she dropped into a chair. With dismay, she accepted she went back in time and the people she met were real and not actors.

When she returned through the mirror, anyone could have followed her back, but who was it? Only the family and their servants would have access to Rosamund's room. Did Jenny do it or Adele? No, not Adele; she was too proper, too afraid to break with etiquette to even think of walking through a mirror. Roz discounted Imogen and Stephen, they would be too busy with their guests, and she discounted the guests. They would not venture to the upper floor because a footman or maid would ask questions. However, Minnie heard someone walking about.

Minnie also said she found the door locked when she arrived, and she hadn't passed anyone on the stairs. Did someone come up the stairs, enter the flat, and walk through the mirror? That person would need a key. Did an earlier tenant still have a key? If that is what had happened, whoever it was probably remained on the other side. Neither she nor Minnie was disturbed during the rest of the night, and they hadn't heard anyone walk across the creaking floorboards when they were in Minnie's flat.

Her mind returned to the frightening question—was it possible someone followed her back? If anyone had come through the mirror last night, he or she would have to go back that way, unless they had hidden somewhere on the attic landing until Minnie entered Roz's flat. If so, where was that person now—on this side or the other side of the mirror?

**

CHAPTER FIVE

The next morning, Charlie Watts, the Nostalgie's odd-job man poked his head around the workroom door. "Any cha going, love?"

Roz looked up from the waistcoat pattern she was pinning to a length of damask. "Come in, Charlie. Agatha's just brewing up." She unwound a tape measure from around her neck and flexed her back and shoulders. "We have digestive biscuits today."

"They'll hit the spot." Grey-haired and in his late fifties, Charlie slouched past Agatha. "So, Roz, you was sick yesterday."

"Not really. I just took a tumble." Roz placed the biscuits on the table and sat opposite Charlie.

"How'd you do that?" Charlie spooned sugar into his tea.

"I stood on a pile of books, fell off and hit my head."

"Don't you have no stepladder?"

"Not in my new flat."

"You don't live with your mum and dad?" Charlie looked surprised.

"They died in a boating accident when I was eight." Roz shoved the memory aside and concentrated on her tea.

Charlie gave a grunt of sympathy and patted her hand before reaching for a biscuit. "So where did you move to?"

"Scarborough Lane, next to the museum," Roz answered.

Charlie dunked the biscuit. "My mate Jim's night watchman there and I stand in for him on Thursdays, on his night off." He slipped the digestive into his mouth just as it threatened to collapse into his cup. "Did you know the museum's haunted?"

"Get away!" Roz grinned.

"It's true!" Charlie insisted.

"Have you seen any ghosts?" Agatha asked as she joined them.

"Nah, but I heard 'em, so has Jim. And I were there the night they brought in them ghost hunters."

"Psychic investigators?" Roz eyed Charlie.

"Them's the ones."

"People took this seriously?" she asked.

"Too right, they did." Charlie slurped his tea. "Had all this paraphernalia—cameras and recording equipment and some sort o' machine what drew lines backards and forards on a roll of paper."

"What did they find?" Roz and Agatha chorused.

"Nothing. The machines didn't record nothing but we heard things."

Agatha shivered. "What sort of things?"

"People laughing and talking like there were a party going on, and music; there were feet crossing the hall and going up the stairs, and doors slamming."

"But the machines didn't recorded anything?" Roz asked.

"Nah. All that fancy equipment and nothing to show for it but a lot o' wet trahsers." Charlie chuckled.

Roz was curious. "You say people were talking. What were they saying?"

"It weren't clear. It were muffled like, as if they was talking behind a thick wall."

"Well, they would be, wouldn't they?" Agatha commented. "Those walls must be over a foot thick in there."

"Two feet in places, they reckon," Charlie said.

Roz sipped her tea. "You said you heard music. What sort of music?"

"Dunno. None o' your rock-and-roll stuff, summat old-fashioned. A bit like *Greensleeves*, only it weren't that. And there were a woman singing."

"Had you heard this before the psychic investigators came?" Roz asked.

"Every time I'm there and Jim says he hears it most nights in summer.

"Aren't you frightened?" Agatha asked.

"Can't say as I am. Mind, the first time I heard it I thought youngsters had broke in and was having a party somewhere in the building. By the time I knew it were ghosts, I'd already searched the whole museum and found nothing. There didn't seem much point in being frightened after that."

Agatha wrapped her arms around herself. "You're braver than I am."

He shrugged. "The sounds are muffled like, as if they come from far away."

Roz was intrigued. "How do you mean?"

"I think what we're hearing is what happened in the past."

"It would be ghost voices," Agatha said in a whisper.

"Nah, the way I reckon it, the past has come close and the walls is thin. Some say different times runs in parallel."

"How do you mean?" Roz asked.

"I don't want to hear any more of this," Agatha said, her voice sharp.

Roz ignored her. "When I was in the museum, I saw a notice about a charity evening. Have you been there when they're holding one, Charlie?"

"Nah. Jim has, though, and they brings in extra guards. Have to shift things around, too, so nothing gets broke."

"What do they do on those nights?" Roz persisted even though Agatha was frowning at her.

"Get theyselves all dressed up like in the old times." Charlie shot a glance in Agatha's direction. "Jim says they looks like ghosts come alive."

"That's it!" Agatha snapped. "No more."

Charlie glanced at Roz, shrugged, and changed the subject. "So you moved into one of them houses in the Lane?"

"It's the house adjoining the museum. I'm in one of the attic flats. You should let me visit you one Thursday so I can hear the noises for myself."

"Any Thursday, love. I work from eight 'til six."

"That's as well as your work here," Agatha commented. "You must find it hard to stay awake."

"I do my rounds every hour on the dot." He gave Agatha a sly grin. "And I take me alarm with me so I don't miss clocking on at every checkpoint."

"They make you punch a time clock?" Roz was surprised.

"How else do you keep a night watchman honest? Mind, they've had a lot of things stolen but never on my shift." He grabbed a final biscuit and got to his feet. "You'll have to come soon though, 'cos they're closing."

"Closing the museum?" Agatha perked up. "When?"

"A couple o' weeks to the public. They already moved some stuff out. Better get going. I hear Old Johnny's on the warpath this morning."

Agatha sighed. "Isn't it the same every Monday?"

Roz got no grief from John Waltham, the theatre's owner. He seemed happy to employ a wardrobe mistress at the pittance he paid her, but he was hard on the other staff.

As soon as Charlie left, Derek arrived in the workroom with another dozen red roses and handed them to Roz with a flourish. "Your illness makes my heart bleed red as these roses."

She accepted them with a strained smile. "I wasn't ill."

"But a bump on the noggin could be serious. You do look wan, sweetie. Let me take you to lunch."

"I brought lunch." Minnie had insisted on packing a ham sandwich and an apple in her holdall.

"You're peeved that I didn't get to see you yesterday, aren't you." Derek looked put out. "I rang your buzzer, but you didn't answer."

"I didn't hear it." Roz wondered if it was working.

"I would have brought the flowers and chocolates up to you, but your dragon of a neighbour and the elderly knight in the front hall wouldn't let me near."

"I wasn't in any condition for visitors." Roz filled a jug with water for the roses.

"Let me make it up to you. Let me take you to dinner tonight," Derek offered.

"I've made plans."

Tonight she would try to go back through the mirror to prove to herself she hadn't been hallucinating. Last night, she'd been too exhausted to do anything but sleep after Minnie brought her a huge platter of spaghetti and a dessert of suet pudding the likes of which Roz hadn't eaten since she left Aunt Lily's.

"Excuse me, Derek. I have work to do." Roz pushed past him and reached for a length of gauze to make into a fichu for Laura.

Derek sighed. "You can't say I didn't try."

"No, you can't say he didn't try." Agatha echoed after Derek left. "*Heart bleeds read as these roses*, indeed. Is your place on Scarborough Lane furnished?"

"It has the basics."

"Did Derek help you move?"

"Derek!" John Waltham's nephew, the Nostalgie's stage manager, spent most of his time wandering aimlessly around the theatre.

"What have you got against him?" Agatha asked in a low voice. "He's very good looking, he's got money, and he—"

"He thinks every woman is fair game, and he drinks too much. Remember the cast party? Derek didn't mix with the rest of us but sat in a corner and got drunk."

Agatha chuckled. "So if someone dried him out, you'd date him?"

"Not likely. All he's interested in is fast cars, booze and horse racing." Roz wanted a man who would treat her like a lady not a one-night stand that, rumour had it, was all Derek wanted in a woman. "Thank goodness Minnie stopped him from coming up to my flat."

"Was that the woman who called here?"

"My downstairs neighbour, Minnie Wilton. She came up to look after me and spent the night in my flat."

"She told them you'd had a fall."

"I was silly enough to stand on a pile of books to check if the hem on Angela's gown was level. I fell and hit my head."

"That's what she told Derek."

Something in Agatha's voice made Roz look up from cutting the gauze. "Is anything wrong?"

Agatha shrugged. "I wondered if you stayed home rather than do Angela's fitting."

"I'm not afraid of her, Agatha."

"I know that."

"Then what's the problem?"

"It's an uneasy feeling. You've just moved into your new place. You don't know the other people in the house, but you let this woman sleep in your flat."

"You're grumpy because you had to come in early." Roz grinned at Agatha. "It's a respectable house. Minnie is an older woman and not in the least threatening—except to Derek—and there's a deaf, retired army major."

"Who else lives there?"

"A married couple occupies the garden flat. I haven't met them yet, but the husband helped Minnie stop Derek from coming up to see me yesterday. There is a woman living in another flat on the ground floor, and a young family in the basement. I don't know who lives in the other attic flat."

"It could be anybody."

"I haven't met all of them; when I do, I'll report back."

"No need to snap. I'm just worried about you."

"I'm sorry." Roz apologised, but Agatha was busy filling the kettle. "You need not worry about me. I'm perfectly safe in that flat."

Like hell she was. She was convinced the mirror offered a way from her flat into the past and vice versa. Could she sleep comfortably knowing anyone might enter that way? The divider would make enough noise to wake her if someone pushed it over, but would she be able to deal with whoever emerged?

If she asked Archie to remove the mirror, would it solve the problem? Would whatever they called it—gateway or portal—still be there? If they took the mirror away, would she ever see David again? Roz was willing to risk almost anything to meet him again.

*

Soon after lunch, the lead actor announced his arrival. "Good afternoon, industrious ladies."

Roz smiled at the man posing in the doorway. "Good afternoon, Granville. I've put your costume in the fitting room."

"Then I shall don it forthwith." He bowed to Agatha. "Good day to you, my dear. Are you well?"

"Yes, thank you, Mr Smythe." Agatha blew a kiss at the actor's back as he swished into the fitting room and closed the curtains.

Roz grinned. Granville Smythe's every action mimicked the larger-than-life movements he made on stage. He was a handsome man and well suited to *The Dandy's* costumes. Dressed in the elegant style of the era when Beau Brummell set the fashion, Granville would do justice to the painstaking measuring and fitting Roz did to make sure the costumes were as close fitting as the originals.

She finished pinning the waistcoat pattern to the damask and picked up the pinking shears to start cutting as Granville re-emerged.

"I think this fits rather well, don't you?" He stood in front of the triple mirror, turning this way and that, flicking the tails of the Regency frockcoat.

Roz gasped and dropped the shears. This is what the man of Sunday night had been wearing—a dark frockcoat over light-coloured trousers. That was what seemed odd about him. Even half asleep, she should have recognised the style of clothing, but she hadn't expected to see it on a modern London street. Where had he come from?

"Rosamund? Is anything wrong, my dear?" Granville picked up the shears and handed them to her with a flourish.

"It's nothing." She smiled weakly. "Now turn around and lift your arms."

The actor smiled at her in the mirror as she checked the strain on the armpit seams. "I think you've done me proud."

"It does suit you, Mr Smythe," Agatha said.

"And the cravat is a masterpiece." Granville lifted his chin and ruffled what appeared to be an intricately tied jabot.

"I'm glad it worked out." Roz spent hours hand stitching the intricate knot of lace and silk so it appeared tied in place around the actor's neck. Beau Brummell would have been ashamed, but Granville's dresser would thank her.

"How goes the shirt for the duelling scene?" Granville asked.

"I'm working on it now," Agatha answered. "It will be ready for a fitting tomorrow."

"Then I shall depart and leave your good hands to their admirable work." The actor sauntered into the fitting room to change and Roz went back to cutting out the waistcoat, her mind on the man she'd seen on Sunday night.

The rest of the morning went without incident as Roz fitted the younger actor with the costume echoing Granville's but made with cheap broadcloth. Granville was to play a wealthy man while Jason would present a poor relation.

Such details were important. When characters first appeared on stage, their clothing gave the audience a lot of information.

On tenterhooks because the leading lady was due, Roz relaxed when Charlie brought a message from Angela Duke. She would not be attending the fitting that day but, typically, she expected both gowns to be ready for the next day.

"How are we supposed to get the last gown done in time?" Roz stabbed a pin into a length of silk and muttered an oath when she pricked her finger.

Close to five o'clock, Derek came to lean languidly against the door to the workroom. "If you're still feeling the after effects of the fall, I can drive you home."

"Thanks but I'm meeting someone." Roz was finding it hard not to be rude to Derek. He was her employer's nephew, and she had to be careful not to lose her job.

"If you are sure. . . ." Derek wandered away.

"Are you ready?" The fastenings on Agatha's raincoat strained across her ample breasts and she wore a plastic rain hat over her greying hair.

"I'm ready." Roz shrugged into her jacket.

They parted outside the stage door. Not in the mood to cook, Roz dashed through the rain towards the chippy. Twenty minutes later, supper wolfed down, she emerged and was happy to find the rain had eased.

Scarborough Lane was in one of the older parts on the outskirts of St John's Wood. At one corner was the Scarborough Museum of Antiquities. It stood a floor taller than the terraced houses that flanked it. They had black iron railings separating them from the pavement with one set of steps leading down to the basement flat and a wider set up to the front door. Once, a butler or a maid would have answered the door but now it stayed locked. Mounted on the wall next to it, a rank of white buttons bore names printed on small cards.

**

CHAPTER SIX

Roz barely arrived home before Minnie came to the door. She glanced at the divider's new position but made no comment. "I've come to take you to meet the others."

Roz was determined to check out the mirror before she spent another uneasy night waiting for someone to push over the divider. "I'd rather not do it tonight."

"Oh, but it's all arranged." Minnie wrung her hands and wore a pained expression. "It's something we do to get to know those with whom we share the house. We usually meet once a month or so, but this is a special get together to introduce you."

"Well. . . ." Roz's hesitation seemed to give Minnie hope.

"Don't you want to know who lives in the other flats?"

"Yes, but—" At least it would set Agatha's mind at rest.

"Are you still feeling unwell? Is your head still giving you pain?"

She could have lied, but it was hard to lie to the woman who had been so kind to her. "It isn't that."

"I told them you'd be there. It's just an informal gathering. Will you come?"

"I'm not very good with crowds." Except, it seemed, when she had to play a spinet without warning and thought she was taking part in a charade.

"There won't be a crowd. Even if Major Middleton comes, there will be only four and me because Sandy Saunders is still out of the country. I doubt Cindy and Elliott from the basement will come, what with the twins teething and fractious. Are you coming?"

45

"I suppose I should." The minute she said it, Roz wanted to bite back the words. It sounded so ungrateful, so ungracious. "I didn't mean that to sound the way it did. I'd like to meet the others, but I usually feel overwhelmed by strangers."

"I'll warn them to go easy on you. They're not insensitive; in fact, I'm sure you'll like them."

Roz got her keys to lock the door and then followed Minnie onto the landing. "There will be four?"

"Reggie Middleton has dinner with other army wallahs quite often and our gatherings usually coincide with some sort of regimental do. I suspect it's an excuse to get out of meeting with us. He's partially deaf, you see; makes it difficult to carry on a conversation. With Sandy away, the only other will be Doris Morris. Funny name, don't you think? Doris Morris. She says she's an archivist in one of the Ministry offices, but I'm sure she's a secretary."

Minnie led the way down the stairs. "Marge and Archie—he's a retired schoolmaster, and she used to be a nurse—have the garden flat on the ground floor. That's where we usually hold our get-togethers. They sort of look after things, you know, act as go between with the agent if any of the tenants have an issue."

"And help you dissuade unwelcome guests from visiting me." Roz said. "Derek told me."

"Are you sure you are feeling better today?"

"I'm fine." Roz answered truthfully. There was a sore spot on the side but at least her head didn't ache now and she didn't feel dizzy.

"Here we are." Minnie tapped on the door bearing No. 1 in polished brass.

An elderly man with thinning grey hair opened the door. He was tall but stoop shouldered. Probably from years of bending over scholarly texts, Roz thought.

He smiled at Minnie and Roz. "Here we are then. Go on in, Minerva." He held the door wider and Minnie scooted under his arm. "You must be Rosamund." He held out his hand. "I'm happy you agreed to join our little gang. I'm Archie. Come and meet Margery."

He closed the door behind her and led Roz into the flat. "Margery, this is Rosamund."

"Oh, what a pretty girl." Marge appeared from behind a table laden with food. She was younger than Archie and stocky, dark hair blunt cut against her neck. "How nice to meet you, my dear. I wish Sandy could be here. He's much more your age and I think you two would get along splendidly. Never mind, when he gets back we'll have everyone down so he can tell us about his travels. I hope you'll have a chance to meet him soon and that you'll be with us for a long time."

"Longer than the other ones stayed there, anyway." A woman Roz hadn't met stepped forward. "I'm Doris Morris. I live in the other flat on this floor."

"Now, Doris, don't go scaring the girl off before she's properly settled in." Marge admonished. "It's a lot of stuff and nonsense."

"What is?" Roz looked from one to the other.

Behind Marge, the smile faded from Archie's face.

"What don't I know about my flat?"

"Just a lot of superstitious nonsense." Marge led Roz to the table. "Help yourself, my dear. You look as though you could do with fattening up."

Added to Agatha's misgivings, the broad hints made Roz uneasy. "I won't rest until you to tell me what you know that I don't."

"See what you started," Minnie said to Doris.

"I shall keep on until you tell me," Roz said.

"At last," said Archie, "a woman of strong character and guts."

"I still say it's a lot of nonsense," Marge insisted. "Bertie Briggs lived up there for over a year and we never had any trouble."

"What sort of trouble?" Roz asked.

"We're not going to tell you until you eat something." Marge put a plate in Roz's hand. "Where would you like to start?" She piled the plate with cheese and crackers and a handful of grapes. "There's a nice spinach dip. I made it myself."

"I'll eat when you tell me what you know that I don't." Roz placed the plate on the table.

"We can't really tell you anything," Doris said over the rim of a glass of golden wine. She turned to Archie. "This is very good, Archie, last year's dandelions?"

Archie nodded and waved a hand to the settee. "Perhaps you should sit down, Rosamund."

"Is it that bad?" She tried to make light of things, but she was worried. "Please tell me nobody was murdered up there."

"No, not murdered, at least, not that we know." Archie sat beside her and twirled a long-stemmed glass in his fingers. "The trouble is we don't have any idea what went on up there. We can only tell you what the previous tenants told us."

"Which wasn't very much," Marge commented. "Minnie knew them better than we did. You were quite friendly with two of them, weren't you, Minnie?"

"With two of the women, yes," Minnie answered. "I can't say I knew any of the men, not even that dreadful Briggs man although he lived there a while before the police took him away."

Roz stared wide-eyed at Minnie. "What did he do?"

"It seems our Mr Briggs wasn't on the up and up." Archie studied his glass. "There was talk of him stealing antiques from the museum next door, but they could never find out how he got in. They have a guard and a custodian during the day and security guards at night, and there are alarms all over the place."

"The police were convinced he was getting in there through somewhere in your flat. They made a lot of noise and nearly tore apart both attic flats," Marge explained.

"It went on for days." Doris said.

"They even cut into the ceilings and tapped all the walls with some sort of gizmo supposed to sound differently if it's rapped against a hollow place." Marge added.

"But they gave up in the end." Minnie said.

"We knew he was up to something," Marge said. "When he came here he was pretty much on his uppers."

"They should never have let him in," muttered Doris. "He looked shifty. Common little man; he didn't belong here."

"As I said," Marge continued, "he didn't seem to have much but, after a few weeks, he had new clothes and a flashy diamond ring on his pinkie. Then a brand-new Rolls arrived outside."

"We wondered why he continued to live here when he had so much money," Minnie said, and a murmur of agreement hovered in the air. "It didn't make sense to us."

They had drawn their chairs into a circle. Roz took her plate, nibbled and listened while they listed the things Bertie Briggs bought with his wealth and argued over the value of each item.

The ability to travel back in time and bring forward antiques to sell would be an easy way of making a fortune for someone with no scruples.

During her time on the other side of the mirror, she saw plenty of things she could have carried back: silver snuffboxes, ormolu clocks, figurines, even the fan she carried. In mint condition, it would be worth a lot of money. The items on the dressing table, too—silver-backed brushes and mirrors; cut glass perfume bottles; and who knew what was inside the jewellery box.

The amethyst pin! Adele thought Rosamund had given it away to the poor but Briggs might have stolen it. Why hadn't Rosamund told them somebody stole the brooch?

"Are you all right, Roz?"

Roz dragged her thoughts back to the present. "I'm okay."

"We should break this up and let you get some sleep." Minnie placed her empty glass on the table.

"Not until I hear the rest of it." Roz took a piece of cheese from her plate. "What happened to this man when the police took him away?"

"Last I heard he was in Wormwood Scrubs *doing time*. I think that's the lingo." Archie got up to refill Minnie's glass. "He should be coming out about now if he's been on his best behaviour."

"Tell her about the foreign student," Doris urged with a hint of excitement in her voice.

"Sammi." Archie returned to sit beside Roz. "His friends came to pick up his things because Sammi wouldn't come near the place after that night."

"What happened?" Roz asked.

"We don't know," Archie answered. "He'd been here only a few days when he ran out babbling one night. His friends spoke very little English so I couldn't find out what happened."

"Something frightened him." Doris clamped her lips into a tight line.

"And we don't know why the others wouldn't even stay one full night up there." Marge said. "The closest we've come to finding out the truth was from Amelia. You knew her best, Minnie. Tell Roz what she told you."

Minnie put her glass down. "Amelia was a nice woman. We became quite friendly, and I thought her a stable sort of person. You know—tweedy, retired army gal with a lot of vim and vigour. A tough one I would have said, always off hiking in the wilds of Scotland. I was surprised when she swore she'd seen a ghost up there."

Roz spluttered on her wine. "A ghost?"

"She came screaming down to my flat one night and refused to go back."

Unbidden, memory of the first night in the flat came to her. Roz heard something, and something or somebody had been in the flat. Minnie had heard something the next night after Roz fell. "Was it the ghost of a man or a woman?"

"A woman, she said. She woke up and saw a shadowy figure in the room, but when she put on the light it had disappeared."

"If it hadn't been for the other incidents, I would have said Amelia had been dreaming," Marge said.

"It might have been an intruder," Roz suggested.

"That's what I said," Minnie went on "but Amelia said she would have heard the door opening and closing if that was the case."

"So she left."

"Never stayed another night," Doris confirmed.

"She's living in Oxford now," Minnie said. "We write to each other occasionally."

"But we've never seen her since," Doris said. "In a way, Amelia disappeared just as surely as the other woman."

"Who was that?" Roz asked.

"Angeline Sauvé." Marge snorted, and all eyes were on her so Roz's start of surprise went unnoticed. "Madame Sauvé if you please. A hoity-toity piece, she was."

"That is not fair, Margery," Archie said quietly.

Marge turned to her husband, eyes flashing. "Isn't it? After what she did to Minnie?"

"Foreigners!" Doris muttered.

"I'm not so sure she was a foreigner," Marge said. "She had an accent, but I wasn't able to pin it down to any of the European countries Archie and I have visited. What say you, Minnie? You knew her best."

"Well, she was always hazy about her origins, and so many of the European countries have dark-haired people with olive skin, don't they? *I am British*, she would say. Like you, I couldn't pin down her accent but, as I don't speak any languages but English, I couldn't test her on any."

"She was an opera singer." Archie offered Roz the dish of dip and she scooped some onto a cracker.

"Opera singer, my eye!" The words burst from Doris.

"She said she was resting," explained Minnie. "I believe it's the term actresses and such use when they're out of work, isn't it? You would know, Roz, because you work for a theatrical company."

"You are an actress!" Doris looked aghast as if Minnie said Roz came from the moon.

"I'm a wardrobe mistress."

"I don't suppose you came across this Sauvé character on your travels?" Doris asked.

"Not in this lifetime." Roz realised what she had said only when the eyes turned upon her were round and staring. "I mean—no, I haven't met her at the Nostalgie."

"She owed three months' rent when she left," Archie said quietly.

"She didn't have much money," said Minnie. "I had her to dinner a few times because I suspected her cupboards were bare. Common decency should have made her say goodbye at least."

"That's foreigners for you." Doris said and earned a disapproving look from Archie.

"She left so suddenly." Minnie took a gulp of wine. She fumbled in her cardigan sleeve for a paper hankie and dabbed at her nose. "Not that we were great friends or anything, but I did try to help her."

"She was a thief." Doris gave Archie a look that threatened violence if he should dispute her statement.

"It upset you when she left." Roz leaned forward to touch Minnie's knee. She could see how distressed the other woman was. Her face was haggard and there were tears in her eyes.

"It's silly really." Minnie spoke through a muffling of tissue.

"It's not silly at all," said Marge. "It was your mother's brooch. And for all you say it wasn't valuable except for sentimental reasons, it was silver set with pearls and amethysts." Marge turned to Roz. "It was shaped like a sprig of heather."

The brooch Madame Sauvé wore. The pathway through the mirror was real and others had discovered it. Was Madame Sauvé trapped in the past?

"The brooch was given to Minerva's mother on her wedding day," Archie explained.

"She said—Angeline said she was going to try out for some opera company or other and needed all the luck she could get. I didn't mind lending her the brooch."

"Then she disappeared with it and nobody has seen her since," Doris added.

"Excuse me." Minnie rose abruptly and hurried from the room.

"Go with her," Archie murmured to Roz and took the glass from her hand. "Minerva can appear nosy at times, but she has a kind heart. Let me know if I can do anything."

Roz caught up with Minnie at the bottom of the stairs. Without a word, she took her arm and together they climbed to the next floor.

"Shall I make you a cup of tea?" Roz asked as they entered Minnie's flat.

"Something stronger." Minnie blew her nose, then tucked the paper handkerchief into her sleeve, crossed to a sideboard, and took out a bottle of sherry. "Will you join me?"

After half a glass of Archie's dandelion wine, Roz wondered if mixing it with sherry would be wise, but Minnie needed company. It shook her to see the woman she thought of as strong enough to face anything break down the way she had.

"I'd like a glass of sherry."

"It's silly of me to get so upset, but the brooch—"

"Your mother's." Roz thrust aside the memory of her own mother's death and the cameo they'd somehow lost at the funeral home. She accepted the glass of sherry and lowered herself onto the couch beside Minnie.

"It was her good luck charm, you see. Mine, too, I suppose. If they hadn't taken it from her in the hospital—" Minnie gulped her sherry. "She was due for an operation. Nothing too serious and she said she'd be all right because the brooch was pinned to the neck of her hospital gown. I found out later that they took it from her after they sedated her. Something about not wearing jewellery in the operating room because of how it reacted to whatever they used. They taped over her wedding ring." Minnie took a deep breath. "She never came round from the anaesthetic."

"I'm sorry." Roz touched Minnie's hand to offer comfort. The woman had been kind to her and she could do something in return: if she could get back through the mirror, she would find Madame Sauvé and get the brooch.

Back in her flat, Roz studied the divider. Although it was late, she stripped down to her underwear, left her watch on the chest, moved the divider and studied her reflection.

It would be dark on the other side and anyone could be waiting for her. However, if thieves were using her flat and this mirror to steal items from the past, they would not necessarily be violent. She had to take a chance and see if Jenny had any information on Madame Sauvé, but she had to be careful not to give herself away.

Roz touched her fingers to the mirror. It was cold and hard. She moved her hands around, smudging the surface, but no part of the glass felt liquid. How had she done it before?

Puzzled by her inability to pass through the mirror, Roz paused to think and leaned her shoulder against the glass. She felt the surface give.

She drew herself upright and touched her hand to the glass. It was unyielding. Roz looked away and stretched a hand towards the mirror. Her hand passed through as if the surface were liquid. She hesitated; wondering what would happen if Rosamund were in that other room. Stepping sideways, Roz crossed through the mirror.

Rosamund's bedroom was in darkness. Outside, the moon emerged from the clouds and in its light she tiptoed to the window. Moonlight passed between the yew trees, basting the lawn with lengths of flickering light under scurrying clouds. Beyond the clipped hedge, white roses embroidered the darkness.

Wondering if she dared go in search of Jenny, Roz was about to turn from the window when a movement drew her attention. She concentrated on the shadow of the hedge and saw a swirl of skirt touch the moonlight. Jenny, with a sweetheart.

Clouds hid the moon and Roz waited. It re-emerged as Jenny and the man kissed and then parted. He began to walk away, then he turned back and Jenny halted as though he called to her. Roz couldn't hear their whispers, but she had a clear view of the man's face. Young, medium build, his hair appeared light brown, tied at the nape of his neck. A good-looking man with strong features and a Roman nose; a face Roz would remember. He hurried away and Jenny returned to the house.

So Jenny had a secret, too. Did Roz dare share her own secret with the maid? Jenny must know Roz wasn't the real Rosamund. Did she dare ask her where Rosamund was? Pondering the questions, Roz returned to her own time.

**

CHAPTER SEVEN

When Agatha arrived for work, she said, "I suppose you know Charlie won't be joining us for tea this morning."

"Why not?"

"They told me when I came in. The police took him down to the station for questioning."

"Why? What did he do?"

"There's a valuable vase missing from the museum and they think Charlie might know something about it."

"Do they think he stole it?"

Agatha shrugged. "I overheard them tell Derek the vase went missing on Sunday night or early Monday morning."

"Charlie told us he only went in on Thursdays."

"Then he can't be charged with anything can he? He'll be *helping them with their enquiries* I expect." Agatha brought the teapot to the table. "Did you bring any biscuits?"

"Sorry, I forgot."

"It was your turn," Agatha grumbled.

"What's wrong, Agatha? You're not usually this grumpy."

"I'm grumpy, but not usually as grumpy as this. Is that what you mean?" Agatha's eyes were sharp over the rim of her cup.

"Is your husband okay?" She knew Agatha's husband had been ill, off and on, for a while.

"He's fine. Why would you ask about him?" The dark eyes were piercing.

"No reason. I'll bring the biscuits tomorrow." Roz moved her cup closer to the cutting table.

Agatha's mood disturbed her. There had been nothing approaching a cross word between them since she started working at the Nostalgie. Something was bothering the other woman, but she'd open up when the time was right. Roz had her own worries.

As Roz worked on Granville Smythe's frockcoat, she remembered the oddly dressed man walking down the road the night she moved into her flat. Why was he wearing a frockcoat? No other theatres existed in the area, so he wasn't an actor wearing his costume home. Who would hold a fancy-dress party on a Sunday night?

Had he found a way into the museum that led back in time? Was it possible he'd come through the mirror into her flat and made the noise that got her out of the bathtub? He was carrying something in his arms that night, and a day or so later the curator of the museum discovered a vase missing. He might be Bertie Briggs, the man the others talked about, but who was the woman Amelia had seen? Was she his accomplice?

Roz had no time to dwell on the possibility. As soon as she finished fitting Jason and Laura, and the alterations were pinned or chalked in place, Charlie arrived for his morning cuppa.

"They let you out, did they, Charlie?" Roz quipped and put the kettle on.

"It were no picnic, I can tell you. Talk about a suspicious lot." He dropped into a chair.

"I suppose they're paid to be that way."

"Wanted to know where I were on Sunday night. Did I have an alibi."

"And did you?"

"I were home in bed wiv the missus. Try proving that to the bobbies."

Roz poured boiling water into the teapot, added two tea bags, and carried it to the table. "What did they say was missing?"

"Some vase or other. It were in one o' them glass cases in the big room, but I don't know as I ever took notice of it."

Roz poured the tea and Charlie spooned sugar into his cup. "It must have been valuable for them to make all this fuss."

"Showed me a picture. It were big wiv flowers painted on it. I said if it were Ming or summat, they shouldn't keep anything that valuable in a small museum."

Vaguely, Roz remembered glass cases in one room at the museum when she went to look at the costumes. "Had someone broken into the case?"

"Nah and that got 'em flummoxed and all. See, Mr Coulter, the custodian, is the only one wiv a key to them cases."

"Was it locked when he noticed the vase missing?"

"That's right. Damned if I know who took it and Jim's in a right state seeing as how he were on duty Sunday night."

"Are you sure he didn't take it?" She studied Charlie over her cup.

"Nah. Jim and me's been mates since we was in the army together. Honest as the day is long, Jim is."

"My neighbours said a lot of things have been stolen from the museum."

"They fingered them thefts to Bertie Briggs. Caught him wiv a few things on him."

"They must have been watching him for a while before they caught him."

"There was a whole week one time when me and Jim had bobbies wiv us. In plain clothes, like." Charlie chuckled. "I reckon one had to go home and wash his trahsers after he heard the goings on in there."

"What things?"

"Voices and such. Hell of a kerfuffle there were one night. Sounded like a fight—people fighting wiv swords. You could hear the clashes. One bobby tried to do a bunk but the other one pulled him back. Couldn't give theyselves away, see."

"My neighbours said the police couldn't figure out how Bertie Briggs was getting into the museum but they thought it was from the flat where I'm living. Apparently they pulled it apart but found nothing."

"They did the same in the museum. Mr Coulter were beside his self over it. They was tapping all the walls and moving the odd bits of furniture in the upstairs rooms, but they couldn't find nowt. They even went into the attic and did damage when a bobby put his foot through the ceiling in one o' the bedrooms."

"Is the upper floor open to the public?"

"Nah, too much dry rot up there. The roof's bad and leaked in some places; turned the floorboards to mush. Mr Coulter, he keeps a fire going all year in the main room to keep the damp off."

Roz hadn't bothered with the museum's other exhibit rooms but concentrated on the display of clothing. "Do you go upstairs on your rounds?"

"Only in the hallways. I looks in the bedrooms, but I don't go in."

"Is there still some furniture up there?"

"A few bits and bobs not worth enough to bring down or send to another museum. I seen it and I got better in me parlour at home."

"I'd love to see what it's like up there. Can I visit you on Thursday?"

"I told yer, I work 'tween eight and six. I do a bit of a changeover wiv the day guard about eight so you could come about a quarter after."

"It's a date."

Charlie chuckled. "Better not let my missus hear you say that. A date! *Heh! Heh!*" He got to his feet. "I'd better get to it or old Johnny boy will be after me."

After Charlie left, Roz sat with a second cup of tea and planned her evening. She'd go through the mirror and scout out the upper floor before going in search of Madame Sauvé. She must find out where the woman lived if the diva was not a regular member of the household, but who would know?

Jenny. Servants knew everything. Jenny was on Rosamund's side or she wouldn't have smuggled Roz back into the house after she ran out into the garden. With that decided, she got up and grabbed her holdall.

In the office, John Waltham's secretary, Sally, was on the telephone. Roz scribbled a note to let her know she was going in search of accessories and left.

The hunt for suitable accessories for period costumes often took her into London's East End where a wealth of junk-, pawn- and second-hand shops jostled with murky and not-so-murky antique shops. Her allowance for costumes for *The Dandy* was running low, but she needed plumes for Angela's bonnet, and a frame upon which to place them. Her wish list also included gold braid and brass buttons. On her visit through the mirror, she'd seen how many gentlemen affected imitations of a soldier's regalia in their formal attire. She had it in mind to make Granville's costume more elaborate.

Covent Garden was a hive of noisy activity. Roz thrust her way through the crowds and stopped to examine the things in the window of a second-hand clothier. A pair of gloves looked promising, as did the nosegay lying next to them. To one side hung a wide-brimmed hat she could make to look an authentic confection for Angela. She studied it and saw a small hole where the brim met the crown. Easily repaired.

The reflection in the window showed a man standing on the other side of the road, staring at her.

Was he watching her? In the sea of people rushing this way and that, his very stillness made him noticeable. He was small with sharp features, looked to be in his fifties, with thinning brown hair cut short. Shabbily dressed, he might be a purse-snatcher or a pickpocket.

She entered the shop and looked out. He held his place at the edge of the kerb as the crowds nudged around him.

"What can I do you for, love?"

Roz swung around at the voice. The woman who spoke was enormous and dressed in what Roz would describe as a flowery tent. "What's the price of the gloves in the window?"

The shopkeeper glanced into the window. "The grey ones? Twenty-five pence, love."

"I'm not sure. . . . What's the price of the nosegay?"

"I'd throw that in with the gloves."

"And the hat on the side—how much?"

"That'd cost you three quid."

"Whew." Roz sidled toward the door. "I don't know if I can afford that. And the hat is damaged."

"It ain't bad." The woman took the hat off the peg and turned it in her hands, showing Roz the edge of the brim. "It ain't busted up."

"There's a hole here," Roz pointed to the damage "and it's grubby."

"Two quid, then—how'd that suit you?"

"If you throw in the gloves and the nosegay, I think I can manage."

"Done." The woman took the items from the window and waddled behind a table serving as a counter.

Roz dug out the money from her jeans pocket. Across the road, the man continued to watch. Perhaps his interest was in the shop.

With the tattered plastic bag in her hand, Roz wandered down the street to a haberdashery that sold feathers. She paused at the window to check the reflection. The man had also moved along the road. Shaken by the certainty he was following her, she entered the shop.

Roz bargained for some sad-looking plumes she planned to rejuvenate with hairspray. All the while, she kept glancing out of the window, almost overlooked a roll of gold ribbon and accidentally upset a small display stand. She left to the accompaniment of grumbling from the shopkeeper who had to rearrange the beads and scarves.

As soon as she emerged, she glanced across the street; the man was still there. She paused at the kerb to take a gulp of air, and dashed across the street, dodging cars, but when she reached the other side he was nowhere in sight. She looked right and left, scanning the crowds, but he was gone.

Holdall and bags clutched to her breast, she made her way to the bus stop and back to the Nostalgie.

Sally handed her a message when she got back to the theatre. Agatha wasn't well and had gone home. It meant Roz had to stay for the first part of the evening performance. It would be nine or nine-thirty by the time she got home and by then she would be too tired to make a foray through the mirror. Her search to recover Minnie's brooch would have to wait.

*

For the first two acts, Roz sat in the wings with a sewing kit. Apart from placing a few a quick stitches in Laura's gown where she'd caught her heel in the hem, there was little to do. Her nearness to the stage meant all Derek was able to do was ogle her from his place as prompt. She tried to ignore him; thankful he would have to stay in the wings until the play ended. As soon as the actors were on stage for the last act, she hurried out.

As Roz entered the house, she met Archie coming out of his flat.

"Ah, Rosamund, just in time. I was about to go up to your floor. Mr Saunders is back, and I wished to take him his letters."

"I can take them up," Roz offered.

"That's kind of you." Archie handed her the envelopes. "And I must thank you for being so kind to Minerva last night."

"She's been very good to me."

"There's a reason for her kindness. I hope I'm not breaking any confidences when I tell you Minerva has always wanted a daughter."

"She looked after me as well as a mother could have," Roz admitted.

"She's a gentle person. She rarely breaks down the way she did last night but the loss of the brooch hurt her deeply."

"I'll do all I can to help her. Perhaps I should call in to see her on my way up."

"She went out earlier. I heard her bid Mr Saunders *Welcome back*. That's when I realised he had returned."

"Well, good night then." Roz stepped towards the stairs.

"Were you been at work until now?" Archie paused at the door to his flat.

"Yes. There's a show on Wednesday evenings and either my seamstress or I have to be on hand. She called in sick, so I had to stay."

"Then it's been a long day and I won't keep you. Good night."

Roz ran up the stairs and tapped on the door to the other attic flat. "Mr Saunders?" When no one answered, she tapped again. "Mr Saunders? I have your post." She waited a few moments. Perhaps he was in the shower and couldn't hear her. She tried a third time. "I'll leave it outside the door, shall I?" She placed the envelopes on the floor and crossed the landing to her own door.

She left the door open and fumbled along the wall behind it for the light switch. It was an inconvenient place, and she intended to buy a lamp to sit just inside. With the flat flooded with light, she closed the door.

Roz smothered a cry. Someone had moved the divider. She'd arranged the side panels to touch the wall on either side of the mirror but they were now a good four inches away from the wall. She pulled the door open again, just in case she had to make a quick escape.

She dropped her holdall and looked around. Nothing else seemed to have been touched. She could see through to the kitchenette and into the bathroom. No one hid there. With her heart in her throat, she crossed to the bed and threw up the cover that hung to the floor: only her suitcase of winter clothing. She approached the wardrobe cautiously, flung the door open and leapt back from whoever might rush out. When no one did, she closed the door on the innocent clothes and relaxed. Whoever had been here was not here now.

She closed her front door and crossed to the divider. Manoeuvring it closer to the wall, she balanced it so the least touch would send it toppling. If someone had knocked it over earlier, Minnie would have heard the crash.

No, Archie said Minnie was out. The Major wouldn't hear it, and if they'd heard it on the ground floor Archie would have mentioned it. Therefore, whoever came or went through the mirror did so cautiously and moved the divider. When returning to the past, it would be impossible to pull the divider any closer to the wall than the depth of fingers or knuckles. By the size of the gap, she decided the intruder was probably a man.

Roz found no comfort in that deduction.

**

CHAPTER EIGHT

Without explanation of the illness that kept her away, when Agatha came back to work, she wasn't her usual cheery self. Roz couldn't forget the way Agatha snapped at her earlier in the week. Until then, there had never been a bad word between them, and Agatha supported her when she demanded an upgrade of the machines they used in the wardrobe department. She made several innovations and Agatha was behind her all the way. In return, Roz often switched work hours to accommodate the older woman when her husband was ill. There had always been give and take but this was an Agatha she didn't know. Something was bothering her but Roz didn't feel she had the right to question her.

Roz flushed at the sharp reply. Perhaps, if she made light conversation, it might ease the tension in the room. "I met the other people in the house."

Agatha looked up from the sewing in her hands. "Oh?"

"They have a tenants' get-together every so often. Minnie took me to meet the couple in the garden flat and the woman who also lives on the ground floor. I didn't get to meet the army man or the young family who live in the basement."

"What about whoever lives in the other attic flat?"

"He was away. He arrived back yesterday but I haven't met him yet."

"Oh."

This was going to be hard; perhaps if she talked about work. . . . "I did a foray to Covent Garden yesterday."

67

"Oh?"

"I picked up this for a lot less than I thought I'd have to pay." Roz held up the hat and gave it a twirl. "What do you think?"

"It's okay."

"It's strange but I'm sure I was followed."

Agatha gasped.

"Did you prick yourself?"

Agatha nodded. "Did you say you were followed?"

"A ferrety-looking man. He might have been a pickpocket. He had a sly look about him."

"Did he talk to you?"

"No, and when I tried to come face to face with him he ran away."

"You should be careful. It isn't safe to wander around the East End on your own."

"In broad daylight?" Roz laughed. "There were so many people about that I was quite safe."

"But if anything happened, nobody would have seen anything. It's like that down there."

"I keep forgetting you live within the sound of Bow Bells."

Agatha rose and went to the sink. "I'll make the tea."

"Sounds good, and I picked up biscuits on my way to work; Bourbon creams. We'll see how Charlie likes them."

The atmosphere was a bit lighter when Charlie arrived. "So tonight's the night I got the date of a lifetime." Charlie grabbed a Bourbon to dunk into his tea.

"What's that then?" Agatha asked.

"You wouldn't think an old codger like me would be going on a date wiv a lovely young lady, would you."

"How much did you have to pay her?" Agatha asked.

"Nothing. She asked me."

"Was she carrying a white stick?"

"Had her eyes wide open." Charlie grinned.

"She was having you on then."

"Oh, she'll be there."

"Don't tease Agatha any more." Roz brought her cup to the table. "Charlie's date is with me."

"You!"

"I'm visiting him at the museum tonight, to see if I can hear the voices."

"I hope they're around so as you can hear 'em. They aren't there every night so I'll keep me fingers crossed for you, love."

"Rather you than me," Agatha said with a shiver. "You wouldn't catch me going to listen to ghosts."

"Maybe they aren't ghosts." Charlie reached for another biscuit.

"What do you mean?" Roz asked quickly.

"They say as old houses keep echoes of sounds in their walls. I think what we hear is the people who used to live there."

Roz held silent as Charlie continued.

"That could be why the psychic people couldn't record nothing on their gadgets. Echoes probably wouldn't register if we was hearing 'em out of time."

"It fair gives me the creeps," said Agatha. "Can't we talk about something more cheerful?"

"Like what?" Charlie asked. "Like the vase that were stolen Sunday night?"

"Why would you mention that?" Agatha asked in a challenging voice.

"Why not? I'm the one the bobbies had in for questioning."

"But they let you go."

"Too right they did. I never saw that vase, never even noticed it in the glass case so they can't pin it on me. Not that they didn't come to my home and upset the missus."

"What?"

"Had a search warrant and all. Did it while I were at the station. Fair gave the missus a fright, I can tell you."

"I'm sorry, Charlie." Roz laid a hand on his arm.

"Did the same to Jim and his missus."

"I suppose they had to do it to could clear you both." Roz withdrew her hand after Charlie gave it a quick pat.

"Mr Coulter put in a good word for us. He knows as we never stole nothing in all the years we worked there."

"He must have a lot of trust in you," Agatha commented.

"Mr Coulter is all right. It'll be a sad day for us when the museum closes."

"Closes?" Roz tried to keep the edge of panic from her voice. If the museum was closing, she had little time to find Minnie's brooch. Worse still, she might never get to know David.

"In a few weeks, a month mebbe. There's no money in it, where it is. It's not what you'd call on the tourist track."

"I wonder what will happen to the building." To where the mirror would lead.

"I can't say. They don't tell Jim and me nothing." Charlie got to his feet and hitched his pants. "So I'll see you tonight, love? About a quarter after eight?"

"I'll be there."

"You shouldn't go," Agatha said after Charlie left. "It isn't safe to wander around on your own at night."

Roz felt a jolt of anger, and her voice was sharp when she spoke. "What's with you, Agatha? I've been wandering around London on my own for a while. Credit me with enough sense not to go into places that could be dangerous. It isn't as if I'm going down to Soho. I'm going next door to where I live, to visit a man I've known for months. I think I'll be quite safe in his company."

When Roz arrived home, she climbed to the first floor where Minnie was miming a conversation with a man Roz decided had to be Reggie. He had a florid complexion half hidden behind heavy side-whiskers that ended abruptly at each side of a pockmarked chin.

"Rosamund," Minnie shouted. "Lives up there." She pointed to the attics.

"*Harumph*! Pleased to make your acquaintance," boomed Reggie.

"Hi." Roz smiled at him. "Nice to meet you."

"What? What was that?" He cupped a hand behind his ear. "Speak up, girl."

"Hello!" Roz shouted and held out her hand.

"What? Oh, yes." He gripped her hand and shook it. "Excuse me." With that, he went inside his flat and closed the door.

"So now you've met Reggie." Minnie had her coat on and carried her handbag.

"Are you coming in or going out?" Roz asked.

"Going out. How are you? No after effects from the fall?"

"None." Roz shook her head. "I'm fine."

"Good. Well, can't stop. I'm meeting the girls for a drink and then we're going to the pictures. They're showing an old Clark Gable film. Now he was a man, Roz. What do you think?"

"Very handsome, for sure. Have a nice time," she called after Minnie as the older woman made her way down the stairs.

The post had gone from outside the other flat. Roz opened her door, dreading what she would find. Before entering, she studied the divider. Still precariously balanced. With a sigh of relief, she closed the door and went into the kitchenette.

As she stirred the soup and buttered bread for a sandwich, Roz checked the divider and kept the bread knife close. It wasn't much of a weapon but better than nothing.

While she ate, she faced the room and left the radio switched off. She washed up making as little noise as possible and watered the plants at the window. Intent on eyeing the divider; she almost missed the man lurking in the shadows across the street. She recognised him as the man who followed her the day before.

Roz stepped back. Why was he following her? Watching her? Should she ring the police? She felt sure Archie and Marge would let her use their telephone.

Roz ran down the stairs and tapped at the door of the garden flat. There was no answer, so they had to be out. She knocked on Doris' door but she wasn't home either.

Should she confront the man? He didn't look too big and Roz could scream her head off if he tried anything. Enough people walked along the Lane, coming from or going to the bus stop, she was sure it would keep him from turning nasty.

Heart pounding, Roz opened the front door and looked out. The man was nowhere in sight.

Roz hurried the short distance to the museum. With a glance behind to see if the man lurked anywhere, she rang the bell and stood with her back to the door as she waited for Charlie.

"Hello, lovely lady. Come for our date?" Charlie grinned as he opened the door. "I weren't sure if you would after Agatha tried to put you off."

"I wouldn't miss it for the world." She waited in the dim hall as he locked and bolted the door.

"Come along then. Our little corner's over here. I make my next rounds at nine. D'you want to come wiv me?"

"Yes, please. I'd love to see behind the scenes." And, she wanted to check Rosamund's bedroom for a mirror like the one in her flat.

"The day guard's only just left. He said as the museum will close at the end of the month when everything's out of here."

"That's only two weeks away."

"Mr Coulter said as he'd put in a word for me and Jim at a couple of other museums." Charlie lowered himself onto a chair behind a table loaded with a Thermos, a packet of sandwiches, an alarm clock, and a heavy-duty torch. "I brought a chair for you from Mr Coulter's office." He indicated a secretarial chair at the end of the table farthest from the doorway. "I reckoned you'd want to be away from the door if the voices start."

"Thanks." Roz sat down but her stomach lurched. "Are they really frightening? The voices, I mean."

"When you first hears 'em, I suppose they are. I've growed used to 'em so they don't bother me."

"What you said earlier today, about the voices being echoes of the people who used to live here, where did you get that idea?"

"It were one o' them psychic people what was here. She were a funny one, I can tell you. Drew some sort of star on the floor in the hall and put candles at all they points. Then she sat in the middle like a yogi. Mind, when the voices started, she were up out o' there like a shot. Never seen a woman move so swift."

Somewhere in the museum, a door slammed.

Roz looked at Charlie; aware her eyes must be like saucers. "What was that?"

"You're in luck. They're about tonight."

"But—but it was so close. It must be from—" She almost said *from this time period.*

"Don't you go getting all squiffy on me now, ducks. I'll be starting rounds in a minute. D'you want me to let you out first?"

He was offering her an escape, but she had to see the layout. She had to see Rosamund's bedroom. The police would say she was casing the joint. "I'm staying." She knew her voice was shaky. "But you won't mind if I make a grab for you once in a while, will you?"

Charlie laughed. "What a story I'll have to tell Agatha tomorrow. She ain't going to believe you grabbed me."

Roz smiled in spite of her nervousness and marvelled that Charlie could stay so serene under the circumstances. He'd heard it all before and come to no harm. She must remember that. Whatever happened, she had to remember that.

Someone ran down the stairs.

"There's somebody here," Roz whispered.

"No, love, there ain't nobody here but us chickens." Charlie took up the torch from the table and unhooked a bunch of keys from the wall. "Here we go. If you're sure. . . ."

"L-lead on, McDuff." Roz got to her feet, knees shaking.

73

"That's the spirit." He led the way out of what would have been the cloakroom in an earlier time.

"Can I . . . ? Can I hold onto your jacket?" Roz squeaked.

Charlie shone the light under his chin, giving his face a demonic look. "Boo!"

"Don't!" Roz shrieked. "Don't do that, Charlie. I'm scared enough already."

In the display rooms, pale moonlight and streetlight penetrated the high. Roz looked over Charlie's shoulder and glanced nervously into the shadows around them.

"Why is it so dark everywhere?" Roz asked.

"'cos the museum's closing, the London Council's been making a row about electric bills, so we don't use the lights unless we have to."

For a moment, Charlie's torch caused the shadows to jump around and Roz thought one of the mannequins in the glass cases moved. Her indrawn breath was a scream.

"What?" Charlie halted.

"N—nothing. It—it's okay." They were dummies, like the ones in the shop windows everywhere. Mannequins. Locked in glass cases. They couldn't move.

Charlie swung his light around each corner and under furniture; he shone it on all the window catches and moved on to the small display rooms leading off the larger one where the glass cases were. Her attention on the figures behind the glass walls, Roz walked backward as they left.

Away from the windows, the only light was the beam of Charlie's torch. Around it, shadows loomed black and menacing.

In one room, a fire glowed in a hearth and Charlie walked across to add a few lumps of coal. "They say as there's a secret passage somewhere around on this floor, but nobody's ever found it."

"Just don't find it tonight, Charlie; I don't think I could cope with spiders as well as all this."

His only answer was a chuckle as he led the way into the rear of the building. At the bottom of the back stairway,

Charlie fed a card into a time clock and moved up with Roz clinging to the hem of his jacket.

Out of the darkness, footsteps clattered down the stairs, the sound ringing on the bare boards. Terrified, Roz pressed herself against the wall. "Charlie!"

"It's all right, love. Just the maid or the footman running to answer a bell, I expect." He stopped and put an arm around her shoulders. "There ain't nobody here. There's nothing that can hurt you."

"I—I want to go back." She shivered until her teeth rattled.

"You can go back but I have to go on wiv me rounds or they'll dock me pay."

"I c-can't go down there on my own."

From the upper region came a shriek of laughter that, to Roz's mind, sounded evil. "Oh, God!"

"There's nothing and no one here." Charlie swung the beam of light up and down the stairs. "I've got to go on. You take a deep breath now to calm yourself."

Roz took a shuddering breath.

"Come on, love." Charlie gave her a little shake. "You're letting your imagination get the better of you. Soon as we finishes the round we can have a cup of coffee."

"Soon as we finish this round, I'm getting out of here."

"That's my girl. On we go." Charlie continued up the stairs with Roz clinging to him like a limpet. He chuckled. "Agatha will never believe this."

"Don't you dare tell her, Charlie Watts!" Roz threatened.

They reached the top of the stairs without further incident. Charlie punched another time card and checked the padlock on a door that looked as if it might lead to the attic before he continued into the hallway.

"Watch your step here. The floor's not all it should be in the middle and to the left side. Keep to the right."

With Roz at his elbow, Charlie shone his torch into three of the bedrooms and said, "I have to check the three on

75

the other side. Do you want to stay here or risk the floor with me?"

"I'm not staying here."

"Let me cross first then."

She clutched his coat. "You lead on." She let him get a step or two ahead of her, the distance his jacket hem and her arms would allow, and then followed.

As he had done on the other side of the hallway, he shone the torch around the room and on the window catches. "All clear here." He led the way to the next bedroom and checked it. Bare but for a broken-down chair, an iron bed frame, and a mildewed table, wallpaper hung in strips amid a musty smell.

"This were the worst damage done up here." He directed the light to the floor and a pile of plaster and rotten boards and then swung the beam up to a hole in the ceiling. "That's where the bobby put his foot through."

"What about the next room?" Probably Rosamund's room.

"It didn't get leaked on as much, but the floor's ready to give way." He opened the door and shone his torch into the room.

"Let me see." Roz took the torch from him. There was no bed; no dressing table with silver brushes and vials of perfume, nothing. Stained and faded wallpaper covered the wall that adjoined her flat. There was no mirror but an outline marked the wall where one had been.

"Seen enough?" Charlie took the torch back. "There's nothing else on this floor. Watch yourself on the stairs. The oak is so worn it's like glass in places." He punched another time clock at the head of the stairs and began to move down.

Footsteps closed in from behind and Roz cried out. For a split second, a waft of frigid air made her shiver. Then it was gone and someone ran down the steps, the sounds muffled. "Charlie!"

From below came a hubbub of subdued voices as if they came from a distance. There was music. A door opened and closed. Someone laughed the deep rumbling laugh of a man and a woman's shrill echo.

"They must be having theyselves a party tonight," Charlie commented and continued down the stairs.

"Wait!" Roz had lost her grip on his jacket and now rushed to catch up with him.

Charlie chuckled. "Agatha'll never believe the tale I have to tell her."

"If you say anything, I'll never speak to you again, Charlie Watts!"

They reached the bottom of the stairs and Charlie shone the light on her crotch. "At least you didn't dirty your jeans."

"Charlie!"

"Strong men have filled theirs. And, you know what? Them psychic people never brung a change of trahsers." He was still chuckling when they entered the cloakroom and he hung the keys on the wall. "Fancy a cup of coffee, love?"

"I think I need something stronger than coffee." Roz ran to the chair and sat with her back against the wall.

"We can have that, too." Charlie went to where his coat hung on the back of the door and produced a bottle. "A drop of rum in your coffee'll steady your nerves."

Beyond the open door, the sounds continued. Roz had thought she might recognise a voice, Imogen or Adele, but they were too distant, male and female voices against the background of a string quartet. Possibly the same piece of music played on Monday night.

"There." Charlie placed a steaming cup on the table. "You get yourself around that."

Roz sipped. It was hot and Charlie had been generous with the rum. "How can you do it? How can you come back here week after week and listen to this, and how can Jim do it?"

"Like I said, the first time I thought kids had broke in and was having a party somewhere in the museum. After that, I didn't see no point in being rattled. I reckon that's why

Mr Coulter's so keen on having me and Jim stay. Not too many night watchmen would stick it out."

"You said you sleep between the hourly rounds. How can you?"

Charlie grinned. "How can I stay awake, is more like. I've been hearing them noises for years. They don't keep me awake no more than would the people down the street if they was having a party."

Roz gulped the cooling coffee. "Did you feel a rush of cold air at the top of the stairs?"

He looked puzzled. "Cold air?"

"Just before we started to come down. . . . This will probably sound silly but. . . .I heard footsteps behind me, then a rush of cold air, and then someone ran down the stairs. Didn't you feel it?"

"Can't say as I did, I never have."

"It was as if someone ran by, very close to me." *Or through me.* Roz shook off the thought.

Charlie shook his head. "I don't know what it could've been, a draught from somewhere, mebbe."

"But you checked all the windows." Roz pointed out.

"In an old building like this, there's gaps and cracks all over the place and the Council ain't of a mind to spend money repairing it. It must have been a draught."

"Didn't the psychic investigators feel anything?"

"Not that they said, and one of them were at the top of the stairs wiv his machine."

"You said something today about the voices being echoes from the past. What made you think that?"

"It were something I read." He took a book from a bag resting under the table. "This bloke reckons as time is in parallel, sort of going on all at the same. He reckons as they sometimes come close together and some people can cross over. They'd look like ghosts, he says."

Roz reached for the book and read the title: *A Rift in the Fabric of Time.* "I never knew you read things like this, Charlie."

"Well, all them things going on in here got me to wondering. Then I saw this on a stall down the market so I bought it."

Roz flicked the pages and found a corner turned down two thirds of the way through the book. "I wouldn't mind borrowing it when you've read it."

Charlie grinned. "But we won't tell, Agatha, eh?"

"Do you think two time periods have come close in the museum?"

"Dimensions, he calls 'em. Yes, I think they have. Jim and me hear what sounds like sword fights, and sometimes we hear horses and carriages outside. I ain't never heard them things in the Lane only in here."

"So if what the author says is true, we could pass into another time dimension."

"That's what he reckons. But he says doing it might be dangerous."

"In what way?"

"He says it might alter history or the dimensions might drift apart wiv no warning."

"And trap somebody in the wrong dimension?" *Like Madame Sauvé.* A flood of ice coursed her back.

Charlie nodded. "And he says people passing from one dimension to another might cause a rift—a break in time—that might be cast-castastrophic."

"Does he say what could happen?"

"He thinks it could cause things like earthquakes or explosions and fires, or something he calls sinkholes."

"Sinkholes?"

"Didn't something like that happen in Cornwall a couple a hundred years ago? Didn't whole houses get swallowed up?"

"I thought they attributed that to some old tin-mine shafts?"

"Mebbe, mebbe not."

"Do you believe what this man wrote?"

"I dunno. Sometimes, when I'm here by myself and the voices start, I tries to get closer to where they are. Once, I thought I heard a name. It were a woman calling somebody."

"For whom was she calling?"

"I swear it were *Jenny*."

Roz shuddered.

"Are you cold?"

"Just a bit." Roz drained her cup. "It was quite an experience, Charlie. More than I expected."

"I'll tell Agatha you enjoyed your date wiv me, shall I?"

"If she doesn't cheer up, I'll drag her here one night and make her go on one of your rounds."

"Going through a bad patch, is she?"

"I don't know what's wrong. I've asked but she won't tell me. Her husband might be ill again, and it's worrying her."

"Ill?"

"He had a bad turn a couple of months ago and she took a few days off to look after him."

"Is that right?"

Something in his voice made Roz study Charlie. His eyes were veiled. "Is there something I should know?"

Charlie shrugged. "Seems to me Agatha would tell you if she wanted you to know."

"But you know something."

"I'll tell you this much—you don't need to worry none over Agatha. She can take care of herself."

"I'll accept that for now, but if there's ever anything I need to know, you'll tell me, won't you?"

"Right enough, love." Charlie got to his feet. "Come on, I'll see you to the door. I can't leave the museum but I can watch 'til you get to your own door."

"Thanks." Roz had forgotten the man who was watching the flat earlier, now she worried if he was still out there. Behind her, the voices had dropped to a faint murmur. "Good night, Charlie." On an impulse, she threw her arms around his neck and hugged him. "And thanks for not making fun of me."

As she ran down the steps and along the street, the thought he was watching comforted her. She paused to give him a wave as she let herself into the house.

She found Archie, Marge and Doris hovering on the attic landing. "What's going on?" she asked.

"We heard a crash," Marge explained, "and we thought you might have fallen and hurt yourself again."

"When you didn't answer our calls, we were trying to decide if we should get the duplicate key and let ourselves in to check." Archie filled in the explanation.

"I think something must have fallen over," Doris said.

Glad to have them with her, Roz unlocked the door and walked in, expecting to find the divider on the floor. She reached behind the door and flicked on the light. Someone had moved the divider again. It stood a few inches from the wall with the side panels arranged to hold it upright.

"Has anything fallen over?" Marge asked, walking into the middle of the room.

Roz shook her head. "Nothing I can see. Are you sure it came from this flat?"

"Well, not for sure, but there was no answer from Sandy either. Perhaps we should get the key and examine his flat," Marge suggested. She looked at Archie. "I'll go and get it."

"Shall I make a cup of tea while we wait for Marge?" Roz asked.

"No, my dear," said Archie. "It's late and we'll only be a few minutes."

Under the pretext of checking things, Roz examined the bathroom and under the bed, and other odd corners where someone might hide. She waited at her door while they checked the flat across the landing and reported nothing looked out of place. When they left to go back downstairs, Roz closed the door and looked around.

Someone had been in the flat. The divider must have fallen over and whoever it was had set it up before they left. If no one passed the others on the stairs, there was only one way out of the flat—through the mirror. Whoever it was had returned to the other side.

It was the last thing she needed after her visit to the museum.

**

CHAPTER NINE

Unless they were in a panic to get costumes finished, Roz and Agatha had alternate Fridays and Sundays off during the run of a play. For *The Dandy*, the costumes were well in hand with only a few things to finish before dress rehearsals. Part of Saturday was free, too, because Roz alternated with Agatha to stand by for the afternoon matinee or evening performance. Occasionally, one or the other of them would work both performances thus freeing the other for a whole weekend. For the upcoming weekend, Roz was to be present during the matinee. Given the mood Agatha was in, Roz didn't dare suggest taking the whole weekend.

She had to decide whom she could ask about Madame Sauvé without sending Imogen into hysterics if she heard. If she asked Jenny, would Jenny tell anyone? Roz was puzzling over the problem when someone knocked at the door. She put on her dressing gown and went to open it.

"I'm off to Southend," Minnie said as she walked in, "but I had to see how you were before I left. Are you quite recovered?"

"I'm feeling fine. You have a good time."

"I'll hardly do that. Wendy has three children and her husband's away working on an oilrig in the North Sea. She works the occasional weekend so I look after the children."

Roz wasn't comfortable with the idea the flat downstairs would be empty. If she needed help, there was no one to hear unless Mr Saunders was in because the Major was too deaf. "When will you be back?"

"Sometime on Sunday night or Monday. You have a nice weekend now. Are you going out?"

"Perhaps, I'm not sure yet." Roz avoided Minnie's gaze and fiddled with the belt of her bathrobe. "But I'll be working this afternoon."

"Well, I'd better be going or I'll miss my train. See you Monday."

After Minnie left, Roz threw off her robe and moved the divider aside. She could not have foreseen that Madame Sauvé's brooch would match the description of the one stolen from Minnie. Was it likely two women who lived two hundred years apart would have the same name and both be singers? Roz looked away, touched the mirror, and stepped back in time.

As before, a gown lay on the bed. This one was made of white embroidered lawn. On the floor, a pair of white slippers sat beside a parasol that leaned against the bed. Roz put the gown on, slipped on the shoes, and went to the mirror to adjust the fichu that completed the ensemble. Everything fitted as if made for her. Not meant for an ingénue, under the fichu the bodice was low cut and the skirt skimmed her hips like a second skin. Clearly, they accepted Rosamund as an adult, and if what Roz knew of fashion history was accurate, they meant the gown to lure a husband.

Behind her, the door opened. Jenny entered silently and Roz studied the maid's reflection in the mirror. The girl knew something. It showed in her eyes.

"This mirror. . . ." Roz touched her hands to the solidity before her.

"It was here afore I come," Jenny answered as she moved into the room. "Shall I do yer hair now, Miss?"

Obediently, Roz sat at the dressing table and Jenny stood behind her with a brush. "Have you worked here long?"

In the mirror, Jenny gave Roz a coy smile. "Eeh, ye know, Miss Rosamund. I come here from the orphanage when I was little."

What Roz knew of the early nineteenth century came from novels and at design school when they studied the effect on fashion by whatever was going on in the world. Society's elite wore different fashions from those of the working class, and the working class had its own levels. They would assign a girl from an orphanage to menial duties, to dishwashing or laundry, to cleaning grates and scrubbing floors; they would not give her a position as a lady's maid. Ladies' maids affected an air of gentility; if only when they were in the presence of their mistresses, but Jenny sounded the way she would if she was scouring the front steps. Why didn't Rosamund have a better class of maid?

"It seems I forget many things, Jenny."

"And no one can blame yer if'n yer want to forget."

"Why is that?"

"Ye know, Miss." Jenny gathered Roz's hair into her hand.

"No, I do not," Roz said . "You tell me."

A wary look entered Jenny's eyes before the girl looked away. "Ye don't 'member the explosion?"

"No."

"Nor yer mum—mother and father?"

"Did they die in the explosion?"

Jenny nodded. "And then yer come here, wiv Mr Old'am."

"Mr Oldham?"

"Yer uncle, Miss." Jenny arranged two combs to hold Roz's hair off her shoulders.

Uncle Stephen. "And you've been my maid ever since?"

"Yer was in the nursery first. I looked after yer then." Jenny poked strategic hairpins into the bunch of curls she was arranging on top of Roz's head. The girl had a knack for hairdressing.

"And you had the skill to continue as my lady's maid?"

Jenny's hands trembled against Roz's scalp and she avoided Roz's eyes. "Madam said I was to."

"Why was Uncle Stephen standing beside Aunt Imogen in the receiving line the other night?"

Jenny's eyes widened. "'Cos he's her brother, Miss."

A much younger brother. Imogen had to be in her forties, but Stephen Oldham could be no more than in his early thirties. "Does he live here all the time?"

"When he's not wiv his regiment."

"And where are Aunt Imogen and Adele?"

"They be gone out for luncheon, Miss. Said as ye was to go wiv them but we couldn't find yer."

"Will they be gone long?"

"Most all afternoon is usual." Jenny placed the last of a batch of hairpins into the complicated topknot of curls and stood back.

"What about Adele's papa? Is he here?"

"Oh, no, Miss. he never come here but stays in the big house in Scarborough proper he does."

"Why are Aunt Imogen and Adele here?" In the mirror, Roz could see that the number of questions were disturbing Jenny.

"For the Season, Miss."

Roz gave a derisory snort. The Season, when they paraded unmarried women like cattle to market. It explained why her gown was designed as it was. Imogen hoped to snare husbands for both Rosamund and Adele and thus forego the cost of two Seasons.

She dared not question Jenny further. Obviously, Rosamund suffered some sort of trauma because they did not make much of her behaviour. If she had blanked out her parents' deaths in the explosion that probably destroyed her home, they would accept a reasonable quirk in her manner. It gave Roz a certain amount of leeway until Rosamund, who was clearly in the habit of disappearing, showed up.

"Will ye be going out, Miss?"

"Perhaps. Later." She had to explore the house to find the exits, in case she had to make a fast escape. "Do you know where Madame Sauvé lives?"

Jenny shook her head.

"Thank you, Jenny. That will be all."

Jenny backed to the door. For a moment, it appeared she was going to say something, then she changed her mind and left.

Roz walked to the open window. Outside, everything was green, unlike the grey pavement and road she saw from her flat window. Manicured lawns surrounded a gravelled driveway that circled a fountain where water cascaded in a glint of sunshine. Flowering trees and shrubs bordered the lawn. A stand of larger trees obscured everything beyond the driveway, except for several spires and towers in the distance. It would be London as it had been at this time before the city encroached upon and engulfed Scarbane House.

Trimmed yews flanked one side of the lawn. The hedge where Jenny met the man separated the grassed area from the rose garden. She breathed deeply, enjoying the perfume and air fresher than in her own London. Behind another hedge, the tip of the kitchen garden with its fruit shrubs and clumps of herbs was visible. It was where Jenny led her the first night, so the kitchen lay in that direction.

A stable boy appeared leading three horses, one of them laden with saddlebags. He stopped beside the steps leading to the front door. Within minutes, Stephen Oldham emerged, dressed in uniform. Another soldier followed, his uniform undecorated by braid and bright buttons. Both mounted and rode away, and the boy went toward the kitchen. With Stephen, Imogen and Adele out of the house, Roz had an opportunity to explore without fear of confronting one of them.

She was about to turn from the window when a movement drew her to look at the yews. A man was studying the house. Not wanting him to see her, she stepped back. He moved from tree to tree, skulking in their shadows as he came closer. Roz recognised the man who had followed her in Covent Garden, the same man who had been outside the house on Scarborough Lane.

P L Crompton

How was it possible for him to be here? Had he also found a way into this time or was he a double of the other man just as she was Rosamund's double? She had to know.

With no clear idea of what she would do when she met him, Roz grabbed the parasol and ran down the carpeted stairs. Her feet made the same muffled sound as the person who ran past her when she was in the museum with Charlie. She wondered if the day guard or visitors to the museum heard her pass.

There was no footman to open the door. She pulled hard on the heavy oak and the door swung open so quickly she almost fell. Then she was outside, running towards the yews, but the man was gone. She looked around, but nowhere offered a hiding place. He was unlikely to enter the house via the kitchen for servants would be present. There had to be another door at the other side of the house. She ran in that direction.

Around the corner of the house, Roz found a stone-floored terrace flanked by a low wall. French windows led into the house and a man in a canvas apron washed the panes. He looked at her in surprise.

Breathless from her mad rush, she asked, "Did a man come by here?"

He shook his head.

Had the man realised she'd seen him and run away from the house or to the kitchen if the staff knew him? If he was a trader, he might have entered the house that way. Roz couldn't barge into the kitchen to ask questions without having questions asked in return. She cursed herself for not having considered it sooner, and made her way down the steps leading to a path around a small lake. Deep in thought, she walked into the tree-lined area and was unaware of the horseman until he was almost upon her.

"Good morning, Miss Oldham." David Ridley dismounted and led his horse forward. "I hoped I would see you."

She wasn't a Scarbane, but an Oldham. "Mr Ridley." In daylight, he was as handsome as in candlelight. He doffed the tall hat he wore, and she saw again that his hair was a shade of sandy blond with no trace of yellow. Skin tanned, eyes the colour of a summer sky regarded her with a warmth that robbed her of breath.

"Permit me to walk with you." He led his mount and walked beside Roz. "On such a sunny afternoon, I thought you would be paying calls with the other ladies."

She would have if she'd been here. "I haven't yet acquired all the niceties of ladies in my position."

"That is to your credit, Miss Rosamund. I find most ladies affect an air of sophistication most unbecoming."

"I hope I shall never become as they." Roz was very aware of him, of the way their elbows brushed. To cover her self-consciousness, she opened her parasol and rested it against her shoulder.

"Do you walk here often?" he asked.

Did she? Did Rosamund? "Some days, if the weather is fine. Do you visit often?" That question was safe. Confined to the nursery, Rosamund wouldn't know who visited the house.

"I have come infrequently in the past, but I shall come more often now. If you permit me, of course."

"If I—" Surprised, Roz looked at him. *Good grief!* He was asking to keep company with her.

"I will come only if it is your wish." He took her hand and raised it to his lips. "I pray you wish it."

"I. . . . Of course." Her heart was doing back flips and her hand trembled in his. "I should very much enjoy your company, Mr Ridley."

His smile was her reward. "I would like to paint you as you look now, with the sun dappling the trees at your back. The curve of your cheek . . . rounded yet, with the innocence of childhood. But your eyes tell me you are a woman."

Roz didn't know what to say. If any of the men she from her own time spoke to her this way, she would laugh and expect them to be teasing her, but in David's eyes, there was nothing but a warm regard. Well, maybe not nothing, there was something; something that brought heat to her face.

"There is to be a ball this evening at Ridley Manor. It is customary for Lady Scarbane and Miss Adele to attend. Shall you accompany them?"

"Yes, I shall attend."

He glanced away from her along the path and then raised her fingers to his lips a second time. "I shall count the hours until we meet again."

Disappointment must have shown in her face. "Are you leaving?"

He looked away and released her hand. "I think it best."

Roz looked in the direction that drew his attention. A horseman galloped towards them. Alex Mindon. He reined in the powerful black stallion and dismounted.

"Miss Rosamund." He touched the brim of his hat to her. "Ridley, I didn't expect to find you here."

"I was on the point of leaving." David bowed to Roz then leapt into the saddle. "Farewell, Miss Rosamund, until we meet again."

Roz watched David ride away and then she turned to Alex Mindon, eyes blazing. "How dare you!"

"And how dare you!" His face was black with anger. "You have always flouted convention. While you were in the nursery this caused no great concern, but you are a young lady now and you must behave with more circumspection."

Circumspection. That word again. *How dare he!*

"To be seen in the company of any man without a chaperone is unacceptable, worst of all, to be seen with David Ridley without a chaperone!" He caught her elbow and forced her around so they walked towards the house. "You will not entertain his presence again."

Roz tugged free of his grip and hurried ahead of him. "I shall see whoever I wish."

"No, you will not." He hauled the stallion forward and caught up with her.

"What is there against Mr Ridley? Is he married? Is he a thief? Is he a murderer? I am aware he is without fortune, but I do consider it a reason why I should not speak to him or be in his company." Roz gained the foot of the steps and started up.

"You place yourself in danger when you are with him." Lord Mindon swung onto the horse and their eyes were on a level when she turned to face him.

"What danger? That of being uncircumspect, of flouting convention? You hint at other things, but you do not speak clearly that I may know what this danger is."

"Accept the advice I give you."

"I understand Mr Ridley is of good family."

"He is the second son. As such, instead of wasting his time with brushes and paints, he should be in uniform."

"A soldier like my uncle? To fight what war?"

"There is much upheaval across the sea. You know of the revolution in France."

"Ah," Roz knew this part of history. "You fear Napoleon."

"He has set his brother as King in Rome. Our regiments are preparing to defend our shores lest he attempt to claim this land for France."

"Napoleon will never invade Britain. He will try to invade Russia, but the cold there will defeat his army and he will turn back." Too late, Roz realised she had said more than she should have. His eyes, the darkest blue she had ever seen, now appeared black, and showed— Was he surprised? Dismayed? Wary?

"Are you now able to predict the future, Miss Rosamund?"

The eyes mocking her and the lips twisted into a smirk, infuriated her. "Perhaps," she challenged.

"Such games should be left in the nursery. I caution you against further revelations or predictions of the future."

Eyes blazing, she cried, "Who are you to tell me what not to do? Just who do you think you are?"

"I am the man you are to marry."

**

CHAPTER TEN

Not on your Nellie!
When hell freezes over!
When pigs fly!

Roz should have hurled those words at Alex Mindon's back as he heeled the stallion away. Instead, speechless for once, she flopped onto the steps, heedless of the dust clinging to the white gown and the way the parasol rolled down to rest in the mud of the path. Luckily, there was no one to admonish her for behaving in a manner unsuitable for a lady or she might have resorted to violence.

Marry him? *Good grief!* He was bossy, arrogant, over confident, more so than men from her own time. He was the last person on earth she would choose as a husband; but women of this time were under their father's control, or in her case, Uncle Stephen's. Poor Rosamund, wherever she was. They would raise her to expect her husband chosen for her; she had none of Roz's freedom of choice. And what of Adele? How would she react when she heard her cousin was to marry the man she adored?

Roz must to put a stop to it. She would confront Stephen Oldham and tell him it was impossible, or—

Did she have to? She could go through the mirror and never come back. If she did, she would never see David again nor retrieve Minnie's brooch from Madame Sauvé. With Alex Mindon's arrival, she hadn't even asked David if he could tell her where the diva lived. Whatever their objections, she must see David again and, though she didn't know when

Rosamund's marriage was to take place, somehow she had to delay it.

Roz retrieved the parasol and continued up the steps. Stephen Oldham had set out for a ride but he might have returned. She would confront him as soon as possible.

Roz entered the house by the French windows and found herself in the formal withdrawing room. Armless chairs and ornate tables filled a room panelled in pale silk. She gave the place no more than a cursory glance but hurried through to the hallway beyond and to the back of the house.

The door where Charlie checked the padlocks and bolts opened at her touch and led into in a glass-walled room with a few chairs placed among several palms. It led to a formal garden with low, boxed hedges forming an intricate pattern around beds of roses and other flowering plants. To her left, an opening led to the kitchen garden. Beyond that, the roofs of other buildings peeped between the trees. She made in their direction.

In the stable yard, a man sweeping the cobbles eyed her in surprise and touched the peak of his cap.

"Is Mr Oldham back?" Roz asked.

The surprise in his eyes deepened. "Major be gone, Miss."

"When will he be back?"

"A week, Miss, mebbe more."

Her shoulders sagged. He must have gone to join his regiment. "Thank you." The man's eyes widen with even greater surprise. Clearly one did not thank servants. She returned to the house.

What now? Stephen Oldham would be away a week or more but his niece's wedding would hardly take place without him there to give her away. She relaxed as the dreaded wedding faded into the future instead of looming imminently. She had breathing space. Nevertheless, the habit of a lifetime, the habit of her own society, settled into her whole being in a wave of indignant anger. How dare they arrange her marriage! How dare they assume she would fall in with their plans without a murmur!

However, this was not her time. This was not her society. Because Rosamund had lived in the nursery, Roz doubted the girl had met Alex Mindon. She might dislike him as much as Roz did, but she would not demur. Rosamund would accept her lot because, in this society, she had no choice.

*

Late in the afternoon, Imogen and Adele flounced in and Roz was waiting in the hall to confront them. Imogen's face bore an expression that boded ill for anyone who wanted to speak to her about something as important as the refusal to comply with an arranged marriage. Behind her, Adele looked ready to burst into tears.

Good. Whatever made her unhappy paid her back for telling Uncle Ruffy Roz agreed to take supper with David Ridley.

Immediately, she felt contrite. Adele was just being true to the way they taught her—above all else, they must consider the family honour. Sorry for the girl, Roz would not add to her misery by telling her they contracted Rosamund to marry Lord Mindon.

Imogen shot a black look in Roz's direction and swept up the stairs. When Adele glanced at Roz, her bottom lip trembled with the tears she obviously wanted to shed but refused to do in public. She walked past Roz without a word and followed her mother.

The attending maid entered the hall. Eyes downcast, she took herself off to the nether regions. Nevertheless, the sly smile on her face told Roz she knew what happened to upset the other two. Maids gossiped. Jenny would learn what happened and Roz would wheedle it out of her. In silence, she returned to Rosamund's bedroom.

Was it possible word of her upcoming marriage had leaked out? It was unlikely a formal announcement had taken place, unless— Would they have announced it at the party given for Rosamund's seventeenth birthday, the night

Roz left early? Would they announce it without her being present? That was days ago. Adele would surely have overcome her shock by now but the girl looked as if she had only just learned something to upset her.

Roz contained her impatience long enough to allow Jenny to hear the gossip, but before she rang the bell to summon her, the maid appeared in the doorway.

"Lady Imogen wishes to see you in her sitting room."

The pattern of speech was not Jenny's and Roz assumed she was quoting Imogen word for word. "Do you know what this is about?"

"No, Miss." Jenny stood to one side at the open door, her eyes lowered, as Roz swept past.

"Which room?"

"The sitting room, Miss."

Roz walked towards the stairs.

"No, Miss," Jenny called after her. "Over there." She pointed along the hallway.

Roz walked back. "Which door?"

"Oh, Miss!" Jenny's face crumpled and her lips clamped together as if she too, were fighting back tears. She walked ahead of Roz, stopped outside one of the doors, and pointed.

Roz tapped and entered.

Imogen stood at the window, her back to Roz, and spoke in a clipped tone. "Close the door."

Roz did as Imogen asked and looked around as she moved to the centre of the room. A book lay on a small table, embroidery rested on a sewing basket, and a half-finished watercolour sat on an easel to one side of the window. "You asked to see me."

Imogen faced Roz, eyes blazing. "I wish to God I had never laid eyes on you. I wish you never entered our lives. You are an abomination. You bring shame upon this family."

Taken aback, Roz stare open-mouthed at Imogen. Recovered, she asked, "What did I do?"

"What did you do? You foolish child, you stupid girl, what did you not do?"

Roz reacted with anger of her own. "Stop talking in riddles. Tell me what I did or say no more."

"Do you dare talk back to me?"

"Say what you have to say."

"I hardly know where to begin. When you first came to us, we excused much of your behaviour and laid it at the door of the ghastly deaths of your parents and the destruction of your home. As time passed, your behaviour did not improve. I blamed it on your mother, poor soul, not knowing what she had to contend with all those years. They spoiled you—my own brother, too; God rest his soul. They gave you too much freedom. They educated you in a way unsuitable for a girl. I excused that, too, believing they did so because there was no son to manage the estate, but they ruined you! I tried to guide you in ways more suitable for a young lady, but all you do is bring our name into disrepute. You are wayward. I tried to curb your excesses, and your penchant for wandering off with total disregard for convention or for the demands society makes upon us all. At times, you have dressed as a man and ridden astride, galloping through the countryside with your hair in disarray. I burned the clothes, and I hope you paid the stable boy well because I dismissed him for giving them to you."

Despite Imogen's diatribe, Roz felt a glow of satisfaction. Rosamund had some spunk. Hurrah for Rosamund! The pride must have shown in her eyes.

"How dare you!" Imogen took a step closer and raised her hand. She let it drop at the look in Roz's eye. "Even now, when this family is the talk of finer society, you show nothing but defiance. Lady Edrington wasted no time in telling everyone you were not in the receiving line at the party we gave in honour of your birthday. She spared no detail when speaking of the way you behaved toward Ridley. Singing to him. Smiling at him. You have no shame!"

"Should I wish to smile at Mr Ridley, I will do so." Roz stood her ground. "And this evening I intend to dance with him at the ball."

Imogen's hand rose swiftly towards her cheek, but Roz was prepared. She caught the older woman's wrist and forced the hand down.

"How dare you! You, who live on my husband's charity," Imogen stepped back. "As for the ball— I shall make your regrets known to Lord and Lady Ridley. You will not be attending."

"I *will* attend. I shall accompany you in the carriage or I will saddle a horse and ride there. The choice is yours, but I will attend the ball." With that, Roz marched from the room.

Her anger abated before she was half way down the hall. Now, Roz was angry with herself. She meant to confront Imogen with the matter of her arranged marriage with Lord Mindon, but Imogen's attack shocked her into forgetting everything but the need to stand up to her. Lord help Rosamund if she'd had to contend with the woman for years, and be forced to do so again when she showed up and took Roz's place.

Roz turned and stomped back to Imogen's sitting room.

At Imogen's answer to her tap, Roz entered and had the impression the older woman, a moment before, had been sitting with her head in her hands. She stood to face Roz.

"Yes? Is there more insolence you wish to throw at me?"

For a moment, Roz pitied the woman. She had every right to be angry. Roz did not belong here and flouting convention brought her to the notice of influential people like Lady Edrington. She had to behave more circumspectly. *Good grief, that word again!*

"I came to discuss the marriage arranged between me and Lord Mindon."

The surprise on Imogen's face appeared genuine. She glanced at the wall separating her sitting room from the next bedroom and kept her voice low. "Marriage? I know nothing of such an arrangement."

Adele's room must be behind the wall and Imogen wanted to avoid upsetting her. Roz lowered her voice. "Then who has arranged it?"

"If what you say is true, it must be Stephen. Did you speak to him?"

"He left before I learned of it."

"Who told you?"

"Lord Mindon himself."

Imogen dropped onto a chair. "It must cost Stephen dearly to make such an arrangement."

"How so?"

"We felt—I felt arranging a suitable match for you would be impossible. Word of your behaviour has spread, I regret to say." She glanced at Roz. "You have no great fortune, although a reasonable dowry can be arranged, but— Alexander Mindon!"

"My sentiments exactly. I will not marry him so Adele is free to make a play for him."

"Make a—? You have the oddest way of speaking."

"Adele adores Lord Mindon and she will be upset to hear of the proposed marriage. Be so good as to tell her I will never marry the man."

"Think carefully, Rosamund. While such a marriage would cause my daughter grief, Stephen has betrothed you to one of the wealthiest men in London. It is an honour he should ask for you."

"I do not love him. In fact, I would go so far as to say I loathe him."

"You have spent little time in his company to form such a strong opinion."

If only Roz could tell her that Alex Mindon reminded her of the men she met in her own era. "Time will not soften my feelings for him."

"If you refuse to marry him. . . ."

"He will be free to ask for Adele's hand. Surely Ste— Uncle Stephen can negotiate an arrangement to allow Adele to take my place."

"Alexander Mindon. . . ." Imogen shook her head as if in wonder. "I never expected such a thing." She looked up at Roz. "You do know arranging another marriage for you will be almost impossible."

"That will please me no end. I do not intend to enter into an arranged marriage."

"Lord Mindon pays you a great honour."

"So you said, but I tell you the wedding will not take place."

"I ask you to at least think about it."

Roz shook her head. "No, I will not."

"Your uncle is not due to return for ten days. Will you agree to say nothing until then, especially to Adele?"

"Of course, I see no reason to cause her unnecessary grief. The betrothal can end without Adele knowing about it. However, I reserve the right to speak to Lord Mindon."

"Be careful. Oh, please be careful."

Roz did not miss the beseeching look in Imogen's eyes, evident in her voice. "Is there something of which I am not aware?"

"Only that Alexander is a powerful man."

"Could he harm the family?"

Imogen looked away. "Perhaps."

"Then I will be careful. I have no wish to harm you."

Imogen stared at Roz. "Do you mean that or are you trying to placate me?"

"I will not knowingly harm you or the family."

"Despite what you have done in the past?"

"I regret any concern I have caused you."

Eyes filled with tears, Imogen gave a shaky smile. "Thank you, Rosamund."

Roz nodded and left.

In her own room, she threw off the fichu and dropped onto the bed. What would Rosamund do? Would she want to marry such a powerful man? They introduced Roz to Alex Mindon on the night of Rosamund's seventeenth birthday party, so the girl had probably never met him.

It was odd she had not seen Rosamund. Did the girl know someone was impersonating her and was taking advantage of the situation? Where would she hide?

"Rosamund, where are you? Where are you hiding?" Roz whispered to the silent room. Then she sat up.

Rosamund must be somewhere in the house. If she had taken a horse and ridden away, the stable hands would know because a mount would be missing. Of course, she could have walked out. Roz sprang from the bed and went to the wardrobe to rummage among the carefully arranged satin slippers. She found a pair of sturdy boots and at the back of an assortment of flimsy gowns hung a travelling cloak. If Rosamund wandered away, she had done so without wearing suitable clothing. So where was she?

Who would blame her for escaping Imogen's dominance? Despite her tear-filled gratitude a moment ago, Imogen had a low opinion of Rosamund. Perhaps Rosamund knew of the intended marriage with Lord Mindon and her only recourse was to keep out of sight. Roz had to find her and help her. Where should she start looking? In the attics? In the cellars? Would she hide in one of the stables or barns? She would have to eat. Did she creep to the kitchen when all were in bed? Did one of the servants smuggle food to her? Jenny? She could hardly ask Jenny if she knew where Rosamund was when Roz herself posed as Rosamund.

As if conjured by the thought of food, Jenny appeared with a tray, and placed it on a bedside table. "Cook said as I was to bring this. Will yer eat, Miss?"

Roz was ravenous. Obviously, she was not to eat in the dining room with Imogen and Adele and Jenny had smuggled this repast to her. She dropped onto the bed and attacked the soup. "Thank Cook for me. I really needed this." She eyed the platter of cold meat and cheese, the hunk of buttered bread, and the cup of cordial. "Which gown should I wear to the ball?"

Jenny paused in her tidying of the room to look at her.

"I see you've been told I'm not going. Well, Jenny, I shall be going, so please take out whichever gown you feel is suitable."

"Yes, Miss."

Roz noted the smile on Jenny's face when the maid crossed to the wardrobe and took out a white gown strewn with pearls about the neckline. Whether she suspected Roz was not Rosamund, Roz's behaviour was in keeping with Rosamund's. Given the way Imogen spoke to Jenny, no doubt the maid revelled in the way Roz defied Imogen as she herself dared not.

"Jenny?" Roz set the empty soup bowl aside. "Did the other maid tell you what upset Aunt Imogen and Adele this afternoon?"

Jenny froze and her face turned pale.

"Come on. Maids gossip and know everything so tell me."

"I heard Madam was told not to take yer visiting as yer would—would taint their daughters' wiv yer hoydenish ways." Jenny stiffened, as if expecting Roz to slap her.

"Who said this to her?"

"Lady Edrington, Miss."

"That pleases me no end because the last thing I want to do is spend boring hours with boring people like Lady Edrington."

"Yes, Miss. I'll go bring water, shall I, Miss?"

Roz nodded her mouth full. She ate quickly; aware Imogen and Adele might take off in the carriage without her. If they did, she would hoof it to Ridley Hall rather than miss the opportunity to meet David again. Surely there, in his own home, no one could keep her from speaking to him.

Jenny returned with a jug of hot water and filled the china bowl behind the screen. Roz washed her face and hands, drying them on the linen towel the maid held. Next, Jenny dropped the gown over Roz's head. *The ingénue*, Roz thought as she studied herself in the mirror. Purity with a promise is what the low neckline suggested. No fichu covered the swell of breasts showing above the neckline but there were fine white stockings to hide her ankles if her hem should rise while dancing. She couldn't help but smile.

"I'll do yer 'air now, Miss Rosamund," Jenny said from behind her.

Roz removed the pins from her hair as she crossed the room to sit at the dressing table. She reached for a brush. "Where are the brushes, Jenny?"

Jenny lifted aside the fichu from where Roz tossed it earlier. The dressing table was bare of brushes and hand mirror. Jenny's mouth trembled. "I didn't take 'em. Oh, say yer believe me. I didn't take 'em, Miss."

"I'm sure you didn't. Can you fetch some from another bedroom?"

"Yes, but, where did they went?"

Did Rosamund come to get them while everyone was out of the house? "Just get brushes from one of the guest rooms, Jenny." Aware of the sharpness in her voice, she added, "Please."

While Jenny was gone, Roz opened the jewellery box. She had no idea what should be in there, probably nothing more than the tangle of amber beads and seed pearls. A girl of seventeen would not have much jewellery unless Rosamund inherited some from her mother. If so, they had disappeared along with the amethyst brooch.

Jenny came back with a set of brushes and began to arrange Roz's hair. The girl's reflection showed she had been crying. She still gave an occasional sniff and rubbed her nose on her sleeve.

Jenny had worked on Roz's hair only hours earlier. The brushes were there then, so somebody stole them while she was out of the house. Did the man she saw in the garden enter the house to steal them? "We won't mention the missing brushes to anyone, all right?"

"Yes, Miss. Thank you, Miss."

"I know you didn't steal them. If anyone asks, tell them I took the brushes and gave them to the poor." Jenny's reflection showed her eyes were like saucers. "I did not. I don't know where they went; nevertheless, I know you did not take them."

"Thank you, Miss."

"Do you know when Lady Imogen is due to leave?"

"After dinner, Miss. Madam and Miss Adele was dressed when they come down."

"Have they ordered the carriage?"

"Timmins brought un to the door when I come with the water." Jenny finished arranging her hair, brought Roz a pair of satin slippers from the wardrobe, and then took an ostrich-feather fan from a chest in the corner. Roz slid her feet into the slippers and held out her wrist for Jenny to tie the fan to it with a length of ribbon.

"Am I all set?"

"Miss?"

"Is there anything else I'm likely to need? A wrap?"

"Oh!" Jenny scurried back to the chest and returned with a silk scarf. Placed over Roz's shoulders the ends reached almost to the floor.

"Right." Roz walked to the door. "Don't wait up for me. I can undress myself." After a quick glance at Jenny's startled face, she stepped into the hallway. From the dining room, the sounds of dishes clattering and utensils clicking against china covered whatever noise Roz made as she descended the stairs and left by the front door.

The coachman slouched on the high seat behind the horses leapt down as she approached. He opened the door and let down the steps so she could enter. Roz thanked him and settled herself in a dark corner.

Minutes later, Imogen and Adele left the house with a maid. Imogen wore a tight-lipped look but Adele looked excited, her creamy complexion flushed. Roz shrank into her corner as a footman opened the door. Imogen entered without a word of thanks to the man who gave her his shoulder to pull against while she climbed into the coach. As she fussed with her skirts, Adele followed Imogen in. When Adele saw Roz, she gave a small cry of dismay.

"Mama! Rosamund is here. You said she would not be coming."

"Hush." Imogen settled herself as the maid entered the coach loaded down with lap blankets and a bag that held all the paraphernalia Imogen and Adele would need during the evening: hairpins, brushes, dusting powder, toilet water, lip salve, clean stockings, peppermint leaves to sweeten the breath and—should Imogen have the vapours—a vial of smelling salts.

"Good evening, Adele. Aunt Imogen." In the darkness, Roz smiled at their discomfort. "I decided to join you after all."

"So I see." Imogen fell silent and Adele followed suit.

It was not late but without street lighting Roz could see only trees outside the rumbling coach. Even with her eyes closed, she would have known they were crossing another road because the coach juddered and jumped over the ruts. Imogen clung to a strap hanging beside the door and Roz followed her example.

What was she to say to Lord Mindon that would not bring down his wrath on the family? She—or Rosamund— had already done enough harm, it seemed. Roz had done nothing that would have been out of place in her own time and she doubted Rosamund was half as black as painted. The restrictions imposed by this society were, to her mind, idiotic. Still, she had to remember this was their world. She wondered if her appearance among them would change the course of history. She had to be careful, and she had to find Rosamund to sound her out on what was best to do.

**

CHAPTER ELEVEN

Charlie's words haunted Roz during the carriage ride and she grew uneasy. What if she was moving too far from the place where the time dimensions met? What if they drifted apart and she had no chance to get back to her own world. What if she couldn't reach the mirror and escape if anything went wrong?

Lost in fearful thoughts, Roz became aware they had reached Ridley Manor only when the coach came to a halt at the foot of steps well lit by lanterns. The maid scrambled out, then, aided by a footman, Imogen emerged and waited for the maid to arrange her gown and drape the long, flimsy scarf across her shoulders. Adele stepped out next and the maid repeated the procedure. When Roz emerged, the maid had already moved off to where Roz suspected the kitchen entrance lay. She fluffed her own skirt and nonchalantly draped the scarf to hang from her elbows. Head held high, she walked up the steps and entered the manor.

A quick glance along the receiving line showed David helping an elderly woman make her precarious way into the ballroom. He glanced over his shoulder and smiled an acknowledgement that brought a grin to her own lips as she approached her hosts.

Lord Ridley was unmistakable. An older version of David, he bowed over her hand when Imogen introduced her. Copying Adele, Roz gave a small curtsy then moved on to Lady Ridley. The woman's eyes were cold and close set above a long nose that seemed to give the world a disdainful sniff. The smile froze on Roz's face. She bobbed her head and moved on. David's older brother was on the stout side. His features were like his mother's and equally cold as he surveyed her down the length of his elongated nose. He stared but didn't attempt to bow over her hand.

An imp of mischief bade Roz give him her sunniest smile and curtsied as low as she could while keeping her balance. "Such a pleasure to meet you, Mr Ridley."

Without waiting for an answer, she rose and flounced after Imogen and Adele. Arrogant men always had an adverse effect on her. What did David's brother think he was—God's gift to women? With features like The Penguin, Batman's arch enemy, no doubt he thought himself a fine catch and expected his wife to be beautiful and slim and—and capable of bearing children by the bucketful.

Good grief," Roz muttered and Adele frowned at her.

Two women greeted Imogen when they entered the ballroom. While making small talk, they cast quick glances at Roz. She ignored them, tried to dismiss the plethora of perfumes, and looked around the room. A group of musicians occupied one corner and a few couples executed a dance Roz could never have named.

"He is here." Adele breathed at her side.

Roz followed the direction of her gaze.

Alex Mindon stood surrounded by a gaggle of women with their daughters in tow. Dressed in sombre black, he was in sharp contrast to the flutter of pastels. The sardonic smile he gave her caused Roz to toss her head and look away.

"He smiled at me," Adele whispered.

"Adele, Rosamund, come." Imogen led them to a vacant chaise and settled herself in the centre. Adele took the chair alongside, forcing Roz to stand.

David appeared with a servant carrying a chair. "Welcome to my home, Miss Rosamund. May I offer you this chair?"

"How kind of you, Mr Ridley." Roz sat. "I am happy to be here."

"Lady Scarbane, Miss Adele; how are you this evening?" Despite the chill evident in his voice, he gave them a small bow.

"We are well." Imogen answered for them both.

Roz smiled up at him. Tonight he was wearing a velvet frockcoat in a shade of blue the exact colour of his eyes.

"Will you do me the honour of allowing me to enter my name on your dance card, Miss Rosamund?"

Dance card? Roz noticed Adele had a small card and a length of charcoal encased in a silver holder dangling from her left wrist. *Damn! Why hadn't Jenny reminded her?* However, Jenny wouldn't know the formalities any better than Roz did.

"I regret, Mr Ridley, I have forgotten my card. However, any dance you wish to claim is promised to you." Beside her, Imogen gasped.

David's eyes held a glint of mischief. "Then I will claim you for the first gavotte and the second waltz if I may."

Gavotte? Good grief, what was a gavotte and how did one dance it? She smiled and hoped her confusion didn't show. "It will be my pleasure." Beside her Imogen cleared her throat loudly.

"The weather is holding out nicely," Imogen said to the air. "It is warm for the time of year."

"If it becomes uncomfortably warm, there is a terrace beyond the conservatory where you may take the air." David suggested.

Roz noted his attention had never left her and the suggestion of taking the air was for her benefit. "I may well take advantage later in the evening." She eyed him intently and saw he nodded. That was it then. Under Imogen's watchful eye, she had arranged a tryst with him.

From behind David, Alex Mindon said, "Good evening, Lady Scarbane. Miss Adele. And good evening to you, Miss Rosamund."

Roz refused to respond.

"Alexander." Imogen held out a limp hand, palm down. She beamed as he took her fingers and bent over them. "How good it is to see you."

"The pleasure is mine." Lord Mindon bowed over Imogen and Adele's hands and threw a mocking glance at Roz before bowing over hers. Then he spoke to David. "Ridley, Honoria Beaumont has some questions for you on the matter of—let me see—watercolours, I believe. It is quite urgent."

An angry flush darkened David's face at the dismissal. He bowed to Roz. "If you'll excuse me."

As David walked away, Roz glared at Alex Mindon and spoke through clenched teeth. "I think you came to claim me for this dance."

"Rosamund!" Imogen's cry, sharp with shock, came from under her breath.

For a moment, he looked taken aback, but he recovered quickly. "You are right, of course, Miss Rosamund. But before we take to the floor, I should like to claim your cousin for other dances." His back to Roz, he took the card Adele held out.

As he entered his name on Adele's card, Roz looked around the cavernous room. People stood or sat in small groups, the women fanning themselves or gossiping behind their fans. There was no sign of David and she had no idea who Honoria Beaumont was or where she would be.

"Young lady." A man in full military regalia stood before her. He was florid of face with a drooping moustache slightly more yellow than the white of his hair. "If you are not spoken for, may I claim this waltz?"

"I should be delighted, sir." She rose and stepped into his arms. From the corner of her eye, she saw Alex turn in her direction as the military man swung her onto the dance floor. She beamed at her partner. "I am Rosamund Oldham, niece to Lady Scarbane."

"Are you, by Jove? Well, I am pleased to make your acquaintance, young miss. I am Captain Josiah Wilmington."

"I thought all military gentlemen had joined their regiments. I am pleased to see one did not." She smiled playfully at him.

He laughed. "A cheeky young minx, are you?"

"I am told I must be more circumspect."

"By Lady Scarbane, no doubt."

"You have the truth of it."

"Thankfully, I have not had the pleasure of making her acquaintance." He leaned closer to her ear. "But not a word to her, eh?"

"Not a whisper of it shall pass my lips." Behind him, Alex Mindon walked away from Imogen and Adele.

Again, the Captain chuckled and waltzed her around the room. "Not just a minx, but a wise one. Your kind is rare, my dear."

When the music ended, he tucked her hand under his elbow and covered it with his own as he led her from the floor. "You started the evening on a happy note for me." When they reached her chair, Captain Wilmington bent over her hand. "I thank you for a delightful interlude."

"How dare you!" Imogen spat the whisper as Captain Wilmington walked away. "Lord Mindon was quite put out."

Roz fixed her with a stern look. "There is a pact between us that precludes this type of conversation, in public or in private."

"How dare you speak to Mama thus," Adele whispered.

"How I dare is known to your mama." Roz stood. "I believe I will take the air."

Roz skirted the dancers and walked quickly to the conservatory. Ignoring the curious glances flashed her way; she moved among the palms, gained the terrace and slowed her pace. Night sounds drowned out the murmur of voices and the muted strains of the string quartet. Apart from an owl's hoot, she could not identify the other bird cries. If she stayed here, she would learn to recognise them. If she stayed here. . . .

Stayed here? Perhaps stranded here. *Good grief.* And marry arrogant Alex Mindon?

However, if she stayed here and avoided the marriage, she might get to know David better. He was so different from any man she'd met. There was gentleness to him; a romantic side he wasn't embarrassed to show. In addition to being considerate, attentive, and respectful, he was gorgeous. He was all a man should be and she couldn't help but wonder what he'd be like in bed; probably loving, gentle and considerate.

Her thoughts on him, when the door behind her opened, Roz expected to see David. Instead, Alex Mindon emerged, the sombreness of his clothes blending with the pools of darkness between the lanterns.

"You!" Roz made to pass him and return to the house.

He caught her arm. "Were you expecting someone else, my dear?

"Anyone would be preferable to you." She tugged her arm free. "But since you are here, there are one or two things I wish to say."

"Evidently these are not pleasant things."

"Your rudeness to David Ridley is inexcusable. You are a guest in this house and should behave as such."

He gave a low laugh. "You are right, of course."

"The idea amuses you?"

"What amuses me is that you of all people should take me to task for a breach of good manners."

"I have never pretended to be other than what I am." Well, that wasn't strictly true but as far as he was aware, she was Rosamund.

"I do not suffer fools gladly and I make no apology."

"David Ridley is no fool," she protested.

"No, he is not. David Ridley is a very clever man."

Roz hadn't expected him to say that. It stunned her into silence.

"Did you feel better when you accepted Captain Wilmington's invitation? Did you enjoy snubbing me after asking me to dance?"

"Yes."

Again he laughed.

"I'm glad you find it amusing," she spat.

"You amuse me, Rosamund. You infuriate me; you amaze, astonish and startle me."

"And we quarrel. Every time we meet, we quarrel. Why do you wish to marry me when we obviously cannot agree on anything?"

"Of all the emotions you arouse in me, boredom is not an issue."

"We have spent little time together. You may discover I am the most boring creature on God's earth."

"Some things are singularly impossible. You could never be boring. You are intriguing and aggravating—"

"And I have acquired a distasteful reputation by all accounts. You would do better to ask for Adele's hand. I will gladly stand aside."

"Adele is a milksop as are so many women paraded before me by their proud mamas."

"You would find any one of them easier to deal with."

"Of that I have no doubt."

"Why would you wish to marry someone with whom you will be in constant disagreement, with someone who flouts convention and thumbs her nose at society?"

"Because the challenge of taming such a woman would be diverting."

She glared at him. "You arrogant, narcissistic, conceited, pompous ass!"

He laughed low in his throat. "I enjoy bandying words with you." He caught her by the shoulders and drew her close. "Even more, I will enjoy making love to you."

Roz kicked him on the shin, sadly aware that, with the soft satin slippers she wore, it hurt her more than it hurt him. But it was enough for him to release her. "You haven't a chance in hell. I would sooner marry the lowliest servant in your house than marry you." She stepped away from him. "I demand to be—" She intended to say *released*, but what would he do to the family? How would they suffer at his hands? She had no knowledge of the intrigues that might exist.

"What do you demand to be?"

What could she say? How could she say anything that wouldn't bring harm to a family that had done her no wrong?

"Rosamund? I hardly expected to find you tongue tied."

"What . . . ? How . . . ?" Roz took a deep breath. "You are aware I have no dowry to speak of."

"That is of no concern to me."

"And I am no great beauty to be thus pursued."

"No, but you have a pleasing countenance."

"And—and because of the tragedy I witnessed, I am—I am prone to—to behave with little concern for what people may think."

"I am prepared to make allowances for you."

She whirled to face the darkness of the garden. *The sod, he'd make allowances, would he?* She wished she had been wearing her winter boots when she kicked him, the ones with the steel toecap. As it was, her toes hurt while he hadn't even flinched.

She sensed he had moved to stand close behind her. Then his hands were on her shoulders and she stiffened. "I remind you, Lord Mindon, propriety dictates you do not lay a finger on me until our wedding night."

"As you wish. But you must be aware of the convention that allows a man to kiss his chosen wife at the announcement of their betrothal." He spun Roz around and she found herself in his arms with his lips on hers. She struggled, aware of his greater strength, and he released her abruptly.

She wiped her mouth with the back of her hand. "Get away from me!" she hissed. "You know I do not love you, that I will never love you. Why do you persist with this?"

He gave no answer. Instead, he said, "After supper this evening, I have asked Lord Ridley to announce our engagement. I shall see you then." With that, he walked back into the house.

**

CHAPTER TWELVE

Tonight? With Adele there to hear. Roz clamped a hand to her mouth to smother the scream of frustration she ached to throw at the night. If only they would be announcing her betrothal to David instead of that detestable man.

It must not happen. If she wasn't there, it couldn't happen. High and mighty Lord Alexander Mindon would be a laughing-stock if he announced his engagement and his intended victim wasn't there for them to congratulate her. She had only to get back to Scarbane House to be safe. She would have time to search for Rosamund and have the girl make her wishes known.

Roz lifted her skirts and raced across the terrace. She rounded a corner of the house and ran into David. He opened his arms and she ran to him. He didn't ask her the cause of her distress but held her until she was calmer. Aware of his arms around her, the strength in the shoulder beneath her cheek, she moaned, "Oh, David."

"Do you wish to speak of the matter that has upset you?" he asked; his breath warm as his voice against her ear.

She dared not tell him, not yet.

When she didn't speak, he went on, "Is there aught I can do to help? Charge me with any course of action to set the matter to right and I will devote myself to the cause."

What could he do? In this world, men called each other out and duelled, but something told her Alex Mindon would prove the better swordsman. She would not place David in danger.

"I must go home." She drew back and looked up at him. "Will you take me?"

"Of course." He brushed a tendril of hair from her cheek and touched the place with his lips. "I will take you anywhere you choose. Do anything you ask of me."

Roz threw her arms around his neck and drew his head down to hers. Their lips met gently at first, and then the passion in his kiss robbed her of breath. Even in the ecstasy and the joy coursing through her like fire, Roz became aware of something else. Like most men, David didn't fumble at the fastenings of her clothes; his hands didn't move to cup her breast; nor did he press her hips against his. Yet, she wanted him to. Every part of her cried out for his touch. She was behaving like the seventeen-year-old she was supposed to be but couldn't curb her feelings, or want to. She had never met a man like David in her own time period.

He released her and ran a finger along the curve of her cheek. "You are so beautiful, Rosamund."

She would have kissed him again, but he placed an arm around her shoulders and led her away from the house.

"Come. I will take you home."

Roz stumbled, as if awakening from a dream, and realised they were walking towards the stables.

Several carriages blocked the driveway and David gave a sigh of dismay. "One o our carriages cannot get through. Will you ride with me?"

Knowing she'd have to hitch her gown up to her waist to mount a horse, Roz hesitated.

"If the nearness to me is unacceptable, I will walk the horse."

He meant her to ride on the same horse. Relieved, she smiled. "I thought we would have to ride separate horses. It is that which caused my hesitation."

He drew her close and kissed the tip of her nose. "Had I my wish, you would never be farther from me than this."

She caught his hand and raised his fingers to her lips. "Your wish is also my wish."

He cupped her face in his hands. "Beloved Rosamund, I will find a way for us to be together."

He kissed her before entering the stables and calling for someone to saddle a horse.

Roz wished the moonlit ride would last forever. Seated side-saddle in front of David, held close to his heart, she huddled beneath the cloak he wrapped around them. Close by, an owl hooted and startled her. David tightened his hold and brushed his lips brushed to cheek. "You are with me. There is nothing to fear."

She snuggled against him. He kept the horse to a walking pace, as if he, too, had no wish to hurry this time together. She wanted to know so much about him; she wanted to ask questions, but what would he want to know in return? What would he ask? She could hardly tell him she came from the future, arrived through a mirror, and was impersonating the woman he thought she was.

"Are you cold?" he asked.

"No," she replied, "but thank you for asking."

He looked down and smiled. "You are like a rosebud trembling to open."

She nuzzled his throat. "And you are my knight in shining armour."

"Would that it was so; I would carry you off to my castle and keep you there, alas, I have only my rooms in London."

"You don't live at Ridley Manor?"

"Only for brief visits, I live in London now."

London. Although she was loath to break the spell, she asked if he knew where Madame Sauvé lived.

Beneath her cheek, he stiffened. For a moment, it seemed he wouldn't speak, and then he admitted, "Yes, I know her house in London. Why do you ask?"

"I should like to meet her again." She felt his tension ease.

"I'm sure she would like to meet you again. She was impressed with your accompaniment."

"You have spoken of me with her? Are you friends?"

"She and I are acquaintances. I have been to her house and I can take you there."

"When?"

"Tomorrow. I can bring the carriage to call for you around noon."

Saturday. She had to be at the Nostalgie for the matinee. "Can we go on Sunday?"

"Madame will not receive us on that day, and it is doubtful Lady Scarbane will release you from attending church."

"But I must speak to Madame Sauvé."

"Is the matter of some urgency?"

Was it? When did Charlie say they were closing the Scarborough? In two weeks. "Perhaps it can wait a few days."

"And there will be some difficulty to overcome if you are to accompany me to London."

"What difficulty?"

"Lady Scarbane would not approve. We would have to visit London in secrecy. If the matter can wait, I suggest we call upon Madame Sauvé a week from tomorrow."

"Why then?"

"It is the day of the Scarborough Fair. Had you forgotten?"

"Madame Sauvé mentioned it but," Roz was confused. "My memory. . . . It isn't. . . ."

"I understand. And after what happened. . . ." His arm tightened around her. "Some years ago, Lady Scarbane was prevailed upon to hold a fair in the grounds here. It is a smaller version of that held in Scarborough town, where your family is from. Usually well attended, in such a crowd they will hardly miss you. We could make our escape unobserved."

Roz smiled up at him. "How clever of you."

"But you must make no mention of it to anyone, else we shall be discovered."

"I won't breathe a word." She felt him stiffen again. "What is it?"

"Another horseman and coming from the direction of Ridley Manor at a gallop." He pulled on the reins and heeled the horse into the trees. "It would not do for you to be seen with me. It would do your reputation irreparable harm."

"Do you think whoever it is might be looking for me?"

"They will have noted your absence from the ball. However, I think Lady Scarbane would take every measure to avoid a scandal and not disclose the matter to any but one she trusts." He drew the horse to a halt behind a stout tree. In silence, they waited.

Scarcely daring to breathe, Roz pressed against David.

"Fear not," he whispered. "We shall not be discovered."

The rider came closer, the horse's hooves muffled by the mud of the road. They watched him pass, cloak flapping as he leaned over the mount's neck to spur it faster.

"Lord Mindon." Roz kept her voice low.

"I suspected it would be he your aunt would dispatch in search of you."

"There is—" Dare she ask? Dare she know? "Do you know what connection there is between Lord Mindon and my family?"

"I know very little, and most of it gossip and conjecture."

"Tell me what you know or have heard."

"Alexander Mindon arrived in this part of the world some time ago." David heeled the horse back onto the road and they continued their journey. "He is from the Americas."

"He doesn't speak like an American."

"And how, pray, do those from the Americas speak?"

Blast! She would have to be more careful and not allow the peace she felt in David's presence to lull her. "I don't know, differently." She shrugged. "How long was he there?"

"To the best of my knowledge, no one has ever questioned him."

"How is he connected with the Scarbane family?"

"They say Mindon is descended from a branch of the family. His advice rescued the Scarbanes from financial ruin."

119

"How?"

"The Scarbanes and Oldhams build ships. They built several ships for the Third Coalition against Napoleon. When some countries withdrew and others were defeated, England stood alone and the ships were needed for Nelson's fleet."

Roz felt a surge of pride in the two families as if they were truly her ancestors.

"England has always been a force at sea as Lord Nelson proved. Although he defeated the French and Spanish fleet, he lost his life and many British ships were damaged."

"You say the family was facing financial ruin, yet Scarbane and Oldham ships were sold to the British Navy, so how could that be?"

"Rumour has it that Hugh Scarbane sold a fleet of ships to both the Royal Navy and a group of East India traders. He intended to deliver them to the navy first, buy them back at a lower price when the navy no longer needed them, and deliver them to the traders. Most of the ships were in the forefront of battle along with Nelson's flagship. They limped home, badly damaged. Scarbane was unable to fulfil his contract with the traders and had to return their money."

"So Lord Mindon lent them money."

"Not he."

"Then how did he help them?"

"The shipyard built sailing ships. With Mindon's knowledge, they concentrated on steam and now they are a force to be reckoned with."

Did they bargain off Rosamund to show their gratitude? Presumably, she would return to America with Alex Mindon, never heard of again, never to be an embarrassment to them. Why Rosamund and not Adele who was the elder? Because Imogen wished to keep Adele close by? Did she fear never to see her darling again?

Weary, she let her head fall against David's shoulder. It had been a long day filled with a range of emotions that had drained her. She still had to meet with Imogen who was certain to confront her as soon as she returned from the ball. Roz could hardly slip back through the mirror until then because Imogen would demand to see her. She could escape and let them think she was in hiding, but the confrontation would come eventually and it might as well be over and done.

"Are you tired?" David asked.

"A little," she replied drowsily.

Even she heard the thudding of hooves this time. "Is he coming back?"

"He has had time enough to question the servants at Scarbane House." David heeled the horse back into the trees. "He will be returning to report to Lady Scarbane."

Would the servants believe Roz had gone into hiding? "They won't know I was with you."

"Even if they do, your uncle is away at the moment and Mindon has no reason to call me out."

Oh, but he did. Rosamund was Alex Mindon's promised wife, and he had every right to challenge David to a duel. They must never learn she had been with David. No one must ever know because it would place him in danger.

*

Roz waited for Imogen in the withdrawing room. She helped herself to a glass of port and sat in the winged chair next to a fire little more than a glow. Toes stretched to the warmth, and sipping the wine, her thoughts filled with David. He kissed her so gently when they parted.

Lost in her memories of him, of what he said, of what he did, the wine, and the day filled with unexpected events, lulled Roz into a doze.

She heard the carriage return; heard Imogen imperiously ask the footman for Rosamund's whereabouts. Roz got to her feet when the door opened and both women entered.

"I told you she would be here, Mama." Adele walked purposefully towards Roz.

"Stop there." Roz put up her hand. "You have no part in this, Adele. Please leave."

"You shall not order me about like a servant in my own home."

"Please leave us, Adele," Imogen said evenly as she moved to the middle of the room.

"But Mama—"

"Go." She spoke sharply, her attention on Roz.

Adele left and Imogen eyed the empty glass on the table. "Have you taken to wine now, young miss?"

"I needed it to calm my nerves and to fortify me for this confrontation."

"So you expected a trouncing."

"I expected to give an explanation for my action."

"What explanation could possibly redeem you in my eyes?"

"You know what was to take place tonight? What Lord Mindon planned? What else could I have done?"

"Speak clearly."

"He prevailed upon Lord Ridley to announce our engagement after supper."

The words deflated Imogen's anger. "Is this true? I knew nothing of this."

"Lord Mindon himself told me. You asked me to say nothing of the matter until Uncle Stephen returned and I saw no way of fending off Lord Mindon except by my absence. I trusted you would agree with me."

"That Stephen should agree to such a thing behind my back is—is inconceivable." Imogen lowered herself into a chair. "And Alexander. . . . He said nothing to me, nothing to prepare me."

"Or prepare Adele. If she has made her feelings for Lord Mindon known to her friends, could she have saved face if the announcement was made in their presence?"

"You are right, of course." Imogen's shoulders sagged; she slumped into a chair and gazed into the fire. "It seems I must thank you once again, Rosamund."

"There is no need to thank me. I did it as much for myself as for you and Adele."

"You have had no change of heart towards Alexander?"

"Alex Mindon is the most despicable man I have ever had the misfortune to meet. I shall never marry him."

**

CHAPTER THIRTEEN

The stench of exhaust fumes assailed Roz as she rushed to work. The dust, the greyness of the streets and the sooty buildings were in grim contrast to the way London used to be.

When she arrived at the Nostalgie, there were two messages. The first informed her Agatha would be absent that day, which meant Roz had to be on standby for both performances. The second was from John Waltham. *My Lord's Dilemma* had played to packed audiences for every performance and he wished to celebrate its success by inviting the players and his executive staff to dinner at *Le Epitomé*, one of London's most exclusive restaurants. He chose Sunday of the following week, the day before final rehearsals for *The Dandy*.

Roz was gathering what she needed to go backstage for the matinee performance when Derek arrived in the workroom.

"You got my uncle's invitation, did you?" he asked.

"I did." She picked up the sewing kit.

"Will you be joining us for the dinner?"

"Of course, but why did he decide to do this? He usually throws a cast party after the final performance." A shoddy affair with several bottles of cheap plonk and a buffet set up on the stage.

"There will still be a cast party for everyone involved with the production, but the success of *My Lord's Dilemma* was phenomenal. This added celebration is his way of making it known the Nostalgie's popularity grows by leaps and bounds."

"So our jobs are safe for a while, is that what you mean?" She made to leave, but he barred her path.

"I believe your contract runs until the end of the year."

She felt a quiver of fear. "I've had no complaints thus far, so I hope it will be extended."

"So do I. By the way, I hope you'll let me drive you home from the dinner next week."

Roz stared at him. Did her contract renewal depend on having an affair with Derek? "If your drunken state at the last cast party is anything to judge by, you'll be in no condition to drive." She thrust past and made for the back of the stage.

In the two hours between the matinee and the evening performances, she repaired a tear on Angela's dress for the last act. Jason lost a button while he scrambled to change and it took a while to find one that matched. By then, she had only a few minutes to grab something from the deli a few doors down and bring it back to the theatre. The first act began as she opened her sandwich, very aware of Derek's scrutiny from his place as prompt in the wings.

When the curtain fell on the first act, Roz tucked her feet out of the way as the actors rushed off the stage to change. She watched as Derek supervised the change of scenery, which involved lowering a new backdrop and swivelling the wings so a different surface faced the audience. A good-looking man, tall dark and handsome, but he couldn't compare with David.

They moved some furniture around and replaced one or two pieces. It went smoothly, and Derek was checking off his props list when Granville Smythe arrived ready to make his entrance. The actor ignored Roz and the stagehands rushing around him. He was detached, already in the world the playwright created.

Was that how she was when she entered that other world? Did she become other than herself, as if she were playing a part, the part of someone who looked so much like her that everyone mistook her for Rosamund? Nevertheless, her emotions were real. Her growing love for David was real as was her loathing of Alex Mindon.

Only Granville Smythe occupied the stage when the curtain came down on the second act. He walked off stage, saw Roz, and smiled as he passed on his way to change for the last act.

She smiled back. "Well done." He accepted her verbal tribute gracefully as laughter and applause wafted through the curtains.

Because the scenery and props remained the same for the last act, Derek left his post when the curtain came down. He returned with two cans of cola in his hand. He passed one to her. "I noticed you didn't have anything to drink with your sandwich."

"Thanks."

Derek sat on the floor. "Why do you hate me, Roz?"

Roz spluttered on a mouthful of cola. "I don't hate you."

"You just dislike me very much."

Laughter exploded from her and Derek grinned.

"I don't even dislike you very much."

"But you don't like me. Why?"

"It isn't that I don't like you. . . . How can I put this? What I don't like is the offer to be one of the women you practice on in the years before you decide to settle down and find a wife."

"Come again?"

"I don't want to be one of the fields where you sow your wild oats."

"In other words, I have a reputation."

"I've seen you with many women."

"Has it occurred to you I'm searching for the right one?"

Roz had done much the same thing. There were many first dates, rarely followed by a second. "But it's so easy for you, Derek. You have the looks and the money. Women fall at your feet."

"And do all the fair maids cry: *I have spread my dreams under your feet; tread softly because you tread on my dreams?*"

"Yeats? You read poetry?"

"Of course, isn't it part of the world of theatre? What I'm trying to say is this—do the women who fall at my feet see my flashy car or me? Do they hear me or the jingle of coin in my pocket?" He glanced to where Angela Duke was making her way up the stairs from the dressing rooms. "And here comes another such woman. Does she see and hear my uncle, or just opportunity knocking?"

"And is that what you are offering me, the opportunity to renew my contract if I agree to date you?"

"That isn't worthy of you, Roz." He got to his feet. "My uncle finds you too valuable for me even to consider such a thing." He walked to his place as prompt without a backward glance and the curtain rose.

Roz left mid-way through the last act. All of the players were on stage. If anything went wrong with the costumes, she could do nothing to repair them until Monday.

She walked home weighed down by Derek's reproach. He might leave her alone now, just when he was beginning to get interesting. She'd never thought of him reading poetry and memorising lines. Although she'd read several poems by Yeats and Longfellow, and even G. K. Chesterton when she was at school, she didn't remember any of them well enough to quote. Moreover, she'd always believed Derek one of Angela's staunch supporters, blind to her scheming.

As Roz entered the house, she met Doris in the main hall.

"Archie," Doris called up the stairs. "Roz is here."

"What's going on?" Roz asked as Archie came down to join them.

"You're here." He looked bewildered. "I swear I heard you running up the stairs not five minutes ago."

She shook her head. "I've been at work."

"And she only just walked in," Doris confirmed.

"Did you want to see me about something?"

"The doorbell rang in my flat and when I came out I found this pushed under the door. It has your name on it. I didn't know how urgent it was, and as I thought you had come home—" Archie handed her an envelope.

She opened it and took out the single sheet of paper. The message was brief:

Stay way from the museem if you now whats good for you.

She gasped, and the note slipped from her fingers.

Doris pounced on it, read it, and passed it to Archie. "This sounds like a threat."

Archie looked angry. "Why would anyone warn you to stay away from the museum? I assume it's the museum next door."

Shaken, she explained as much as she dared. "I've been there twice. Once to research costumes and once to visit Charlie, the night watchman, who is a friend of mine." The message probably didn't refer to the present-day building but to Scarbane House. Somebody knew about her visits through the mirror and warned her to stop.

"I think you'd better come and sit down." Archie indicated the door to his flat. "Margery is out, but I can manage a cup of tea, or something stronger, if you feel the need."

"Give her a glass of your elderberry wine," Doris said. "That always sets me up."

Archie guided Roz into the garden flat. In a daze, she accepted the wine he brought her.

"Should we ring the police?" Doris asked.

The last thing Roz needed was the police tearing her flat apart. "This note doesn't really make a threat, does it?"

"It does." Archie disagreed. "It intimates that if you continue to visit the museum some harm will come to you."

"Then I won't go to the museum again." Did she dare go to Scarbane House? Yes, she had to. If she didn't, she'd never see David again, and she'd never recover Minnie's brooch.

129

She eyed Archie. "You said you thought I'd come in earlier. Could it have been Mr Saunders you heard?"

Archie shook his head. "They were the footsteps of a much lighter person. When you've lived in this flat as long as Margery and I have, you learn to recognise a person's footsteps. I know the sound of Mr Saunders' steps so I assumed the ones I heard were yours."

"There has to be somebody else up there." An edge of hysteria entered Doris' voice. "Somebody has broken in."

"Did you see anyone?" Roz asked Archie.

"I had barely reached the attic landing when Doris called that you were down here." He hesitated, then continued, "Whoever it was could have entered your flat, Rosamund, or gone into Mr Saunders' place."

"I shan't sleep a wink until I know there isn't someone lurking about up there; we could be murdered in our beds! I say we ring the police," Doris urged.

"I don't think we need to go that far," Roz said.

"Well, I do." Doris said firmly. "Will you ring them, Archie, or shall I?"

"If you think it wise. . . ." Archie took one look at Doris' determined face and walked across the room to the telephone. He dialled 999 and Doris kept glancing nervously at the door.

"I don't think there's anything to worry about," Roz whispered. "They may not have been footsteps Archie heard."

"What else could it be?" Doris hissed. "Mice? There have been too many strange things going on in this house and they must stop; otherwise, I shall find another place to live."

"They said they'd be along as soon as they could." Archie returned to sit beside them.

"It's Saturday night. They'll be rushed off their feet," Doris commented. "I don't know why most criminals do their deeds on weekends."

Though shaken, Roz repeated the explanation Charlie gave once. "Because it doesn't interfere with their day jobs."

Sober disbelief met her effort to inject humour into the situation.

"I don't think it's anything to be flippant about," Doris said. "You may not have anything worth stealing but I have my mother's silver."

"We all have things we don't want to lose," Archie said quietly. "They may not always have a monetary value but they are just as precious to us."

Roz shot him a grateful look. "Like Minnie's brooch."

"That had some value." Doris pointed out, "And we know who stole it, but did the police find the woman? No. They don't care."

The doorbell rang as Doris spoke.

"That will be them." Archie went out to the hall with Roz and Doris at his heels.

"They don't usually respond so quickly," Doris said, as if to reinforce her earlier statement, and Archie echoed her words as he let the police in.

"You came very promptly."

"We were in the area when the call came in. You said there was an intruder." Two plain-clothed policemen walked in, filling the small vestibule with their bulk and battered raincoats.

Roz studied them as they questioned Archie. If ever she had to dress an actor as a detective, this would be how.

"You live in one of the attic flats, Miss?" A policeman towered over her.

"Reid. Rosamund Reid."

"The other flat is empty; Mr Saunders is away at the moment," Archie explained. "I have a spare key to his flat, and to the flat below Miss Reid's. Mrs Wilton is also away this weekend."

"What about Major Middleton?" Doris asked. "Is he in, do you think?"

"Yes." Archie explained. "His flat is directly above ours and I heard him moving about up there. He's quite deaf so he can't have heard anything to help you with your enquiries."

"Perhaps you would be good enough to get me Mrs Wilton's spare key," the younger of the policemen said to Archie, and then he turned to Roz, "If I can have your key, Miss Reid."

Roz dug in her pocket and produced the key. "I can come up with you."

"You will be safer down here. If the man is cornered, and he turns violent, you could be hurt."

"Are you sure it's a man?" Doris asked.

"Most burglars are men, ma'am," the older policeman answered. "Where is your flat?"

"I'm on this floor, on the other side of the hall."

"And what is your name?"

"Doris Morris."

Roz watched intently for a reaction to the name. To their credit, neither policeman gave even a hint of a smile.

"Archie said the footsteps were those of a light person, someone about my size. It might have been a woman."

"I doubt it, Miss Reid."

Chagrined, Roz looked away. How could he be so sure? Amelia had seen a woman, and the woman might be back.

Archie brought the spare keys and handed them to the older officer. "Should I accompany you?"

"If we need your help, sir, we'll call out."

"How insolent," Doris muttered as the two men climbed the stairs. "Who would know better than Archie if anything was missing or had been moved? I don't care for policemen."

"But they are the first people we call if we're afraid," Roz pointed out. Thereafter, Doris kept her mouth shut as they listened for shouts or scuffles from the upper floors.

What would they find in her flat? Roz wondered. Would the divider be in place before the mirror or would it be on the floor?

Archie said the footsteps were of a light person; someone close to her weight. Was it the man she had seen on both sides of the mirror, or the woman the earlier tenant saw? Unless whoever it was had crept down the stairs and left while Roz and Doris were in Archie's flat drinking wine, he or she was on the other side.

They came and went when the flat was empty, but how had they known she would be out tonight?

From the floor above, Major Middleton demanded to know what they wanted and insisted they show him their identification. A few minutes later, the policemen came back.

"Do you want to search down here?" Archie asked.

The senior policeman shook his head. "No need, sir. Unless you feel he might be hiding down here."

"No one came down the stairs while we waited for you."

"Then it's a mystery where he may have got to. We searched everywhere someone could hide." The older policeman handed Archie the keys and led the way to the front door.

"Before you go. . . ." Doris ran forward to grip an officer's sleeve. "The man you took from here, the Cockney who looked like a weasel, Bertie Briggs, is he still in prison?"

"No, ma'am, he was released a month ago."

Bertie Briggs, the man who used to live in her flat. Things were falling into place. "Is Mr Briggs still in London, officer?" Roz asked.

"He's on parole and has to report every week. Unless he's doing a lot of commuting, yes, he's still in London."

Bertie Briggs was small and skinny, and probably weighed little more than she did. Could he be the person who ran up the stairs earlier?

"Is there something you wish to say, Miss Reid?"

She shook her head. "No, nothing."

"Yes, she does," Doris said. "Show them the note you got earlier."

"A note?" Both officers halted on their way to the door.

"It's in there." Roz pointed to Archie's flat.

"I think they should see it, it's quite threatening. Coupled with the intruder who was here, I think they have to see it." Doris led the way into Archie's flat.

Roz took up the note from the table and handed it to the older policeman. Both read the note, and then the older one asked Roz: "Do you mind if we keep this?"

"Are you going to investigate it?" Doris burst in.

"I would hardly be keeping it for its literary value, ma'am," came the answer. To Roz, he repeated his question.

Roz shrugged. "I don't think it's of any significance."

"Do you consider it a threat?"

"Not really."

"The museum referred to—would that be the Scarborough next door?"

"I don't know. I think so." She looked away; disconcerted by the intent looks both officers were giving her.

"Do you go there often?"

"I've been there twice in the past month. Once to research costumes, and—"

"Once to visit the night watchman who is a friend of hers." Doris interrupted.

"What is the night watchman's name, Miss Reid?"

"Charlie Watts. He and I both work at the Nostalgie."

"The theatre? Are you an actress?"

"I'm the wardrobe mistress and Charlie is, well, basically he's the odd-job man who builds scenery."

"Does Mr Watts also work at the museum?"

"Only on Thursday nights."

The older officer took a card from his pocket and handed it to Roz. "If you get more notes of this nature, please let me know."

Roz glanced at the card: *Detective Inspector Morgan.* "I don't think—" She was about to say the note and any future notes were unimportant, but he interrupted her.

"It isn't a request, Miss Reid, but a demand." The face that had a minute before seemed concerned and friendly turned icy.

Roz nodded. "All right."

When they left, Archie said, relief evident in his voice, "Well, at least we know there is no one in the house who shouldn't be here."

"You said Mr Saunders is away?" Roz asked.

"He left me a note, but he didn't tell me where he was off to this time. He must lead a very exciting life, always off to foreign parts." Archie made for his flat. "Margery will be home soon and I'd better get the kettle going for tea. Do you wish to join me Rosamund? Doris?"

Roz shook her head and Doris echoed the movement. "It's been a long day. . . ."

"Goodnight, then." Archie handed Roz her keys, went into his flat and closed the door.

"I can't believe Bertie Briggs is out of prison. He might still have a key to this place," Doris said as she walked across the hall.

He must still have a key to her flat. Roz wondered why Archie hadn't changed the locks when Bertie Briggs moved out, and who was responsible for doing it. Either way, she had to change the lock, and soon.

**

CHAPTER FOURTEEN

Roz waited to give Imogen and Adele time to leave for church so it was late on Sunday morning when she stepped through the mirror. From the window in Rosamund's bedroom, she watched them ride away in the carriage. Behind the carriage, a pony and trap carried several servants, Jenny among them. There would still be a few servants in the house. The cook would be preparing the midday meal and she probably had a scullery maid to help her.

Roz slipped into the demure gown left on the bed. They must have searched for her to accompany them to church, but Rosamund had set up a scenario of disappearances that allowed Roz to return through the mirror without having awkward questions asked.

Before crossing through the mirror, she had placed a candle and her lighter in a linen bag. When she searched for the lighter, she couldn't find it. Had she dropped it? She turned the bag inside out, but it wasn't there. The silk chemise she wore and the linen bag and candle came through unscathed, as had the brooch Madame Sauvé had stolen from Minnie and brought back in time, but all of those materials existed at the beginning of the Nineteenth Century, lighters hadn't.

With no means of lighting the candle, she began her search for Rosamund on the upper floor where there were windows. Although there was little chance of discovery, she took every precaution to be as silent as possible as she tiptoed to the door leading up to the servants' floor.

One room had three beds with chests holding washbowls and jugs to separate them. Another room held empty trunks and valises.

The contents of one room were familiar—the sewing room. Bolts of silk, cotton and muslin filled the shelves, and a basket held all manner of trimmings. In this era, unless there was a resident seamstress, they would summon one to the house to make gowns for the ladies and the servants' clothes. Tailors outfitted wealthy men.

None of the rooms offered a place where Rosamund could hide; nevertheless, Roz called out as loudly as she dared, "Rosamund? If you are here, please answer me. I want to help you."

Silence followed her cry.

One floor down, although she doubted Rosamund could remain hidden in one of the bedrooms, Roz made a determined search of every one, opening each wardrobe and cupboard and checking under every bed. Nothing gave her reason to believe Rosamund had ever hidden there.

With no means of lighting the candle, a search of the cellar was out of the question. Instead, she went outside and checked the stables and barns, climbing into the lofts where the menservants slept, and then to the dairy and fly-ridden outhouse. Periodically, she called out Rosamund's name, but no one answered. Satisfied the girl wasn't hiding in any of the satellite buildings, she returned to the house to search the main floor.

As she saw on her tour with Charlie, there were a surprising number of small cupboard-like rooms leading off the main reception areas. Some were little more than alcoves with panelled doors. In one, the maids kept their cleaning equipment: brooms and mops, buckets and dusters, and bars of evil-smelling lye soap. Another proved to be a water closet that smelled none too fresh. Most of the others held a variety of paraphernalia. None hid Rosamund or contained anything in which she could hide.

She remembered Charlie mentioning a secret passage, but that may be nothing more than a rumour. It was unlikely to have remained undiscovered in her time because workmen would have torn into several of the walls when they installed electrical wiring.

Her search brought her to the back stairs with one flight leading up and one down. From below came the sounds of voices and kitchen clatter, and the aroma of roasting meat.

Leading off the small landing was the cellar door. She turned the heavy iron ring and the door opened with a creak. Beyond, a flight of steps led down into darkness. She closed the door as voices came from the front part of the house. Imogen and Adele had returned.

Quickly, Roz ran up the back stairs. In Rosamund's bedroom, she struggled out of the grimy gown with bits of straw clinging to it, and donned a robe she found behind the screen. Before Imogen walked in, Roz slipped the candle into the robe's deep pocket.

"Your absence was noted in church, Rosamund." Imogen eyed the robe. "Were you about to wash? You have dirt on your cheek."

Roz raised a hand to her cheek then hastily withdrew it and hid it behind her back. Her hands were black with dust.

"Why do you constantly behave in a manner that draws unfavourable attention to this family?"

Roz shrugged.

"I told Lord and Lady Ridley you were unwell at the ball and returned home."

Roz nodded.

"They asked the nature of your affliction. I told them it was a female problem."

"Good."

"You are supposedly indisposed; therefore, you will not attend the boating party this afternoon but remain in your room. Is that understood?"

Roz nodded again.

"I will have luncheon brought to you," Imogen said as she left.

Roz relaxed. She was to be a prisoner in her room. So be it, but who would be at the boating party? Would David be there? She determined to make a speedy recovery from the imaginary illness and join them.

As she washed her face and hands, Jenny arrived with a tray. Still in the robe, she sat at the small table next to the bed and ate as Jenny bustled about. The maid took the dirty water away, then came back and gathered up the soiled gown. Wordlessly, she picked off the bits of straw clinging to the skirt.

"Will you do my hair, Jenny?" Roz moved to sit at the dressing table.

"Miss?"

"I feel quite recovered and I shall be joining the boating party."

In the mirror, surprise showed on Jenny's face when she came to stand behind Roz. "I'm glad yer feelin' better, Miss." She began to brush Roz's hair.

"Tell me, Jenny, how do you light a candle?"

The look on Jenny's face told her this was something even the smallest child would know. Something a woman of her position would have a maid do.

"If I wanted to light a candle, how would I do it?"

"With a taper from the fire, Miss. Do ye want to light a candle now?"

"Not now, maybe later." Although it was a warm day, there had been a small fire in the withdrawing room. She mentally kicked herself for not thinking of it. Perhaps she should forego the boating party and continue her search for Rosamund. However, David might be at the party.

"What time does the boating party start?"

"I heard as Miss Adele will be going out after luncheon."

"Isn't Aunt Imogen going?"

"Oh, no, Madam never goes. Lady Ridley will chaperone Miss Adele."

When Jenny went to the wardrobe to take out a gown and slippers, Roz slipped the candle from her pocket into a drawer in the dressing table. She allowed Jenny to dress her and accepted the parasol the maid held out.

"Do I need anything else?" Roz asked, remembering the forgotten dance card.

"Sometimes ye do take yer sketchbook."

Drawing was a skill she developed at design school. "Then I'll take it now."

From the chest beside the window, Jenny brought her a sketchbook and several lengths of charcoal in a leather case.

"Thank you, Jenny. You may go."

Jenny left and Roz opened the sketchbook. Rosamund had talent but made mistakes involving perspective common in the sketches of the untrained. To a layperson, Roz's sketches would look no different from those of Rosamund's. Not for the first time, she wondered at the similarities between them.

She tucked the sketchbook and leather case under her arm, picked up the parasol, and left the room.

As Roz reached the front hall, a servant opened it to admit Lady Ridley. Her eyes widened when she spied Roz. "I understood you were indisposed, Rosamund."

"I am quite recovered, Lady Ridley, and I humbly beg forgiveness for having left so abruptly the other night. You see, Aunt Imogen and Cousin Adele were enjoying themselves immensely and I was loath to take them away from such an excellent ball."

The compliment seemed to mollify the other woman. "We should be grateful to Lord Mindon for ensuring your safe journey home."

"Indeed, ma'am." So that was the story spread around. If Lord and Lady Ridley were aware of the forthcoming announcement of her engagement to Alexander Mindon, perhaps they would see little harm in allowing her to be in his company without a chaperone.

Imogen emerged from the dining room with Adele in tow. "Rosamund?"

"Aunt Imogen." She faced the older woman. "I am quite recovered and bent on joining Adele for the boating party."

Behind Imogen, Adele's glowing face turned a ghastly shade of grey. "Surely you are not well enough, cousin."

"On the contrary, I am completely well." Roz stepped towards Lady Ridley. "Shall we depart, ma'am?"

"Just a moment." Imogen moved closer. "I insist you take a day longer to recover, Rosamund."

"But—"

"I think Lady Scarbane is right. One should not hurry the convalescence period."

"Yes, Cousin Rosamund. You do not want a relapse."

Roz wondered what sort of female complaint she was supposed to have. However, faced with three women who opposed her joining the boating party, she could do nothing but accede. She nodded. "Perhaps you are right."

All three were visibly relieved and she wondered what they planned that wasn't to include her. She stood aside to allow Adele to join Lady Ridley, and then they left.

"I shall not be joining them," Imogen said, "but I shall take the air on this side of the lake." In her eyes was a challenge that dared Roz to leave the house.

"And I shall return to my room," Roz informed her. *To get the candle and search the cellar.*

When Roz felt Imogen had enough time to exit the house, she took the candle from the dressing-table drawer and went downstairs. From the withdrawing room window, she saw Imogen's parasol bobbing above the low wall separating the terrace from the garden. She crossed to the small fire banked to keep it alight until the evening, held a taper to the glow, and lit the candle. Shielding it with her hand, she moved quickly to the cellar door.

The steps were of stone and wet, the air musty. Roz stayed close to the wall, one hand touching it to guide her, the other holding the candle aloft. It gave very little light, especially to someone accustomed to electricity, but the flame held steady as she descended. In a couple of places, torches were set in sconces on the wall, but she dared not light them. At any moment, one of the servants might come to the cellar and she could easily extinguish a candle, even though it meant she'd have to feel her way back up.

The earth floor was damp, as if water from the lake seeped in, and there was a stench of stagnant water. Wooden trestles raised bins and sacks of vegetables off the ground. Beyond them were racks for bottles of wine, most empty. Bricked pillars rose here and there to support the structure above, casting dark shadows Roz had to check. She examined the cellar from one corner to another but found no trace of Rosamund. Despite that, she whispered the girl's name from time to time, but there was no answering call.

As she reached the top of the stairs and stepped onto the landing, she met Jenny. The maid's eyes widened and her mouth hung open as she studied her. Roz looked down. Her gown was filthy and her slippers encrusted with mud. Jenny made a quick motion with her hand and Roz obeyed, moved back onto the cellar steps and closed the door. As she did so, she heard one of the menservants upbraid Jenny for not being quicker in fetching the mistress' posset. Roz waited; then, hearing no more sounds, opened the door and ran up the back stairs.

Roz had been in the bedroom a few minutes before Jenny appeared.

"What be ye a doing in the cellar, Miss?" Jenny helped her out of the soiled gown and then wrapped it around the stained slippers.

"I wanted to see what was down there."

"There be rats down there."

Roz shuddered. "I didn't see any."

"Alfred says as he heard them down there, one time. Crying just like a woman, he says."

Crying like a woman. . . . Was Rosamund trapped down there somewhere? "Have they set traps?"

"Yes, a while ago, but Donald got his foot caught in one so they took they up." Jenny smothered a laugh. "It be the only rat caught down there."

"Has Aunt Imogen returned to the house?"

"Yes, Miss. Drinkin' a posset in her sitting room, she is. Says as it was cold in the garden and she caught a chill."

Imogen's sitting room overlooked the front of the house. If Roz left by the French windows and kept under the trees, she could come out on this side of the lake opposite where the boating party was to take place. She pulled another gown from the wardrobe. "Help me with this, Jenny."

"Are ye going out, Miss?"

"Yes. You won't tell anyone, will you? And you won't tell anyone I was in the cellar?"

Jenny shook her head. "No, Miss."

"Good girl." Gown changed, Roz took up the sketchbook and leather case. "If anyone asks, I'm in my room lying down."

When she reached the terrace, laughter rang across the water. Anxious that no one should see her; she kept to the trees and checked who was at the party.

There was no sign of David, but Lady Ridley was ensconced in a chair with a rug wrapped around her knees. Beside her sat the mother of the twins who played the spinet during Roz's first visit this side of the mirror. One twin lolled dejectedly under a tree while the other slumped in a punt being poled across the lake.

Another punt followed the shore. In it, Adele sat beneath her parasol, languid hand trailed in the water. The man poling her along was Alex Mindon.

Now Roz knew why she wasn't welcome to join them— Adele was to have her chance to captivate the man she adored.

Roz lowered herself onto a tuft under an oak, opened the sketchbook and took out a stick of charcoal. In quick strokes, she drew the likenesses of Adele and Alex.

"Rosamund?"

The whisper came from behind her. Roz looked around but saw no one. "Who's there?"

"David Ridley."

Her heart skipped a beat. "Where are you?"

"Behind you and to your left."

She packed the charcoal away and closed her sketchbook. Unhurriedly, lest anyone be watching, she rose and made her way up the bank to where David waited.

"I was hoping you would come out." He took her hand and raised it to his lips.

"Why are you not with the boating party?"

"I said I wanted to take a walk. I hoped I would see you if I came to this side of the water." He led her farther into the trees where no one could see them from the lake or from the house.

"I tried to join the party but Aunt Imogen stopped me and your mother agreed with her. There was nothing I could do."

"I understand." He drew her into the shadows, took the sketchbook and case from her and placed them on the grass. "They will do everything in their power to keep us from seeing each other."

She stepped into the circle of his waiting arms. "But we will see each other, won't we?"

"Nothing can keep me away from you." He bent his head and kissed her. "You are everything I have searched for. You are all I need in my life, dearest Rosamund."

Her heart leapt at his words. Too overcome with emotion to speak, she threw her arms around his neck and laid her cheek against his.

Against her ear, he whispered, "Say you have some regard for me."

"Yes. Oh, yes." She held his face between her palms. He was more than she had hoped to find. He was gentle. He treated her with respect. He didn't paw her or demand she go to bed with him or else he would move on to the next woman who took his eye. She stood on tiptoes and kissed him.

He caught her to him, returned her kiss, and they heard his name called from across the water.

"I must go." He released her after another kiss. "If I can, I will come tomorrow."

"Yes. Please come."

"Farewell, my love." He touched his hand to her cheek then he was gone.

Roz hugged her arms around herself and watched until he was out of sight. She never thought to find a man like David, but she didn't belong here. This was not her time. Unless—

Madame Sauvé came through the mirror and stayed. If Roz stayed, they might force her to marry Alex Mindon, unless she eloped with David. That he was penniless meant nothing to her. She was an expert dressmaker. She could design and make clothes for a living. Maybe they could open a shop where she could sell ready-made gowns and hats, a concept not widely adopted at this time. They wouldn't be rich, but they would be happy.

She picked up the sketchbook and case and walked towards the house.

Without warning, a car's horn followed by a squeal of brakes blasted the silence. For a second, she paid the sounds no heed, but then she realised they didn't belong to this London but to her own.

Knees trembling, she ran to the house and raced up the stairs to Rosamund's bedroom. She leapt back to her own time and collapsed shivering on her bed.

**

CHAPTER FIFTEEN

LAST WEEK posters pasted over the playbills advertising *My Lord's Dilemma* greeted Roz when she passed the front doors of the theatre. She entered the alley leading to the stage door and let herself in.

Sally Jones was on the telephone when Roz walked into the office to get her pay packet. She signalled Roz to wait while she finished her call. "They've picked him up again."

"Who's that?" Roz asked.

"Charlie. He just called from the police station to say he'd be late. Something else was stolen from the museum over the weekend."

"Did he say what was taken?"

Sally shook her head. "By the way, John wants a word with you if you have a minute."

Roz nodded. "Is he in now?"

Sally waved a hand towards her boss's door as the telephone jangled again.

Roz tapped on the door of John's inner sanctum and entered when he called out. "Sally said you wanted to see me."

He looked up from the spreadsheet he was studying. "Just to ask how the costumes are going for the next production."

"Most are finished, apart from a few accessories."

"Good. Are the fittings done?"

"All done."

"Can we look forward to seeing you for dinner on Sunday?"

"Absolutely." By then she would have retrieved Minnie's brooch from Madame Sauvé.

"Good. Good. Carry on then." John hunched over the spreadsheet again and she left.

In the workroom, Roz checked several bolts of fabric and then rummaged for a length of silk jersey to duplicate the wrap she had worn to the ball. Cut in half lengthways, it would make wraps for both Angela and Laura if she added an opulent trim for the leading lady. She was rooting through the drawer of trims when Derek appeared.

"Good morning, Roz."

"Good morning." She eyed the fabrics draped over his arm. "Is there something I can help you with?"

"I have a choice of colours for the draperies in Lady Amberley's boudoir and I wondered which would go best with Angela's gowns." He spread the fabric over the workroom table.

"These are her gowns." Roz lifted three from the rack and brought them to the table. "From the audience's perspective, I think the red would work best."

"Right you are. It will work well with the pastels of the gowns. I'll have these draped on the window frames." With that, he gathered up the fabrics and left.

Roz gazed after him. She must have really upset him on Saturday because this was the first time he hadn't propositioned her. The change in his behaviour was disconcerting. Although she hated to admit it even to herself, she missed his attempts to get her to go out with him.

At eleven, Agatha arrived with an apology for leaving Roz with both performances on Saturday.

"Is your husband ill again?" Roz asked. Agatha nodded before she hung up her coat. "It's no big deal, but I have something planned for next Saturday so you'll have to work both performances."

"Going anywhere nice?" Agatha moved to the table and took up her sewing.

"I think so. A friend is taking me to a fair and to visit a friend of his."

Agatha looked up. "This sounds serious."

"It might be."

"What's his name? And when do I get to meet him?"

"His name is David and I don't know when I'll get the chance to bring him to meet you." *Probably never.* For an instant, she tried to picture David in her time. He would fit in no better than with his own society.

"Where did you meet him?"

"At a party; some friends introduced us."

"Is he good looking?"

"He's drop-dead gorgeous."

"So Derek is out of the picture?"

"He was never in it. Derek and I had a chat on Saturday. I don't think he'll be sweet-talking me again." Roz looked up as Charlie walked in.

"I know I'm late, but is there any tea in the pot?"

"Always, Charlie, come on in." The kettle still contained hot water. Roz flicked the switch to let it boil. "I hear they took you in for questioning again."

"Oh, Charlie," Agatha let the sewing fall into her lap, "what was it about this time?"

"Same thing, some stuff got stolen over the weekend." Charlie dropped into a chair beside the table.

"What was taken this time?" Roz asked.

"Some silver brushes; went missing from a glass case, same as before."

"But you weren't on duty, were you?" Roz asked and her hand shook as she poured boiling water into the teapot.

"Nah, Jim were."

"You look as if they gave you a hard time." Roz placed a cup of tea before Charlie and brought a packet of biscuits to the table.

"The bobbies was okay, but they had this other one wiv 'em. In plain clothes, he were. Detective Inspector bloody Morgan."

Roz slopped tea onto the table.

"What did he do?" Agatha asked.

"What didn't he do, short of hitting me. Ranted and raved. Cussed like a navvy. But I couldn't tell him what I didn't know, could I?"

"Did they question Jim, too?" Roz asked.

"He had it worse than me, 'cos he were on duty." Charlie shot a quick look at Agatha and said, "Asked if I knew Bertie Briggs."

Roz fought down her start of surprise, but Agatha gasped.

"I used to know him, I says." Charlie continued. "Him and his missus lived down our road, and she still lives there, though he's been gone for more'n a year. Been in prison, I heard."

"Did Jim hear the voices over the weekend?" Agatha asked.

Roz glanced at her. Was Agatha changing the subject?

"He says it were all quiet early on last night, then there were a bit of a fuss later, like two women was having a go at each other."

"Could he hear what was being said?" Roz asked.

"Funny thing, he could make out a lot of the words. Two women were talking about a man called Alexander, and he heard something we ain't never heard before. A horse galloped up the steps to the front door and then the door opened and a man shouted something. Couldn't make out what it were, but he says whoever it were was in a temper. Fair gave him the willies, it did."

"Why? You've both heard voices before." Roz pointed out.

"Not like this, he says he felt a draught, though the door were closed and locked, and the voice were like it were next to his ear." Charlie looked at Roz. "You said something Thursday night. You said as you felt cold air, as if somebody'd run past you."

"You went to the museum?" Agatha peered at Roz over the rim of her cup.

Roz nodded. "And I felt something. Like a cold draught."

"Same as Jim did. Can't say as I've ever felt nothing like that." Charlie grinned at Agatha and chuckled. "See, I had my date wiv this lovely young lady. Grabbed me, she did and hung on like I was the last man on earth. I daren't tell the missus, though."

"Charlie!" Roz cried. "You promised you wouldn't say anything."

"No, I didn't," he argued with a twinkle in his eyes.

"Was she going to fall, Charlie? Is that why she grabbed you?" Agatha asked.

"Fall, nothing. Hung onto me like she were drowning, she did."

"I was frightened," Roz explained.

"Did you hear the voices?" Agatha asked.

Roz nodded. "And I heard doors slamming, and people running down the stairs. But I didn't see anything, and that was the scary part."

"Had to get her drunk to calm her down," Charlie said with a grin as he got up to leave.

"I had a tot of rum in my coffee," Roz protested.

"Do I take it you won't be going there again?" Agatha asked.

"Never at night. If I go there, it'll be in broad daylight." It was something she might have to do because it occurred to her the museum might have family records to give her an idea of what happened to Rosamund.

As Roz stitched the gold braid to Granville's frockcoat, her mind revolved around several questions that in some odd way seemed tied together. The man in the garden at Scarbane House probably stole the brushes and he might well be the Bertie Briggs she kept hearing about, the man who used to live in her flat.

Did Agatha know him, too? She reacted in a strange way when Charlie mentioned the man's name, and Charlie hinted he knew something about Agatha's husband. Could there be a connection between Agatha's husband and Bertie Briggs?

What did Jim hear and feel? It had been quiet earlier in the evening because they were at Ridley Manor. The horseman riding up to the door must have been Alex Mindon searching for her after she left the ball. The two women quarrelling were herself and Imogen. Jim experienced a rush of cold air as she had; but Charlie had never felt it.

In Charlie's book, there was mention of a catastrophe if two time dimensions collided. Was it possible she and Bertie Briggs were causing a rift in the barriers of time? And what of the ghost woman Minnie's friend had seen? She was forgetting about her.

In addition, Detective Inspector Morgan. . . . Was it a coincidence he was investigating the stolen property or were the police watching the museum? It could explain how they were able to arrive so promptly in answer to Archie's call.

The intruder could be the woman or Bertie Briggs, but how had they known Roz wasn't home? It was true no light would have shone from her window, but she could have been in bed.

On Thursday evening, when she was with Charlie in the museum, who had known? Charlie and Agatha. Agatha would know when Roz was at work. Was she passing information to Bertie Briggs or the mystery woman? Agatha could be the mystery woman, except she was overweight and unlikely to run up stairways.

Would the thieves risk passing through the mirror during the day when they could run into a family member or one of the servants? She saw Briggs in the garden at Scarbane House on Friday. The night before that, she discovered the divider moved. He must have seen her at the window in Rosamund's bedroom and he had only to wait until she went outside before he made his escape.

On Friday Doris would have been at work and Minnie might have gone out. That left Major Middleton, Archie, and Marge the only people to slip past. Archie hadn't mentioned hearing anyone on the stairs as he had on Saturday when he thought Roz ran up them.

Was it possible Bertie Briggs or the woman saw her walking down the Lane and taken a chance? Why had they waited so late to get into the house? If they had seen Morgan or one of his men watching the museum, how had they given the police the slip?

Agatha seemed wrapped in her own thoughts, too, as she sewed the pearl trim on Angela's wrap. When they emerged from the theatre, they wished each other good night and Roz walked home, head down and deep in thought.

A light rain began to fall when she entered Scarborough Lane. Roz stepped off the pavement to cross the road and heard horses galloping towards her and the rumble of carriage wheels. She leapt back and looked in the direction of the sounds. There were no horses in sight, but she smelled fresh horse droppings.

She arrived home damp and miserable. On the doormat lay a plain white envelope with her name on it.

**

CHAPTER SIXTEEN

Roz's cry brought Archie rushing out of his flat. He began to speak but fell silent when he saw the envelope in her hand. She opened it and withdrew the sheet of paper. It bore five words:

Get out of yer flat

Wordlessly, she handed it to Archie.

Archie read the note and passed it back. "Why would anyone want you to leave your flat?"

Roz shrugged and scrunched the note into her pocket. She couldn't tell Archie about her forays into the past. If the museum were to close soon, the thieves would want to make the most of their time. With Roz in the flat, they couldn't come and go as they pleased, but how did they know the museum was closing? Did Agatha tell them?

"One of the policemen gave you his card the other night. You were to let him know if you got another note." Archie placed a comforting arm around Roz's shoulders. "Come on. You can use our phone."

Marge looked up in surprise from the dough she was kneading when they walked in.

"Rosamund has another note. This one tells her to get out of her flat." Archie guided Roz to the telephone. "Do you want to ring the police or shall I?"

More frightened than she expected, Roz rummaged in her holdall and came up with Morgan's card. She handed it to Archie. "Y—you do it."

Marge wiped the flour from her hands and led Roz to a chair. "You've had quite a shock. Sit down and I'll make you a cup of tea."

Roz sat and hugged her holdall. How far were Briggs and the woman willing to go? She knew nothing about the woman but from everything she'd heard Briggs was a thief. If she were—what was the term—queering their pitch—how far would they go to get her out of the way?

"Here you are." Marge placed a cup of tea on the table beside Roz then took the holdall from her nerveless fingers.

"The policewoman at the station said she'd get a message to Detective Inspector Morgan right away." Archie sat beside Roz. "Why don't you stay here until they arrive?"

Roz nodded.

"Drink your tea, love," Marge urged.

"And take a few deep breaths." Archie patted Roz's hand. "You'll be all right here with us."

Roz took a sip of the tea. "I was going to ask you about changing the lock on my door."

"We can do that," Archie said. "We always keep a few spare locks around, so I can do it tomorrow or tonight if that's what you want. But you know Margery and I will have to keep a duplicate, don't you?"

"I don't mind if you have a spare key."

"We should have changed the lock when the Briggs man was taken away," Marge said, "but, with one thing and another, we never got around to it."

"The flat was empty for several months before I moved in, wasn't it?"

"Yes, indeed," said Archie. "The police made quite a mess up there and it took time to set it to rights. I did most of it myself, when I could."

"And when you weren't in hospital." Marge added.

"You were ill?" Roz looked at Archie over the rim of the cup.

"Nothing serious, my dear, but it meant I had to delay getting your flat finished."

"It was months before we were able to show it." Marge got to her feet when the front door bell rang. "That'll be the police. I'll let them in."

"Margery," Archie called after her and got to his feet. "Be careful, dear."

Roz noticed the fear in his voice. "Are you afraid it might be whoever is sending me these notes?"

He shook his head. "Not really. Anyone who sends anonymous notes has to be too cowardly to show up at the door and ring the bell, but it pays to be cautious."

If it were Bertie Briggs sending her the notes, a swift kick where it hurt would put him out of action, Roz decided, and she felt she would be a match for most women. She put the cup down and prepared to stand as Detective Inspector Morgan and the younger police officer entered the room.

"Don't get up, Miss Reid." Morgan pulled a chair away from the table and swung it around so he could straddle it facing Roz. "I hear you've had another note. May I see it?"

Roz pulled the crumpled paper from her pocket and handed it to him.

Morgan read it and passed it to the other man. "It might be a good idea if you stayed with a friend for a while."

"I am not leaving my flat. No one is going to drive me out."

The vehemence in her voice caused Morgan to lean back. "Your bravery is laudable, but there are times when discretion is the better part of valour."

How could she tell him she felt she could handle scrawny Bertie Briggs? She couldn't even hint at who was behind the notes because she could give no explanation that wouldn't see her checked into a looney bin. Who would believe her? She could show them how they went through the mirror, but what would that do to the delicate balance of time? She suspected the barriers were crumbling. Who knew what catastrophe would follow if more people used the portal. It was better to say nothing.

"Miss Reid?"

She looked at him and had the uncomfortable feeling he had been watching her intently. "Yes?"

"Are you quite certain you don't want to move out for a few days?"

"Yes."

Morgan stood up. "Very well, but you must keep us informed of anything that happens, especially if you get another note like this one."

"Of course."

"And I will keep this. It may give us a clue to who is doing this."

"How could it?" Roz asked. "There is nothing to lead you to anyone."

"There are ways." He moved towards the door with the younger man at his heels. "Good evening, Miss Reid, Mr and Mrs Pym."

"I'll see you out." Archie followed them into the hall.

"Are you sure you don't want to stay somewhere else for a while?" Marge asked. "If we had a spare room, I'd have you stay down here with us."

"I'll be fine." Now she was reasonably sure Bertie Briggs and his accomplice were behind all this, Roz lost some of her fear.

"You must come down or call out if anything frightens you. Minnie will be back soon. If you bang on the floor, she'll hear you and know something is wrong."

"Thank you." Roz grabbed her holdall and headed for the door.

"I'll be up in a few minutes to change the lock." Archie called after her.

The first thing Roz checked when she entered was the divider. Someone had moved it, but on which side of the mirror was that person now? Whoever it was could have gone through and come back during the time Roz was at work. There was no way of knowing. However, once Archie changed the lock, they could only leave through her flat; they wouldn't be able to get back in.

"Here we are." Archie announced his arrival as he reached the landing.

Roz opened the door wider. "Would you like a cup of tea while you are changing the lock?"

"I'd better not." Archie carried a plastic bag filled with an assortment of locks. "Margery is making Cornish pasties and they don't take long to bake."

"You have so many locks," Roz commented.

"I usually change them when a tenant leaves." He extracted one and examined the tag tied to it. "This was the one we used when Sammi was here. He hasn't been near the place since so it will be safe to use it. And, anyway, he turned in the front door key."

"Wasn't Sammi the one who wouldn't even come back to collect his things?"

"That's right." Archie took a screwdriver from his pocket then looked around. "It's a nice little flat. I don't know why we've had such a problem keeping tenants, but you seem to be settling in all right, Rosamund."

"The flat suits me fine." Nevertheless, if her feelings for David grew, she might be another woman who would disappear like Madame Sauvé.

"I'm glad." Archie removed a screw. "We all took to you the other night, especially Minerva."

"She's a caring lady."

"Margery and I think so. I think Doris likes her, too, but it's hard to tell with Doris."

"What about Mr Saunders? Does he like Minnie?"

"I couldn't say. We've seen so little of him that we hardly know what he thinks about any of us." Archie took out the old lock and fitted the new one in place. "He's very polite, but we really don't know too much about him."

"Only that he works for Oxfam."

"Yes. Well, we like to know something about the people who live in the house."

"You don't really know anything about me, either." Roz pointed out.

Archie grinned. "Haven't you noticed how nosy we are?"

Roz laughed. "There isn't much to tell about me. After my parents died, I lived with my Aunt Lily in Gravesend before I came to London to study fashion design. My job at the Nostalgie is my first real job."

"Do you not have brothers or sisters?" Archie put the last screw in place and tried the key.

"None."

"Well, I hope you'll look upon Margery and me, and Minerva of course, as your family in London."

"I shall be proud to do so. I'm very lucky to share a house with people who care. I would hate to live in one of the new multi storeys; they always seem so cold and impersonal."

"We think so, too." Archie took the key out. "There you are—a new lock. And here's one of the keys to it." He passed her a key then took the tag marked Sammi and attached it to Roz's old lock. Then he took a pen from his pocket, scratched out Sammi's name and wrote *Rosamund* on the tag before dropping the lock into the plastic bag.

"Thank you, Archie. I appreciate it."

"Anything we can do to keep a tenant happy. you'll let me know if you need anything else." He paused in the doorway and looked directly at her. "With your family so far away, Rosamund, if you ever need to talk to anyone about anything, anything at all, you know you can come to Margery or me."

"I'll remember that." As she closed the door, Roz wondered how much Archie and Marge knew about what went on in her flat. Many tenants were frightened into leaving, and Madame Sauvé disappeared never to be seen again, not in this world anyway. It must make them wonder, and it must make them speculate, but she doubted their speculations came anywhere near the truth.

Amelia told Minnie she saw a woman's ghost. She'd lived in the flat before Bertie Briggs, so who was the woman using the mirror at that time?

Roz had barely finished eating when there was a knock at her door.

"It's only me." Minnie called out.

"You're back." Roz opened the door wide. "Come in. How was your weekend?"

"Busy, busy. You know what young children are like, they never seem to stop." Minnie stepped inside. "I came to tell you that Doris has called an emergency meeting of the tenants for tonight. Now, actually."

"Is that usual? I thought we met only once a month or so."

"Yes, but she has some bee in her bonnet and she wants us all there."

"Did she say what it was about?"

"No. And it's not about the intruder or the two notes you got because Archie asked her."

"So he told you about that." Roz picked up the key to her new lock.

"I think it's frightful." Minnie waited on the landing while Roz locked the door. "I'm glad I'm back where I can keep an eye on you. Next weekend, I think you should come with me to visit my niece."

"I'll probably be away next weekend." *In a different London.*

"I worry about you being up here alone when I'm not home. Major Middleton couldn't hear you if you called out and the others are two floors down."

"I'll be fine." Roz followed Minnie down the stairs. "I suppose Archie told you about the police being here."

"Twice, he tells me. I wonder if they were the same ones who came to arrest the Briggs man that time."

"I know the name of only one of them—Detective Inspector Morgan."

Minnie paused with one hand on the rail. "A big man? In his early forties with a scar on his lip?"

"Yes."

"It's the same man. There couldn't be two with the same name and description. Archie didn't say he recognised him."

Roz shrugged. "He probably didn't think about it. It isn't unusual to have the same policeman answering calls if they're in his district."

"For uniformed police, I'd agree, but not a Detective Inspector. Don't they usually cover murders and violent crimes, or things like that?"

Murder? Good grief! Did they think Madame Sauvé was murdered? Were they watching the house rather than the museum? Did they think Bertie Briggs would—?

Fear bumped and tumbled down her back like a fall of ice cubes. If forced to, would Bertie Briggs kill to gain access to the mirror?

Archie was waiting for them. "Hello, you two. Go on in, Minerva, Doris is already here." He held Roz back. "You are looking pale, Rosamund. Are you all right?"

Roz nodded, too shaken to speak. If her life was in danger, they could do nothing. If she told the police, would they believe her?

"Good. Now we're all here." Marge was at the table pouring wine into glasses. "Doris brought a bottle of sherry and insists we all have a drink before she says what she has to say." Marge handed glasses to Roz and Archie, and they went to sit on the couch as Minnie and Doris accepted their wine. Marge took the last glass for herself and sat in a chair beside the table.

"I suppose it's too much for us to expect Major Middleton to join us," Doris said.

"I knocked on his door earlier but there was no answer." Minnie informed them.

"He wouldn't come, even if he was in," Marge commented. "Now, Doris, what's this all about? Are we celebrating something?"

"Hardly." Doris looked around. "Has everyone taken a good drink of the sherry?"

"Yes," said Marge. "Now get on with it."

162

"You know how I sometimes have to courier papers from one government office to another?" Doris looked around to see who was nodding. "Well, today I had to take a file to Scotland Yard." She took a sip of sherry.

"And?" Minnie prompted.

"You'll never guess who I saw." Doris paused.

"Out with it, woman," Marge said in a voice that was almost a shout.

"Our Mr Saunders."

"So?" Marge asked.

"Didn't he tell you he was going overseas again, Archie?" Doris asked.

"Well, no, he didn't. He pushed a note under my door saying he'd be gone for a few weeks. He didn't say where."

"Well, it wouldn't be abroad, I can tell you that."

"Stop being coy, Doris. Say what you have to say." Marge's voice was growing sharper.

"When I got to the Yard, Mr Saunders went out one door as I went in the other. I called after him, but he didn't hear me. He had a couple of men with him. One was the younger police officer who was here on Saturday night."

"I still don't see what is so important you had to call an emergency meeting," Archie said.

"Oh, but you will." Doris took another sip of sherry and looked at them over the rim of her glass. "I thought I might have been mistaken so I asked a police officer in the foyer who the man was. He said he wasn't sure of the man's name but he knew he was a detective with one of the special units."

There was silence for a moment while they all looked at each other, then Archie said slowly, "So Mr Saunders is a policeman."

"Why would he lie to us?" Minnie asked.

Roz knew why. They weren't just watching the house; they had an undercover man planted in it, but why was he away so often?

"You'll have to contact the agent and ask for an explanation, Archie," Doris said.

"Oh, don't tell me you are prejudiced against policemen, too." Marge said with a sigh.

"I'm concerned the agent isn't taking his job seriously," Doris explained. "First he lets in the out-of-work opera singer, then we had that ferret of a man the police took away, and—"

"And now you have me." Roz said. "Is that what you were going to say?"

"Actually, I was going to say *now he lets in a police officer*."

"What's wrong with that?" Roz asked. "It should make us all feel safer in our beds."

"Not if one of the criminals Mr Saunders arrests decides to take his revenge. Then we'll all be in the line of fire," Doris pointed out.

"You've been watching too many cops-and-robbers shows on the telly," Marge said.

"Did you know he was a police officer?" Doris asked Archie.

Archie shifted position. "I told you what he told me. He goes off on assignments for Oxfam."

"That isn't a straight answer." Doris persisted.

"Are you accusing me of lying?" Archie asked in a calm voice.

"Of course she isn't," Minnie said. "I think we're getting off the subject here. As Roz pointed out, we should feel safer with a policeman in the house. And I don't believe some criminal would attack us so he can get at Sandy."

"Nor do I." Marge agreed. "If Sandy doesn't want us to know he's a policeman, he must have a good reason."

"I heard policemen don't like to tell their neighbours what they do for a living. They could be compromised in some way," Minnie said.

"How?" Doris asked.

"Well. . . . I suppose they're a bit like doctors." Minnie answered. "Doctors don't like it when people come up to them at parties to ask their opinion on some ailment or other. Policemen must feel the same way. When they're off duty, they need to relax not deal with problems that should be dealt with through official channels."

"Are you saying I would take advantage of Mr Saunders?" Doris bristled visibly.

"As a matter of fact, yes, I am." Minnie fixed Doris with a glare.

"Well, I never!" Doris glared back indignantly.

"Ladies," Archie said, "you are arguing over something that is merely hypothetical, since Mr Saunders spends very little time here."

"So he can't be working undercover here or he'd be around more often," Marge said.

Roz glanced at Marge. What she said was true. An under-cover policeman would be in the house most of the time.

"It's much too cloak-and-dagger for me." Doris put her glass down and got to her feet. "And another thing—I saw that Briggs man at the end of the Lane this morning. He crossed the road when he saw me, but I recognised him. And he wasn't wearing his fancy clothes or driving his Rolls either." With that, Doris left.

"I don't like it that Briggs is hanging around," Marge said as the door closed. "Do you think you should change the lock on the front door, Archie? I seem to remember he didn't turn in his key when he left."

Archie nodded. "I was thinking of doing that, but I don't have a lock to fit and I'm waiting for the agent to approve the cost of a new one."

"Bugger the cost," said Marge. "Buy the lock and we'll all chip in, right, girls?"

"Right," Minnie said.

"I agree," Roz echoed. That would make it even more difficult for Bertie Briggs to get to the mirror and have his thieving ways with Scarbane House.

"But it's a surprise about Mr Saunders being a policeman. I wonder where he goes when he's away." Marge looked at Archie. "Any ideas?"

"None." Archie answered. "Unless he goes under cover, and I don't mean here, but somewhere else."

"You know," Minnie said thoughtfully. "I often wondered why he didn't have a suntan, if he's supposed to be working overseas I mean."

"I doubt we'll ever know where he goes," said Marge.

"Let's leave well enough alone," said Archie. "He pays his rent on time and doesn't cause any trouble. Are we all agreed?"

Roz and Minnie both said yes, as did Marge, who added, "But I can't speak for Doris."

"You leave Doris to me," Archie said quietly.

"What're you going to do, gag her?" Marge asked with a laugh.

"I can have her thrown out." Archie answered.

"Hear, hear," said Minnie "and now I have to go. I still have unpacking to do. Are you coming, Roz?"

Roz nodded and put her glass down.

As she rose, Archie caught her hand. "Will you be all right, Rosamund?"

"She'll be fine. Won't you, love?" Marge began clearing the glasses away.

"Yes. I'll be fine." Especially behind two new locks.

**

CHAPTER SEVENTEEN

Roz stopped for a cup of tea with Minnie and she was late leaving after looking at photographs of Minnie's niece, her children, and their absent father. Included in the album were several photographs of Minnie's mother wearing the sprig-of-heather brooch. She examined it closely while Minnie made fresh tea. It was the one Madame Sauvé wore.

Nervous because of the second note, Roz was uneasy about going through the mirror at night. It didn't mean she was afraid of the woman, she was sure she could handle her, and she'd handled bigger men than Briggs who thought *No* meant *Okay, if you insist.*

She'd risked going through at night once and been lucky. Next time, the thieves might be waiting for her. The attack could come as soon as she entered Rosamund's bedroom. No one on this side would ever know what happened to her. It was safer to go through in daylight when servants scurried here and there about the house. Thus far, no one had seen her emerge, but there was always a chance Rosamund would be in the room, or Jenny. She had no idea what she would do if that happened.

In the meantime, she must decide whether to contact Detective Inspector Morgan. After they arrested Bertie Briggs, was it conceivable the police had torn her flat apart in an effort to discover the way to the past and found nothing?

She found it by accident. Surely, one of the investigating officers had also found the entrance and the world beyond.

So much of what was happening didn't make sense, but dealing with the mystery was easier than talking to the police and have them think she was a pin short of a box. If only *she* knew how much *they* knew.

Roz undressed for bed, but her attention was on the mirror. She seemed to think more clearly when she was on the other side, and she needed to clear her thoughts.

If she went through now, and Rosamund was in her bedroom, she'd probably be asleep. Few servants would be up and about, and she'd have to take a chance that Briggs and the woman wouldn't be waiting for her. She pulled on the gown and slippers worn during her hurried return, took a deep breath, and stepped back in time.

She stood still, listening, and peering into the gloom. The bed was empty; Rosamund hadn't returned. Her gown shimmered in what little moonlight there was. Roz stepped to the wardrobe and took out a dark shawl to place over her shoulders. Cautiously, she walked to the door and cracked it open. All was silent, the hall and stairway dimly lit by a solitary candle. She crept down the stairs, footsteps muffled by the carpeting, and crossed through the withdrawing room to the French windows.

It was lighter outside, the moon shining intermittently among dark clouds. Roz walked across the terrace and turned to study the upper windows. No candles glowed to show someone was awake and might see her.

Beneath the terrace, the path leading to the treed walk beckoned. David would hardly be there, but thoughts of him drew her down the steps and along the path to the lake.

"He won't be coming."

Roz gasped and spun around. Out of the dark trees, Alex Mindon walked towards her. What was he doing here at this time of night?

"Ridley has returned to London."

David had left. Though her heart skipped a heavy beat at his words, she feigned disinterest. "It is of no concern to me."

"Were I a dunderhead, I would believe that."

He stood in a patch of moonlight and the half smile on his lips made her angry. "Are you calling me a liar, sir?"

"Yes."

Roz tried to pass him, intent on returning to the house. "I do not need your insults."

"Nor I your lies." He blocked her way. "It is late for you to be out. Were you going to see the preparations being made for the Fair?"

"They are of no interest to me."

"That surprises me. Last year, so I'm told, you enjoyed the fair immensely and ran hither and thither, falling into conversation with all manner of people."

"And no doubt I was chastised for behaving in a manner that brought shame to the family."

"You would know better than I. Lady Scarbane's idea of correct behaviour is legendary."

"Does that mean not everyone agrees with her?"

"On the contrary, most are of the opinion you should be horsewhipped."

"I'd have her guts for garters if she tried."

"Only a father has that right, or a husband."

"Hah!" Roz glared at him. "And as my husband, you would take a horsewhip to me?"

"I have always believed a horse learns better with gentle handling."

"Supposing, of course, the horse believes what you want her to do is also what she wants to do."

"Then we must compromise."

"And if a compromise cannot be reached?"

"Then I use the horsewhip."

"Fat chance!"

"My dear, the words you sometimes use are not in keeping with the way others speak. I caution you to be careful of what you say so as not to be misunderstood."

Angry with herself for using a modern idiom, Roz started up the steps to the terrace. "How do you know Mr Ridley has returned to London?"

"I spoke with him regarding it the night of the ball. I made our association known and asked him to withdraw." He kept pace with her.

"You mean you challenged him to a duel?

"How perceptive of you."

Roz shot him a quick look. *The sod! He was enjoying this.* "Why do you persist in this? I shall never marry you. You could be free of me, Lord Mindon, and I am sure my uncle would arrange a more congenial wife, like Adele."

"I doubt she would ever argue with me or raise her voice to me as you do."

"Then ask for her. She will be ecstatic."

"Unfortunately, I am smitten with you for all your bad temper."

Roz glared at him. "I am not bad tempered!"

"Argumentative, then."

"I speak up when I feel the need to do so."

"It is the way your father taught you to be. And for that I thank him."

Roz looked at him in astonishment. "You agree a woman should speak her mind?"

"And with women being educated as you have been."

"That is an admission I never expected to hear you utter."

"Why? One can hold a conversation with an intelligent woman. One can discuss matters with an educated wife. After all, what is one to do with her outside of the bedroom?"

Shocked, she stared at him, her mouth open in a silent *O.*

"I see you have not been educated in the matters that take place behind the closed bedroom door. It will be my pleasure to teach you."

Roz closed her mouth with a snap. "Never!"

She pushed past him, ran to the steps and entered the house, pausing in Rosamund's bedroom to catch her breath.

Whatever else she did, she had to get out of the marriage arranged for her with that detestable man.

*

On Tuesday, with the braiding on Granville's costume finished, Roz met with John and Sally to go over the accounting. Thanks to her haggling in Covent Garden, the wardrobe department came in under budget. Content, John handed her a copy of the script for the next play. Although happy to be kept on, it presented her with a new challenge because the Victorian play was set in a country town in the north of England. Even as John gave her a thumbnail description of the play, she visualised bonnets and multiple petticoats under wide skirts. Men wore mismatched jackets and pants, because the suit didn't become common wear until years later. She left the office with her mind already on the intricacies of early Victorian dress.

"You're deep in thought, Roz."

She looked up. Derek.

"What do you think of the new play?"

"I haven't had time to read the script yet."

"If I can be of help, please let me know."

"Thanks." Roz walked on. That wasn't the Derek she knew. It had to be an act and he couldn't keep it up indefinitely. In a way, she missed the old Derek.

Agatha and Charlie were drinking tea when she arrived in the workroom.

"There's my young girlfriend," Charlie said with a grin.

Roz squeezed his shoulder affectionately as she walked around him to the other side of the table. "Any tea left?"

"In the pot," Agatha said, "but we ran out of biscuits."

"Oh, well. . . ." Roz poured herself tea and sat. "How are you, Charlie? Has anything happened at the museum we should know about?"

"Funny you should say that," said Charlie. "Jim said as there were a kerfuffle going on last night. A lot of shouting and people running about all over the place as if they was chasing somebody. He heard the front door open and slam shut, and then open again. He could even feel the draught, but when he checked the door it were locked."

Roz wondered about the chase. Was that the reason Alex Mindon was up and about that late?

"It's odd none of you can understand what's being said, even when there's shouting," Agatha commented.

"I know, but Roz'll tell you the sounds are muffled, like. Isn't that right?"

"The voices sound as if they're coming from far away."

"Hundreds of years away, I reckon," said Charlie.

"Shut up, you two," Agatha shrilled. "You fair give me the willies."

Roz and Charlie grinned at each other and Charlie got up to leave. "It's something me and my girlfriend will discuss another time."

"You're not going back into the museum are you?" Agatha asked after Charlie left.

"How do you mean?" Roz studied Agatha. If there was a connection between Agatha and the thieves, was she checking if Roz would obey the note?

"I mean that you shouldn't go at night ever again. It's dangerous. Things could happen to you."

"What sorts of things?"

"I don't know! You might get hurt."

"How? Charlie would never hurt me, and as for the voices—or ghosts if you like—they can't hurt me." Unless she was in a time when the ghost wasn't a ghost but alive and well.

"It's up to you, but you can't say I didn't warn you."

"No, I can't say you didn't warn me," Roz snapped.

"Does that mean you'll be going again?"

"I'm thinking about it."

Agatha snorted and rose to clear away the teacups. Defiance sharpened her voice: "And another thing—if I'm working both shows on Saturday, you can work the Wednesday night show."

"Fine, but you'll have to work the Wednesday matinee."

Roz brought a pad and pencil to the table and opened the script. She read the list of characters and two more actors were included in the cast. Unless they performed badly, the Nostalgie tended to hire the same actors if there were suitable parts. Pleased Laura Whaley would be in the next production, because she was fond of the young actress, Roz studied the stage layout. There would be two sets of scenery: a farmhouse kitchen and a forest, so none of the clothes could be green.

The words faded. . . .

Was Agatha warning her against something? Did she know Bertie Briggs was making threats? Would he try to get into her flat on Wednesday night? He could try, but there was a new lock and another would be on the front door, so it would not be easy.

Roz forced her thoughts back to the script. She was making notes and drawing preliminary sketches when Sally popped her head around the door.

"Roz? Can you come up to the office for a moment?"

Roz placed the pencil inside the script to mark her place, then stood and went out. "Does John want to see me?" she asked as they walked along the corridor.

"No. It's—" Sally glanced behind them and kept her voice low. "It's two police officers in civvies. They said to keep it confidential. What is this about, Roz?"

"We had an intruder at the house where I live. I expect they want to ask if I've remembered anything more."

"Was anyone hurt?"

"No. We never saw the man, at least we assume it was a man, but one of the tenants heard him."

"Was anything stolen?"

"Not that we can tell."

"How odd that the police would follow up on it if no one was hurt and nothing was stolen." Sally led the way up the stairs. "I've put them in John's office. He went for an early lunch so it will be private."

"I don't think it's that big of a deal but I suppose we'd better do as they ask. I don't know why they want to keep it confidential unless—" Unless they knew Agatha was connected with Bertie Briggs and they didn't want her to know.

"Unless what, Roz?"

Roz evaded the question. "Perhaps you shouldn't mention any of this to anyone, except to John, of course. He has a right to know."

"As his secretary, I can't keep something like this from him." Sally walked into the office and crossed it to open the door to John's sanctum. "Here she is."

"Thank you, Miss Jones." Detective Inspector Morgan rose from the chair behind the desk. "Please come in, Miss Reid."

Sally left and Roz entered. The younger detective stood with his back against the wall. She nodded to him then sat in the chair facing the desk as he closed the door. "Why do you want to see me, Inspector?"

Morgan dropped back into the chair. "Have there been any more notes?"

"No."

"How about uninvited visitors?"

"None I'm aware of."

"Nothing unusual happen? You would tell me, wouldn't you?"

"Of course and in return I want you to tell me why a police detective is living in the house."

Surprise showed briefly in Morgan's face. He masked it so quickly she couldn't be sure it had been there. "So you've discovered Saunders is an officer of the law."

"One of my neighbours saw him at Scotland Yard and made enquiries."

"I see."

"Why is he there?"

Morgan shot a quick glance at the other officer. "We don't crawl out from under stones, despite what some think. We must all live somewhere. I assume it's what Saunders is doing."

"That answer doesn't satisfy me. He told no one he was a policeman."

"I'm sure the agent is aware of Saunders' occupation."

"Oh." Roz remembered the form she filled out when she wanted to rent her flat. She had to list her occupation, but— "He told the other tenants he worked for Oxfam and would be away much of the time. Why would he lie?"

"You must understand—and this is strictly confidential, Miss Reid, I don't want it passed on to the other tenants—Detective Saunders is attached to Special Branch. He is sometimes involved in what could be dangerous situations. When this happens, to safeguard his home and his neighbours, he will take up temporary residence somewhere else. That is why he is rarely at home and invented the Oxfam connection."

It was plausible. So why didn't she believe him? The doubt must have shown in her face.

"I'm asking you not to pursue this."

Roz bit her lip and studied him. If only everything could be out in the open. Before she could risk earning the name *lunatic,* she had to know what they knew. "Something is going on, Inspector; I'd be a fool not to realise that. Why don't you tell me?"

His eyes were bland, emotionless. "Tell you what?"

"You are a senior officer, aren't you? I don't mean to be rude but at your age, and a Detective inspector, you must be a valuable member of the police force. Why are you answering calls about an intruder?"

"I happened to be in the area."

"Then tell me this. As a senior officer, why are you investigating petty thefts from the Scarborough Museum?"

Morgan didn't show the surprise Roz expected. "So you know about that."

"You know I work with Charlie Watts, and you know he would probably tell me you participated in his interrogation. Why do you think I wouldn't make the connection?"

Morgan didn't answer, but he glanced at the other man and then eyed Roz.

"You are watching the museum and the house aren't you?"

"What makes you think that?"

"Feminine intuition?" Roz watched him smile. "Perhaps you'd prefer to call it logical deduction. I know Bertie Briggs used to live in my flat, and you tore the flat apart in an effort to find out how he got into the museum from there. I also know Briggs is watching the house, and he may be the intruder we had the other night. Is that what you thought? Is that why you came yourself and why you arrived so quickly?"

"You are putting two and two together and getting five and a half."

"No, I'm not."

Morgan rubbed a hand across his chin as he studied her. "Miss Reid, we're conducting a delicate investigation."

"The investigation of the theft of antiquities cannot possibly be so delicate it requires the attention of a senior officer. You arrested Bertie Briggs once, do so again, or arrest his accomplice, and we can all rest easy." Behind her, the sergeant cleared his throat but Morgan's eyes didn't leave her face.

"Are you telling me Briggs is working with someone?"

"A woman."

Morgan looked puzzled. "Who is this woman?"

"I don't know," she admitted.

He took a notebook and pen from his pocket. "Describe her."

"I've never seen her but Amelia did."

"Who is Amelia?"

"She used to live in my flat before Briggs. She lives in Oxford now."

Pen poised, he asked, "Do you have her address?"

"No, but Mrs Wilton does."

"Ah." He made a note.

"Look," Roz said, "why don't you just arrest Briggs?"

"On what charge should I arrest him?"

"Theft of course. Surely he's tried to fence the goods."

"Fence? Goods?"

"Don't treat me like an idiot, Inspector. We both suspect Bertie Briggs and this woman are stealing from the museum. If they aren't keeping the things for their own use they have to be passing them on to someone."

"And who might that someone be?"

Roz didn't have an answer.

"The matter isn't as cut and dried as you think, is it? We know nothing about the woman, but if Briggs is the thief, the stolen articles are not in his possession and he hasn't contacted his usual outlets."

"What are they doing with the things they steal?"

"You seem sure he is the thief."

Roz studied him. He had the look of someone who had just gained a victory. Why? Quickly, she went over the conversation. *He'd side tracked her*! "I still don't understand why a senior officer would be in charge of an investigation involving petty theft."

The victorious glimmer faded from his eyes. "Can I rely on your discretion, Miss Reid? On absolute confidentiality?"

"Of course."

"While our cover is the investigation of the thefts from the museum, the real investigation involves a possible murder."

Roz gasped. "Murder! Who was murdered?"

"I can't tell you."

"Was it a woman?"

"Miss Reid, please! This is a delicate matter and I cannot give you any information."

"Was it the woman who once lived in my flat?"

A sliver of ice entered Morgan's eyes and voice. "I told you—"

"Are you by any chance investigating the disappearance of Madame Sauvé who used to live in my flat?"

He looked away. "We closed that investigation some time ago."

"So you found her?"

"We know where she is."

That was impossible, unless— "Where does she live now?"

"Still in London."

Technically, that was true but . . . . His answer sent Roz's mind into a turmoil. How much did he know? Before she could decide what to do, he asked:

"About the threatening notes you got, who do you think sent them?"

"Bertie Briggs."

"Why?"

If only she could tell him the whole truth. "It stands to reason, doesn't it? When he lived in my flat, he had access to the museum. I live there now so I'm in his way."

Something flickered in his eyes and was quickly gone.

Good grief, she'd confirmed there was a way from her flat into the museum.

"But you won't consider moving out temporarily?"

"No."

"By staying you place yourself at risk."

"Perhaps, but there's a new lock on the door to my flat and another is being installed on the front door today."

Morgan leaned back in the chair. "You're a feisty little thing, aren't you?"

"Don't patronise me, Inspector." Roz stood in a wave of indignation. "If this interview is over I have work to do." She stomped across the room, hesitating only while the younger man hurriedly stepped away from the door.

"Miss Reid?" Morgan's voice halted her. "I leave you with this thought. Briggs is a burglar and burglars have a way with locks."

**

CHAPTER EIGHTEEN

Detective Inspector Morgan's parting shot left Roz with no appetite for lunch.

"What did Sally want you for?" Agatha asked when she got back to the workroom.

"Just a question on the accounting." The answer satisfied Agatha and Roz hoped she wouldn't ask for details.

It was difficult to behave in a natural manner around Agatha when she suspected such terrible things of the woman. After an hour of trying, Roz stuffed the script and notepad into her holdall and announced she was off home to do some research and make preliminary sketches.

A note attached to the row of white buttons beside the front door instructed tenants to press No. 1. Roz did so and saw scratch marks on the wood, probably made when Archie installed the new lock. It looked the same as the lock on Aunt Lily's front door. Once, when Uncle Nick forgot his key, and no one was home to let him in, he opened the door with a penknife.

Marge answered the door with several keys in her hand. "You are home early," she commented as she gave Roz a key.

"I decided to work at home where it's quieter." Roz slipped the old key off her chain and passed it to Marge.

"What are you going to sew?"

"I'm not." Roz shook her head. "I'm making notes about costumes for the play they'll be staging in September."

"You start this far ahead?"

Roz nodded. "I have to design the costumes according to the characters' status in society and know their actions so I can make allowances for their movements." She walked to the stairs.

"That policeman rang Archie earlier."

Roz paused with her foot on the first step and turned. "Did he have any news?"

"No, but he suggested Archie install a certain brand of lock on the front door. He said it was the best type to foil burglars." Marge chuckled. "Half an hour later a courier turned up with the lock."

Was it possible Morgan was setting a trap and supplied a lock Bertie Briggs would be able to open easily? He told her burglars could open most locks. So much for police concern. "I didn't know police did that."

"Nor did I. The others will have to ring our bell, too. I hope you won't be disturbed."

"Is everyone out?"

"Except for the Major, we've heard him moving about up there."

Saunders was still away. Perhaps it was as well because Roz wasn't sure what she would say to him. She continued up the stairs and entered her flat.

The divider was as she'd left it.

Roz found it impossible to concentrate and her attention kept straying to the mirror. Feeling guilty, she set the sketchpad aside, took off her watch, and stripped to her underwear before picking up the gown and shawl she had brought back from the other side. She hesitated for a moment before sliding the divider to one side and stepping into the past.

*

On the bed were piles of neatly folded clothes and an open trunk sat on the floor at the foot of the bed. Several articles of clothing lay swathed in linen in the bottom. It looked as if Rosamund, or even the whole family, were about to move.

Roz checked the wardrobe. Only three gowns hung inside, matching footwear paired beneath. She slipped a gown over her head and then donned a pair of slippers before walking to the window.

Beyond the formal yews and the hedge around the rose garden, a patchwork of gaily-striped awnings fluttered in the breeze, ready for the fair.

If she walked under the trees beside the lake, would David be there? Perhaps, but she couldn't go out with her hair hanging over her shoulders, and the two-pronged pins Jenny used were more than she could manage. She went to the bell pull to summon her.

A girl who came in answer looked ten years old. An apron, spotlessly white, hung almost to her bare feet. The hands she wrung together were chapped and red, perhaps from being too long in water. She was probably the scullery maid.

"Where is Jenny?" Roz asked.

The girl shied away from the words as if expecting Roz to hit her. "She be gone."

"Gone where?"

"Ta help in they field, mum."

"The field where the fair is to be held?"

"Yes'm."

"Thank you. That will be all." She'd have to manage her hair somehow. She twisted it into a rope, caught it up in a knot on top of her head and inserted several of the pins. It was lopsided but it would have to do. She was about to leave when there was a tap on the door and another woman appeared.

"Who are you?" Roz asked.

Surprised by the question, the woman answered calmly. "I am Hilda, Miss Adele's personal maid. I intercepted the kitchen maid on her way from your room and she said you had need of Jenny. She thought it was to do your hair."

"Clever girl." Roz went back to the dressing table and sat. "I can do nothing with it. Will you try?"

"Yes, Miss Rosamund." Hilda stood behind Roz and removed the pins from the haphazard arrangement. Deftly, she swept Roz's hair up and around her fingers and secured the curls with several pins. Then she opened a drawer and took out a box of powder.

"What is that?" Roz eyed the powder with suspicion.

"For the complexion, Miss; your skin is darkened by the sun and it is not becoming."

"Give me that." Roz took the box and gave the contents a cautious sniff. Beneath the rose perfume, there was a faint odour of rotten eggs. "What's in it?"

"I am sure I do not know all the contents. Attar of Roses, of course, and powdered arsenopyrite to—"

"Arsenopyrite. . . . Wait a minute. . . ." One of the courses she took at design school referred to dyes and leather treatment. They said. . . . "That's a form of arsenic! Deadly poison!" Roz handed her the box. "I will not use it."

"Miss Adele uses it to enhance the complexion."

"Then tell her to stop. That powder will kill her."

"Yes, Miss." The maid replaced the box in the drawer and stood back. "Will there be anything else?"

"Nothing, thank you." In the mirror, her hair looked great.

Before she left, Hilda brought her a parasol. "To protect your complexion from the sun, Miss Rosamund."

Roz took the parasol and left.

She met no one as she went downstairs and exited the house via the French windows. Nor did she see anyone when she ran across the terrace and down the steps to the path alongside the lake. She dawdled and watched the direction from which David rode that first day, but when someone joined her it was Alex Mindon.

He came from the direction of the house. He must have walked across the grass under the trees because she didn't hear him until he was within a few paces of her and spoke.

"I told you he has returned to London."

"And I told you it was of no interest to me." She turned to face him. "I also told you I would never marry you whatever harm my refusal may cause the family."

"Harm? What harm?"

"Am I not the pawn in a ridiculous game whereby you can bring the family to financial ruin if I do not marry you?"

"Who told you this pack of lies?" His eyes were piercing.

In many ways, Roz preferred the mockery she usually saw there. "Lady Imogen believed it to be so but she has not questioned my uncle on the terms of your contract."

"Nor will she; Stephen Oldham died last night."

Startled, Roz asked, "What?" How would this affect Rosamund, who was his ward?

"I do not have all the details but there was an accident with a carriage. It overturned pinning Stephen beneath. I came here *post haste* with the news to find Lady Imogen and Adele are paying social calls somewhere in the vicinity."

"Oh." Tears filled her eyes. She'd met Stephen Oldham only once but she imagined the effect on Imogen and Adele.

"I'm sorry to have broken the news in such a way but I had not thought you had strong feelings for your uncle."

"This makes me a ward of Sir Hugh and Lady Scarbane doesn't it?"

"So that is why you are upset. I thought better of you, Rosamund."

"Stephen Oldham's death releases you from any contract he arranged, doesn't it? This is your opportunity to be free of me, Lord Mindon."

"If it were my choice." He took her arm. "While we wait for Lady Imogen and Adele to return, let us see how they have progressed setting up the booths for the fair

"I should prefer to return to the house," Roz squeaked.

"Impossible. If we return now, it would look as if we are trying to avoid Lady Ridley who is bearing down on us." He greeted the other woman when they were within speaking distance. "Good day to you, Lady Ridley."

"And good day to you, Lord Mindon." Lady Ridley's long nose pointed in Roz's direction and her sharp eyes scrutinised her. "Are you crying, Rosamund?"

"I have just made Rosamund aware of her Uncle Stephen's death."

"Stephen Oldham dead? How?"

"An unfortunate incident with a carriage. I have not yet acquainted Lady Scarbane of the accident for she is not at home."

"Oh, my dear child." Lady Ridley held out a hand to Roz.

Alex Mindon placed an arm around Roz' shoulders and a handkerchief in her hands. "I am sure you will excuse us, Lady Ridley. Rosamund needs to grieve in private."

"Yes, yes, of course. If I can do anything I can do. . . ."

"Thank you. I shall acquaint Lady Scarbane with your kind offer." He kept his arm around Roz and they walked towards the house. "Keep your head down and the handkerchief to your face."

"You think my grief is not real?"

"I know your grief is not real, but you are in shock."

"Is she still watching?"

"I will not look back and neither will you." His arm tightened as if to make sure she wasn't able to turn her head even if she wanted to.

When they entered the house, Roz pulled free of him and made for the stairs.

"Rosamund?"

She whirled around, one hand on the rail to steady herself. "What now?"

"Lady Imogen and Adele will need your comfort and support. It would be unkind to hide from them at such a time."

Roz nodded then continued up the stairs. She could be here tonight and tomorrow morning but she had to be at the Nostalgie tomorrow night. It might make her appear callous in their eyes but, with David gone to London, perhaps her visits through the mirror should cease. But if they did, how could she hope to recover Minnie's brooch?

*

Roz went through every drawer and cupboard in Rosamund's bedroom in search of a clue to the girl's whereabouts. If only she could ask Jenny. She was almost certain the maid knew she wasn't whom she pretended to be, but until she was sure, she dare not ask.

The only corners of the house she hadn't searched were the kitchen areas. Even if one of the servants were to help Rosamund, she wouldn't be able to stay hidden there for long.

Wheels crunched up the driveway. Imogen and Adele had returned. Roz opened the bedroom door and crept along the upper hall as they entered the house.

Alex Mindon met them and Imogen expressed surprise at seeing him. She asked where Rosamund was and he replied she was in her room. He then said he wished to speak to them in the withdrawing room. They left the hall and Roz returned to the bedroom. Even through two closed doors, she heard Imogen's anguished cry and her heart ached for the woman.

Roz didn't know what to do. Should she extend sympathy even though Stephen was her uncle? Should she allow Imogen a time of private grief? What of Adele? How had she taken the news? Roz had no way of knowing how close Stephen Oldham had been to Adele. She paced the room, and it began to grow dark.

Jenny brought a lighted candle to light the other candles. "Lord Mindon asks if yer be going to dinner, Miss."

"Is it necessary for me to go down? Can't I eat up here?"

Jenny spoke haltingly, as if trying to remember the exact words she was to repeat. "Lord Mindon says as he is a guest and one of the family should eat wiv him, Miss."

"What of Lady Scarbane? Or Adele?"

"They be gone to their rooms."

185

"I see." Roz studied Jenny. "You've heard my uncle is dead?"

Jenny nodded.

"Is there anything suitable in the wardrobe I can wear? Anything black?"

"No, Miss, but there be a band ye wore when—"

When Rosamund's parents died. "Very well, you choose something." With Imogen and Adele both overcome with grief, it fell to Roz, as Rosamund, to step in as hostess. Dining alone with Alex Mindon didn't appeal to her but under the circumstances she could do nothing else.

Jenny took a gown of deep blue from the wardrobe and helped Roz dress. "I'll do yer 'air now."

"Don't bother." Roz tucked a stray curl into the cluster at the top of her head. "I'm sure Lord Mindon won't expect me to look my best." If she looked a disaster it might put him off. "When is dinner to be served?"

"Soon as ye go down, Miss."

"Thank you." Without even a glance in the mirror, Roz left the room.

The door to the dining room was ajar and Roz entered silently. Alex Mindon stood beside the fireplace; one elbow on the mantel he stared into the flames. He was unaware of her presence and she had the opportunity to study him.

He was a handsome man, as Adele said. His nose was aquiline above lips full and sensual and his black hair had a deep wave long enough to curl onto the high collar of the frockcoat. He still wore the dark coat, leather breeches and knee-high, tight-fitting boots he had worn earlier. He looked so tired, so desolate, Roz had an urge to hold him to offer comfort.

Good grief! What was she thinking! She detested this man!

"Good evening, Lord Mindon." Roz walked forward.

He straightened and turned to her. "Good evening, Rosamund. Are you recovered from the news of your uncle's unfortunate accident?"

"I am well enough." She moved to the table and sat. "I am told dinner will be served immediately."

"I am glad you have an appetite after such tragic news." He took a chair across from Roz and sat down.

"I am told you asked, nay demanded, one of the family undertake to play hostess for you. The duty fell to me." His jaw tightened. Did he seriously think she would enjoy dining alone with him? "I didn't realise you were to stay on once you acquainted us with the sad news."

"Unfortunately, there is no male member of the Scarbane family here to attend to the arrangements."

"The arrangements being?"

"Stephen will be returned to Scarborough for burial in the family vault. First, the casket will come here because London is *en route*. I will accompany him to Scarborough."

"When?"

"If all goes as planned, the casket should arrive here late on Friday and we shall begin the journey north on Saturday morning."

"We?"

"Lady Imogen, Adele, you and I."

David would take her to see Angeline Sauvé on Saturday.

Roz dare not go to Scarborough. If she travelled so far away from the mirror, would she be able to get back if the dimensions should collide? In addition, she would never get back in time for the celebratory dinner on Sunday evening and might lose her job. Vaguely, she was aware of a servant ladling soup into the bowl before her. Her mind elsewhere, Roz spooned the soup around.

How was she to get out of this? The situation wasn't one in which hiding away would be accepted. They would tear the place apart looking for her. Dishes of meat, potatoes and peas arrived at the table. She transferred some to her plate but shook her head at the gravy boat hovering at her shoulder.

Alex' voice cut across her thoughts. "Lady Imogen planned for the family to leave for Scarborough immediately after church on Sunday, so preparations for departure were already underway."

Now the half-filled trunk made sense. "The fair was to take place on Saturday."

"Naturally, it has been cancelled. Were you looking forward to attending?"

"Yes." To meet David, go to London, and find Madame Sauvé. Would she be able to find her own way to the city? Could she commandeer a coach or a trap? Even if she arranged it, when she got there how would she find the opera singer?

A stemmed dish of sherbet took the place of the plate.

If she went to Ridley Manor, would they give her David's address? Then, if she got to London, would he be home? Someone took the stemmed dish away and only the cloth remained. White damask, with a fingernail, she traced the pattern of roses.

She must find Rosamund and acquaint her with the news of her uncle's death and the family's imminent departure. She had searched every possible place where the girl could hide; her only recourse was to speak to Jenny. The maid must know where Rosamund was, but how could she explain who she herself was? How could she explain she came from the future?

"Shall we adjourn to the withdrawing room?"

His voice jerked Roz into lifting her head. So deep had she been in trying to solve her problems that, for a moment, she couldn't focus. She nodded and rose unsteadily, resting her hand for support on the back of each chair as she walked by. When she reached the end of the table, Alex Mindon took her elbow to guide her from the room.

As they emerged into the hallway, the candles flickered and dimmed. A static crackling came from an area near the front door and a man's voice announced *This is the nine o'clock news.*

Roz swayed and would have fallen if not for the supporting hand under her elbow. She turned to Alex, wild eyed. Had he heard?

He looked at her in enquiry. "Are you unwell?"

Roz shook her head in reply. How close were the two time periods; how close were they to forming a rift with catastrophic results?

When they reached the withdrawing room, she sank gratefully onto a chair beside the fire. She heard him issuing orders to a servant in a low voice. Aware of not being a good hostess, Roz tried to pull herself together.

"I assume you'll be staying the night, Lord Mindon. I shall arrange for a room to be prepared." Was her voice slurred? Her words were running into each other as if they had no energy to space themselves out.

Then he was before her, kneeling on the rose carpet. Roses or peonies? He covered one of her hands with his own. She studied it dully; saw the strength in it and the heavy gold and onyx ring on his finger.

"Do not be concerned for me as I have arranged everything with the housekeeper."

There was a housekeeper? How little she knew about the household. How little she knew about anything. She had been behaving. . . . How? As she had when she was a brash seventeen-year-old? Like a spoilt brat? Like Rosamund? What was she to do now—desert Imogen and Adele when they needed her? How could she not desert them? She couldn't go to Scarborough. She dare not leave London.

"This has affected you more deeply than I had expected."

Roz looked into his face. He showed every sign of exhaustion. He must have ridden all night to bring them the news. There were fine lines around eyes that showed his weariness and she had shown him nothing but hostility. He was doing all he could to help the family yet he couldn't have known them long. They were business associates, nothing more. She wondered why he was so concerned. "You are going out of your way to be kind to us, Lord Mindon. Why?" There, now she was being an ungrateful, impertinent brat again.

He had no time to answer because a servant entered and placed a tray on the table. When he left, Alex Mindon brought Roz a cup of hot milk. "This will help you sleep." He wrapped both her hands around the cup.

Roz raised the cup and took a sip. "There's something in this."

"Some brandy. To help you sleep." He went to the table and came back with a glass of wine. He sat in the chair at the other side of the fire. "You ate nothing at dinner."

"I wasn't hungry." When did she have her last meal? Roz took a drink from the cup and felt warmth course through her.

"Have you spoken to Lady Imogen or Adele?"

Roz shook her head. "Not yet."

"In the morning, perhaps, when you are all feeling stronger."

"I heard Aunt Imogen cry out. Was Adele very upset?"

"Your aunt was naturally distraught. Adele fainted when she heard the news. She hasn't your strength, neither of will nor of character."

Roz looked at him, wondering if he mocked her, but saw no glint of humour in his eyes. "I don't feel very strong right now."

"That is understandable, but I am here, Rosamund. Lean on me. Use my strength."

Roz looked away, fighting the tears brought on by his concern and shame at her ingratitude. "Why are you being so kind when I have shown you nothing but hostility?"

"Isn't it obvious?"

"No, it isn't."

"When I first saw you, I saw someone different from the other women who are thrown at me at every turn. You were not taught to faint at the drop of a hat or to sew a fine seam."

Roz giggled into the cup. "Oh, but I assure you I can sew a very fine seam."

"No doubt you can, but you must know what I'm trying to say."

"I'm not sure I do. You don't know me."

"Perhaps not all there is to know, but I shall in the future."

No, he wouldn't. In the future, in her time period, he would have been dead for over a century. Dust to dust. All that strength and male beauty mouldered away. "Ashes to ashes," she said quietly and let her tears flow.

"Rosamund?" He set the glass down and came to her side. "Perhaps it is time I helped you to your room."

In a final burst of strength and gathering of senses, she said, "I don't need your help."

"As you wish." He stood back.

Roz put the cup down and rose to her feet. She swayed and her view of the room blurred.

As she began to fall, he caught her and lifted her in his arms. He carried her from the room and up the stairs, laid her on the bed, removed her slippers and drew the cover to her chin.

Half asleep, Roz felt something brush her cheek. It could have been a kiss or it could have been his fingers. She only half heard his murmured, "Sleep well, my Rosamund."

**

CHAPTER NINETEEN

Roz had no idea of the time when she woke. It was light outside but clouds stood like a barrier before the sun and she couldn't gauge the time by its position. She felt groggy as she went to the washbowl behind the screen to splash water on her face. She was drying herself on a square of linen when Jenny entered carrying a tray of rattling china.

"What time is it?" Roz asked, ignoring the look on Jenny's face when she noted Roz was still wearing the gown she'd worn for dinner.

"Just after seven, Miss. Lord Mindon. . . . He said as I were to bring yer tea." Jenny poured a cup from the pot.

Roz took the tea and dropped onto the stool at the dressing table. "Where is Lord Mindon?"

"He be gone, Miss; left at six this mornin'."

"Do you know where he went?"

"No, Miss."

"Is Lady Scarbane awake?"

"Yes, Miss. Her took tea with Lord Mindon."

Roz had time to visit Imogen before she had to leave for the Nostalgie, but she dare not go looking as she did. "Find me something to wear."

Jenny went to the wardrobe and Roz wondered what she should say to Imogen. Should she offer condolences? Stephen Oldham was supposedly her uncle and Imogen should be offering her condolences. Still. . . .

"Shall I do yer 'air, Miss?"

"Just tidy it. When I've spoken to Lady Scarbane, I shall go back to bed. I don't want to be disturbed after that, not even for luncheon."

"Yes, Miss." Jenny stood behind her and fiddled with her hair.

"What of Adele? Is she awake?"

"She were given a potion, Miss. Madam says as she'd be sleeping most of the day."

Jenny was taking too long with her hair. It still had a bit of a *drawn-through-a-hedge-backwards* look about it, but it would do.

"That will be all. Thank you, Jenny." Roz got to her feet, went out, and walked along the hallway to tap on Imogen's door.

"Enter."

Imogen was standing at the window with her back to Roz. She was still in her wrap, her hair flowing to her waist.

"I came to say I'm sorry."

"You are sorry." Imogen swung around and cast upon her such a look of red-eyed hatred that Roz took a step back. "You are sorry. Now he is dead, you are sorry. After the trouble you caused Stephen when he was alive; the shame you brought on him. The shame you brought on all of us. We are forced to leave here because of you. Were you aware of that? We shall be leaving earlier than intended, which is a blessing, for neither Adele nor I will have to put up with the whispers a day longer. Get out of my sight, you miserable creature! Stay out of my sight! I do not wish to see you until we leave for Scarborough. It is unfortunate I must see you then."

Faced with such vehemence, Roz could say nothing. Eyes filled with tears, she turned to the door and rushed out. In the hallway, she ran into Alex Mindon.

"You came back. I thought— Jenny said—"

"Rosamund? What is it?"

"Imogen. She said. . . . She said. . . ." Roz had never before faced such hatred and it shook her. "Am I so bad?"

"Tell me what this is about." With a hand under her chin, he raised her head. "Why are you crying?"

"Imogen said I brought shame to Stephen. She said I brought shame to all of them." Looking up at him, she implored, "What did I do that was so bad? What did I do?" She buried her face in her hands, and in despair she repeated, "What did I do?"

"Nothing. You did nothing."

"I must have." What had Rosamund done that she didn't know about?

"You have done no more than be true to yourself. You are who you are, Rosamund. You were your father's only child, his heir. With no son to take over the business, he trained you. He took you to the shipyards almost as soon as you could walk. He taught you about running a business He also made you spend time with a tutor he hired to educate you as he would a son. You can tell a mast from a yardarm, a sheepshank from a reef knot."

"He expected a woman to run the shipyard?"

"Not an easy thing in this world, I'll grant you."

Suddenly, Roz was alert. "What do you mean *in this world*?"

He hesitated before answering. "In the Americas it is easier. There are women there who run farms and hostelries, they own shops and stables, but here—" He looked into her eyes. "To be brought up as you were, is it surprising you find the life here confining? From the freedom of the shipyard, you have come to spending your days having luncheon with neighbours or being at home to them. Is it any wonder there are times when you must break free?"

"But what did I do that they should be shamed by me?"

"You did nothing but be yourself. You harmed no one, and in the Americas your behaviour would go unremarked."

She took a shuddering breath.

"Do not change, Rosamund. Always be true to yourself."

In that moment, a carriage rumbled along the.

"That will be either Lady Edrington or Lady Ridley come to pay their respects. Imogen is in no state to receive them and neither are you nor Adele, so it falls to me." He touched his hand to her cheek. "Rest, my love, the days ahead will not be easy ones."

*

Roz was late getting to work. After Alex left to greet whoever arrived, Roz rushed through the mirror. Even as she took off the gown and removed the pins from her hair, Imogen's hate-filled outburst rang in her ears. In the shower, her skin prickled as if with ice, and tears welled and fall with the water. As for her hair, it wouldn't lie as she wanted, and she tied it back at the nape of her neck. Nothing was working out right. The milk for her coffee was sour, the egg she cracked was rotten, and she broke one of the laces on a trainer. Snuffling into a wad of paper hankies, she left the house.

Aware of the curious glances cast her way, she tried to stem the flow of tears. Logically, it was ridiculous for her to feel the pain Imogen and Adele were feeling. They and Stephen Oldham had been dead nearly two hundred years. They were nothing to her and she was even less to them. She had no ties to them beyond the mirror that allowed her into their world.

It didn't help when she arrived at the Nostalgie and have Sally, going through receipts with the stage door manager, see her.

"My, but you look peaky, Roz. Is everything all right?"

"Fine." Tears blurring the way, Roz rushed past them and down the stairs to the workroom.

Thankfully, although she was late, it was still too early for Agatha to be there. She put the kettle on and took a handful of biscuits from the packet. When the water boiled, she made tea and sat to drink it.

Imogen's face hovered before her, the eyes livid in the grief-ravaged face and the anger-twisted mouth a hard line. No one had ever before looked at Roz in that way. Dislike, she could cope with, but hatred, loathing—that was something else. What did Rosamund do to deserve it?

If what Alex Mindon said was true, Rosamund was a woman ahead of her time. In this world, women ran businesses, they went down mines, and they became fire fighters. Rosamund would fit in well.

Oddly, when she went over the previous twenty-four hours in her mind, the only feeling of warmth came from Alex's kindness.

But wait— What had he called her? *Love?* He spoke of taming her, hinted at sex, but never mentioned love before. In this world, the word meant no more than chum or pal. Charlie called her love all the time, but it didn't mean he loved her as a man would love a woman.

Don't be silly, Roz, she told herself. Alex Mindon didn't love her, but perhaps he loved the thought of the shipyard Rosamund may have inherited.

Did she inherit anything? Imogen said she had no dowry to speak of, so what had happened to the shipyard? Was the money in trust until she was older or married?

Roz blew her nose and looked around when the door opened and John Waltham walked in.

"Sally said you didn't look well." He perched a distance away on a corner of the worktable. "I must say you look washed out. Is there anything I can do?"

Roz shook her head. "I didn't sleep well last night." She sniffed back her tears.

"Starting a cold, are you?"

Roz wiped her nose and cleared her throat, but before she could speak, he continued.

"In our business, a cold is the last thing we want to spread through the cast and Angela's particularly susceptible. We can't have our leading lady ill, can we, not during the last week's run of the play. I insist you go home to bed."

"I'll be fine."

"But we can't take that chance. I must insist you leave immediately."

They both looked towards the door as Agatha came in.

"Ah, Mrs Grey. Our Roz isn't very well so I'm sending her home. You'll have to cope on your own."

"Going home?" Agatha reacted more vehemently than Roz expected. "But she can't!"

"We can't have the cast catching whatever it is, and I'm sure you could do with the overtime to make up for the time you've lost in the past week." John looked at Roz. "Oh, yes, I know you handled both performances last Saturday, so it's Mrs Grey's turn, don't you think?"

"I'm supposed to do both performances today?" Agatha asked, not sounding too happy about it.

"That's what I said." John Waltham hopped off the table. "Come along, Roz. I'll see you to the stage door and Derek can drive you home."

Good grief! That was all she needed to cap off her morning. And she didn't want Derek to see her in the state she was in. "What if he catches what I have and passes it on?"

"I suppose you're right. We'll get you a taxi."

Feeling guilty, Roz allowed him to escort her from the theatre. She huddled miserably in the back of the taxi while John Waltham passed money to the driver.

John ducked his head into the open door. "Don't come back until you are no longer infectious, all right?"

For the short journey home, Roz let her head fall onto the back of the seat. Why did other people's misery affect her? This time, was Imogen's hatred of her the cause or was she upset at Stephen Oldham's death? Had Rosamund been fond of her uncle? Could she be picking up vibes from her? What of Alex? He hadn't seemed upset by Stephen Oldham's death even though he was doing all he could to help Imogen. It could be because he had a lot to gain.

"Here we are, love." The driver drew up in front of the house. "Do you need any help to get out?"

"I'll manage." She emerged from the taxi into bright sunshine. "Thank you."

"You take care now."

As the taxi drove off, she climbed the steps to the front door and glanced at the museum. Perhaps the answer to Rosamund's disappearance lay there, in this time period. She was in no fit state to go there now, but perhaps later. . . .

As always, when she first entered her flat, she checked the divider. Certain no one had moved it; she went into the minuscule bathroom to bathe her face with cold water. The mirror reflected her blotched face and red eyes. Having her hair tied back didn't help, it added to the drawn appearance. Impatiently, she tugged the elastic band away and let her hair fall about her shoulders.

This was who she was, not Rosamund Oldham but Roz Reid, yet the draw of the world on the other side of the mirror was strong. If only David hadn't gone back to London. Had he truly cared for her or was he, too, interested in Rosamund's shipyard?

Roz pushed the doubts aside. David loved her, but faced with Alex Mindon's presence what else could he have done but leave? If only she could have gone with him.

Could she live on the other side of the mirror? Could she live a life knowing what she knew of the future? Could she sew everything by hand, knowing a functional sewing machine was only a few years away? Would her love for David be enough to make her forget all she knew? Did she know him well enough? The sexual attraction was strong. Was that all there was between them?

Roz threw herself onto the bed. It was no good thinking of that possibility now, not when David had deserted her. She hadn't thought his feelings shallow and believed him when he said nothing would keep him from her. Nothing and nobody but Alex Mindon.

David was the gentler soul of the two. He'd stand no chance in a fight of any kind with Alex Mindon, yet the gentleness was what endeared him to her.

How could he have run away!

Roz allowed the pillow to soak up what she had no strength to stem.

**

CHAPTER TWENTY

Roz awoke in mid-afternoon. For the second time that day, she showered and put on fresh clothes. Feeling calmer, but with no appetite for lunch, she let herself out of the flat and walked the few steps to the museum.

The Scarborough wasn't one of London's largest or most famous museums. Even the name was foreign to a southern city. Scarborough was a town on the north coast of England, but here was the museum, plopped in England's capital. She had never questioned the name, but now it intrigued her. She paused at the top of the steps to read the tarnished plaque she had ignored earlier: *Donated to the City of London by Rufus Scarbane.*

Uncle Ruffy donated the house to London, and they named it after the family's hometown. What had become of Imogen and Adele? How had Uncle Ruffy come to inherit? With that puzzle on her mind, she paid the entry fee and walked in.

During her earlier visit, she'd studied the costumes. Now she drank in everything, the curving staircase bare of the red carpet, the marble floor of the entry hall, the hole in the ceiling where a chandelier once hung, and the dull suit-of-armour standing in one corner. She could imagine Imogen saying: *remove it at once!*

Before, Roz had gone straight to the ballroom and the costume displays, now she walked into what was once the withdrawing room. How different it was. Glass cases sat in the middle of the room and columns along one wall held busts of Roman emperors. Landscape paintings decorated the walls.

No other visitors were present so Roz wandered slowly past the glass cases. Gaps showed where stolen items once rested. Of Rosamund's silver-backed set of brushes and combs, only one small comb remained. Perhaps it hadn't been with the others on the dressing table so the thieves missed it. Satisfied their profit would be less because the set was incomplete, she moved on.

One glass case held gloves and velvet nosegays; snuff boxes with silver or enamelled lids; a small clock set in an ivory carving; an ostrich-feather fan; and two lace-trimmed and monogrammed handkerchiefs. In one corner on the lower shelf sat a pair of lavender slippers, perhaps the ones she had worn.

For a moment, the other world intruded. Feeling dizzy, Roz closed her eyes and clutched the glass case for support.

"Are you unwell?"

Roz opened her eyes to find the custodian standing beside her. "I'm fine. Thank you." She waited until he moved away before continuing her examination of the contents of the glass case, but she was aware of him hovering in the doorway while she went to another case.

It held mostly paper. Visiting cards fanned across a silver tray. The top one bore an engraved name: *Lady Jemima Ridley.* Pages of sheet music lay beside old newspapers and a few books. Menus spoke of the wealth of a family who dined on ten-course meals of pheasant and salmon and out-of-season strawberries while much of London's population lived in near starvation. Open account books showed prices that seemed laughable until one realised how little the average working family lived on during those days.

Her gaze flickered over the faded folder of sketches that poked from between the covers. Most of one sketch was visible—a charcoal rendering of this room as it once looked.

On the shelf below were invitations to masquerades and balls, programs of operas and theatrical productions. Roz crouched down for a better look at a stack of concert programs. On one of them, four letters of the artiste's name were visible: *auvé*. So Madame Sauvé became famous back in—Roz checked the date on the program—1805.

Hand on the glass top of the case for support, she stood and studied the portraits arranged on the wall. She recognised Imogen standing with the man who, by the names engraved on brass plaque under the portrait, was her husband, Sir Hugh. The next portrait was of Adele, elaborately gowned and curled. She held an ostrich-feather fan, the same fan resting in the glass case.

Roz turned to the custodian who was still hovering, suspicion in his eyes. "Are there other family portraits?"

He walked towards her. "Do you know of the family?"

"Not really, but a friend of mine is a night guard here. Charlie Watts."

He warmed visibly. "Ah, yes, Charlie, one of the few willing to stay on as night guards."

"Because of the voices?"

"He's told you about them."

"Yes. He says he and his friend, Jim, have been hearing them for years."

"I've heard them myself on occasion." He held out his hand. "I'm Vincent Coulter, the curator here."

"Roz Reid." Roz shook his hand. "Charlie said the museum is to close soon."

"Unfortunately, yes. I'm in the process of checking the catalogues to make sure we have the entire inventory we borrowed from other museums."

"Charlie says many things have been stolen."

"Fortunately all of the things taken were from the original Scarbane collection so we won't have to explain the loss of items on loan to us. Some things, such as the portraits, will be shipped north to a museum in Scarborough."

"Is there a portrait of Rufus Scarbane?"

"Of both Rufus Scarbanes. They are in the next room."

Roz followed him.

A fire spitted and sparked in an ornate fireplace. Despite the fireguard, a cinder escaped and Vincent Coulter rushed forward to kick it from the wood floor back into the hearth. "It seems terrible to keep a fire going, but this is a damp old house and the exhibits must be kept dry."

Roz barely heard him as she looked at the two portraits above the mantel. One of them was Uncle Ruffy, the other a younger man. Both wore dog collars. "They were both clergymen?"

"Rufus the Younger gave up the church when his father inherited Scarbane House."

"What happened to the family?"

"We know very little of course even though I did some research when I became custodian. The main family history is in Scarborough itself, in Scarbane Hall, donated to the city there. All we have here is a bare-bones account of the family."

"Those would be the people in the other portraits?"

"Yes. Come with me." He led her back to the room with the glass cases and halted in front of Imogen and Adele's depictions. "Lady Scarbane visited London each year for the Season. Sir Hugh rarely came. It's said he had no taste for the social rounds but no doubt he would have come if a husband was found for their daughter." He pointed to Adele's portrait. "That's Lady Adele Scarbane. Quite pretty, isn't she?"

"Did she ever marry?"

"Unfortunately, no. It's rather a sad case and it is what brought about the downfall of the Scarbanes in my opinion."

"Why? What happened?"

"Lady Adele was an only child and doted on. When she died, Lady Imogen took to her bed never to rise again. Hugh

Scarbane, or so I'm told, began to drink heavily and was killed a few years later in a riding accident."

Roz stared at Adele's portrait, her mouth opened in dismay. "H-how did Adele die?"

"There's no proof of course, but it was assumed she was poisoned."

"Poisoned? How?"

"Arsenic, they say. Women of that period often used arsenic to whiten the skin." He sighed. "No doubt Lady Adele achieved her complexion at the cost of her life. It was a tragedy that could have been avoided, whereas the other tragedies—" He studied Roz. "Are you really interested in this, or merely being polite?"

"I'm interested. You say there were other tragedies?"

"Lady Scarbane, or Imogen Oldham as she was before she married, lost an older brother and sister-in-law to a fire. Then her younger brother was killed in a carriage accident."

"Did either of the brothers have children?"

"Yes, I believe it was the older brother, the one who died in a fire. There was a daughter and her name was Rosamund. Mind you, I'm only going by the things found in the house when Rufus Scarbane turned it over to the city. There are several sketches in a book bearing the name of Rosamund Oldham. According to the letters we have, letters Sir Hugh sent in reply to Lady Imogen, Rosamund was a wild one. The black sheep of the family you could say. She disappeared."

"They never found her?"

The custodian shook his head. "In the letters we found, some thought she ran away with a man she'd met, others thought she accompanied Madame Sauvé to Italy. Madame Sauvé was one of the foremost opera singers of the time. She was a frequent visitor to the house and she may have taken the girl with her. Others believed Rosamund met with an unfortunate accident in one of the poorer parts of the city because she frequently went into the slums to hand out money or food."

"I see." This was in keeping with what Adele said about Rosamund giving away her jewellery.

"Although there is no portrait of Rosamund, there are sketches she made and one or two are self-portraits. Would you care to see them?"

"Very much."

The custodian walked to a glass case and opened it with a key he took from his pocket. He put on white cotton gloves, took out the sketchbook and opened it. "Please do not touch the drawings, they are easily damaged." He showed her one of the sketches. "Rosamund added names to her sketches, and we believe the un-named ones may be self-portraits."

Roz leaned over the drawing. It could have been her likeness. If she piled her hair on top of her head, she would look exactly like the girl in the sketch. No wonder they accepted her as Rosamund so easily. "Are there others?"

In answer, the custodian showed her more drawings. "There are two more we believe are of Rosamund. In one of them, she is ten or eleven years old, dressed like a boy, with sailing ships in the background. She also sketched other people but didn't always add names." He brought a couple of others to the top. "This is a young servant girl."

The first sketch was of Jenny with her name printed at the bottom—Jennifer Beach.

One drawing caused Roz to utter a cry she covered with a cough. It was of Adele twirling a parasol and lying languidly in a punt while Alex Mindon poled them on the lake. The drawing Roz herself made on the day they barred her from the boating party.

Again, the room whirled, and she swayed.

The custodian placed a firm hand under her elbow. "Are you sure you are all right?"

"Yes, I'm all right." She steadied herself as he put the sketchbook back. "Thank you for showing me the sketches, Mr Coulter. You said Rufus inherited."

"He and his son were the last of this line of Scarbanes. Rufus the Elder continued to act as clergyman for several years before retiring to Scarbane House. Rufus the Younger

206

had barely begun his vocation when his father came into the inheritance. They sent him north to handle the family's shipyard but, within five years, he ran it into the ground. He lived more like a wealthy member of the upper class than as a clergyman.

"He ruined his father and earned a name for himself as a gambler and lecher. They found him murdered in one of the fleshpots for the few coins he carried. Rufus the Elder was the last of the family. He kept the house going for a while, selling bits and pieces to eke out a living. He sold most of the land around the house as the city encroached and on his deathbed he endowed London with Scarbane House and all it contained."

"Which wasn't much."

"It held even less than this. We have been lucky to have a few pieces donated over the years and we borrowed items from the storage rooms of other museums. We've already returned some items and others will leave here in the next few days. We will ship the more personal family items to Scarborough and donate everything else to museums throughout the city. The Scarborough hasn't made any money for years and it is no great historical landmark."

"Has a date been set for the closure?"

"It will be closed to the public a week from now but it will take weeks before everything can be packed up and transferred." He sighed as he looked around. "I shall be sorry to see it close, but we can't be sentimental about such things, can we. The London Borough Council certainly isn't."

"I'm glad I visited before it closed, and I thank you for telling me the history of the family who lived here."

"Few people bother to ask so it was a pleasure to talk about them before—" He shrugged. "I shall miss the old place. I've been its custodian for fifteen years."

He escorted her to the door and waited until the guard unlocked it. It was only then she realised the time and that the museum had closed fifteen minutes earlier.

"If you care to visit again, ask for me. We can forego the entrance fee for our only visitor in years who has shown any interest. Make sure you come back before the end of next week."

It was something Roz intended doing, in whichever time period.

**

CHAPTER TWENTY-ONE

On her return from the museum, as Roz reached the landing outside Minnie's door, Minnie emerged with a foil-wrapped plate balanced on top of a casserole. She looked at Roz in surprise, glanced up the stairs, and then looked back at Roz.

"I heard you walking around up there just a minute ago." Minnie looked puzzled. "The floorboards were creaking."

Roz shook her head. "I've been at the museum for over an hour."

"You went to the museum after the note told you to stay away?"

"I won't be bullied."

Minnie grinned. "That's my girl. But I worry about you."

"There's no need."

"Well, at least I can make sure you're fed." Minnie held out the plate and casserole. "I was hoping we could share these."

Roz smiled. "Your place or mine?"

"Mine's closer."

"Okay, but let me drop off my bag and freshen up."

"Don't be too long. These are ready to eat now."

"I won't be a minute." Roz ran up the stairs and found the door to her flat locked. She opened it cautiously and pushed it wide so it touched the wall, leaving no room for anyone to hide behind it.

209

The divider stood to one side of the mirror. Whoever went through had not bothered to hide the way they were using her flat. By now, Roz should be at the Nostalgie, and they thought the place would be empty for several hours. If Agatha was informing them of Roz's movements, she probably hadn't been able to let them know Roz would be at home. It was a fluke that she'd gone out.

There seemed little point in putting the divider back in front of the mirror. If they returned, she'd hear their footsteps from Minnie's flat. She might even be able to waylay them on the stairs. Determined to listen, Roz went downstairs and tapped on Minnie's door.

Minnie had prepared a chicken casserole with parsley potatoes and a medley of peas and carrots. Roz couldn't remember when she'd eaten her last meal, and she tucked in under Minnie's smiling gaze.

"You were really hungry, weren't you?"

"Starving." With her fork, Roz pierced the last pea on her plate. "This is wonderful. How many meals do I owe you now?"

"It can't be easy cooking on that little gas thing you have. I told Archie he should install a full size cooker up there. You'd like that, wouldn't you?"

"I'm not much of a cook."

"Then I shall teach you. When you get married, you'll need to cook for a man."

"If I ever get married."

"Nonsense, there must be dozens of men looking for someone as pretty as you."

"If there are, I haven't met any."

"Let's sit somewhere more comfortable." Minnie headed toward the red-velvet couch and chairs.

"What about the washing up?"

"That can wait until I don't have someone to talk to. Would you like a glass of sherry?"

"That sounds good." Roz sensed Minnie had something she wanted to discuss so searching for Rosamund would have to wait. It was getting late, too, and she didn't relish going back now she had proof someone had only just gone through.

"Are you settling in all right?" Minnie handed Roz a glass of sherry.

"Yes. Everyone's been very kind, especially you."

"Does anything up there bother you?"

"Are you thinking of the two women who were frightened into leaving?"

"Only one. Angeline wasn't in the least bit frightened. Amelia's happy in her little flat in Oxford and she has a gentleman friend."

"That's nice."

"You've been through, haven't you?"

Roz choked on the sip of sherry and her eyes watered. "What?"

Minnie was studying her. "You've found the way into the past."

"What are you talking about?"

"I looked for you last night, but you didn't answer your door."

"I went out."

"No, you didn't. At least, you didn't go down these stairs." Minnie leaned forward. "Where were you, Roz?"

"You mustn't have heard me leave."

"No, I didn't hear you leave, but you did, didn't you? You went through time."

Hand shaking, Roz put down her glass. "What do you mean?"

"I know there is a way from your flat into the past."

"Oh? How do you know that?"

"I'm not dumb, Roz. Perhaps I've read too many novels by H. G. Wells and Jules Verne, but I knew Briggs had a way of getting into the museum. I went down to the police station when they took him in and I looked at the things they found on him. Old pieces in mint condition. Now, if he'd stolen them from the museum, they'd have a veneer of age, so I asked myself how he managed to steal brand new things. The only answer was that he had found a door to the past. And that door is in your flat."

"That's absurd!" Roz protested uneasily.

"Then I thought of the others who had lived up there. Most of them didn't stay a full night, and Amelia was certain she'd seen a ghost. What she saw was someone from the past who came through the door for a visit."

"If anyone came from the past wouldn't that person be a ghost or just a pile of bones?"

"Isn't a ghost what Amelia said she saw? Don't be flippant, Roz, I'm trying to help you." Minnie went to get the bottle of sherry. She refilled Roz's glass and then her own. "While at the police station, when they arrested Briggs, I talked to Detective Inspector Morgan about it. Although not convinced about the time travel part, he suspected there might be a way into the museum from this house. I'm responsible for having the flats up there torn apart."

"They didn't find a door as you suggest."

"But neither they nor I had anything to point the way. Now I do. It has something to do with the mirror, doesn't it?"

Roz forced down her jolt of surprise. "What makes you think that?"

"By the way you've moved the divider to stand in front of it. I've noticed the way you look at it when you enter the flat. It was the divider falling that caused the crash the other night, wasn't it? Who's using your flat, Roz? Is it Briggs?"

Roz couldn't look at her and deny or lie any longer. Minnie's guesses were spot on. "I don't know. I think so."

"Is he the one sending you the notes?"

"I think so."

"Are you in cahoots with him?"

"No!" The thought made Roz shudder.

"You know he's friendly with the husband of the woman you work with, don't you?"

Roz looked up. "I suspected as much. How do you know?"

"I stopped in for a cup of tea at a café a few days ago. Briggs was sitting in the booth next to mine and I heard him talking to a man and a woman. The woman mentioned she had to be at work and her husband said she worked in the wardrobe department at the Nostalgie. He boasted about being able to get in free to see the shows."

"That would be Agatha."

"Did you know her husband was an ex-convict?"

Roz stared at Minnie. "No, I didn't."

"It came up in the conversation I overheard. He'd just come out of prison and he and the Briggs man compared notes on the guards."

"Agatha told me her husband was often ill."

"Perhaps he is, but he's also on the wrong side of the law."

"Do you—" Roz bit her lip. "Is it possible Agatha's husband is receiving stolen goods from Bertie Briggs? Detective Inspector Morgan said they didn't find any in his house but he hadn't passed things to his usual contacts."

"It's possible. Have you mentioned this to the police?"

"How could I? I wasn't sure Agatha was involved."

"What made you suspect her?"

"She wasn't happy I'd moved in here. She questioned me on who else lived in the house. Then I found the thieves came when I was at work and I put two and two together."

"Thieves? Plural?" Minnie tilted her head and studied Roz.

"Briggs and the woman Amelia saw."

"Oh, my." Minnie's eyes widened. "But you weren't at work this afternoon, you were at the museum."

"Agatha didn't know until late this morning that I would be at home. Normally, I'd leave here about five-thirty to be at the Nostalgie by six. When did you hear someone upstairs?"

"About six, or soon after; a few minutes before you arrived."

"I left the museum just after it closed, at about ten past six."

Minnie nodded. "So they would expect you to be at work."

"I was supposed to be on standby for the evening performance. John changed the schedule at the last moment." Roz wasn't about to explain her crying fit.

"And this Agatha woman probably couldn't get a hold of Briggs. Is that the way it went?"

"It sounds like it. Have you told the others what you suspect about my flat?"

Minnie shook her head. "I had no proof. If I'd told them what I suspected they'd think me barmy and you can imagine what Doris would say."

"So they don't know."

"I have said nothing."

"Have you had contact with Detective Inspector Morgan recently?"

Minnie shrugged. "Not really."

"What does *not really* mean?"

"I've seen him sitting in different vehicles outside the museum and outside this house. He pretended not to see me, so I followed suit. I suspect he's watching for the Briggs man and whoever the woman is."

"I'm supposed to keep this confidential, but— He's investigating a murder." Roz surprised Minnie into sitting bolt upright.

"Murder, did you say? Whose murder?"

"He wouldn't tell me."

"You don't think— No, that's too much to believe, but you don't think Angeline Sauvé was murdered, do you?"

"That was my first question to Morgan. He said she is living in another part of London."

Anger sparked in Minnie's eyes. "Did he tell you where? I should like to find her and get my mother's brooch back."

Roz squirmed. If she told Minnie she knew where Angeline Sauvé was, Minnie might go through the mirror to look for her. "No, he didn't tell me."

"If the police are watching the place because of a murder, they're no longer interested in how those people travel from your flat into the museum. We must tell them they're still getting into this house, though."

"They already suspect. Morgan more or less told me the new locks wouldn't keep Bertie Briggs out."

Minnie shivered. "That horrible little man, he looked like a rat—skinny, with a pointed nose and sharp little eyes."

"I thought the same when I first saw him. I've seen him outside here and I think he followed me in Covent Garden." Roz remembered Agatha lived in the East End. Bertie Briggs may not have followed her that day, he might have been visiting Agatha's husband. She couldn't tell Minnie she'd also seen him on the other side of the mirror.

"You don't seem perturbed," Minnie commented.

"He's a small man."

"But probably vicious."

"I'm not afraid of him." Not on this side of the mirror.

"I'm afraid for you, Roz. I don't like the thought of you up there all alone when anyone could walk into your flat, either through the door or—the mirror is the doorway, isn't it."

"Yes."

"How did you find out?"

"By accident." Roz kept her eyes averted. Would Minnie ask to go through the mirror?

"And all that time the police were up there, they didn't find it. What's it like over there?"

"It's a private home, owned by the Scarbane family."

"Luxurious, I suppose, with lots of servants." Minnie drained her glass. "Another sherry?"

Roz smiled. "Are you trying to get me drunk?"

"On three sherries? I'm working up the nerve to ask you to stay down here for a few nights. There's a camp bed I can make up for you."

"I won't allow Bertie Briggs or his accomplice to drive me out of my home."

"If you won't come down here, let me come to stay with you."

"Absolutely not. I won't have you inconvenienced because of those people."

"Very well, but we must inform Detective Inspector Morgan."

If they did that, Roz would never find Madame Sauvé and retrieve the brooch. "Not yet. Give me until the end of the week."

"Why do you want to delay?"

"I have something I want to do."

"On the other side of the mirror? Please be careful, Roz. You could be in great danger."

"I don't think so." Not if Alex was at Scarbane House.

With surprise, Roz realised she wouldn't come to harm if he was there. If she mentioned people were stealing from the house, she was certain Alex would hunt them down. She found it strange that she looked to him for protection when it should be David.

"I don't like this, Roz." Minnie poured sherry into their glasses. "If I agree to wait, will you tell me when you next go through the mirror?"

"If you are here. I prefer to go through during the day."

"You went through last night. I tried to reach you, but you weren't there."

"I went through early in the day and remained overnight."

Minnie blanched. "Weren't you afraid?"

"Afraid of what?"

"I don't know—something. You don't know those people."

"No more than I know you or Archie or Marge."

"But we're so ordinary," Minnie protested.

"So are they, in their own way. They are society people, no more frightening than you are."

"If you are sure you are safe. . . ."

"As safe as I am right now, here with you." Roz couldn't mention the danger of the two dimensions colliding. She had no proof a catastrophe would happen.

"I worry so much about you. You will be careful, won't you? I mean—what would happen if you couldn't get back? What if you had to stay there?"

"Then I would. Apart from missing a few of our modern conveniences, living there would be no hardship." Please God, Minnie wouldn't try to rescue her if that happened, wouldn't bring Detective Inspector Morgan and his big feet to investigate. Despite her unease, she smiled as she visualised a confrontation between Morgan and Imogen.

"You are quite sure?"

"I'm sure. Nothing bad will happen to me there."

**

CHAPTER TWENTY-TWO

Thursday dawned dark and gloomy. For once, Roz didn't spring out of bed eager to go to work. She'd had no time off in the six months she'd worked at the Nostalgie. If she wasn't at the theatre she was researching costumes or working on her notes and designs. The costumes were well in hand so taking the day off didn't seem like such a bad idea, especially when John Waltham was convinced she had a cold.

She showered, drank coffee, but couldn't face breakfast. The mirror seemed to demand her attention, and she kept glancing at it. Imogen told her to keep out of her sight, but during her forays through the mirror, there were times when she hadn't run into Imogen.

Tomorrow they were leaving for Scarborough with Stephen's casket. Before they left, she wanted to warn Adele about using the face powder. Could she change the course of history, save Adele's life, and forestall the disastrous events that followed the girl's death? There was only one way to find out.

The trunk was gone. Roz opened the wardrobe, bare of all but one gown, a pair of slippers, and a heavy travelling cloak, she dressed quickly and went to tap at Adele's door. No one answered her first knock, she tapped again and the door opened.

A gaunt woman informed her: "Miss Adele will see no one."

"I am her cousin, Rosamund."

219

"I know who you are and you are the last person she wishes to see. At any rate, she's resting in preparation for the journey north so please go away."

As the woman closed the door, Roz wondered about her. Alex had spoken of a housekeeper. She had an air of authority and could well be the iron hand that ruled the servants.

Roz returned to Rosamund's room. If they wouldn't allow her to speak to Adele, she could write her a letter. From the chest by the window, she pulled out the sketchbook, tore out a page, took one of the sticks of charcoal and sat at the dressing table to write.

> *Dear Cousin Adele,*
>
> *It is with the deepest concern for you I write these lines. I hope you will accept them in the spirit of friendship and love.*
>
> *I implore you not to use the face powder that whitens the skin. It contains a derivative of arsenic, which is a deadly poison.*
>
> *This is my last and only request of you. I beseech you to do as I ask. I am certain any apothecary you consult will confirm what I tell you.*
>
> *If we do not meet again, I beg you to think kindly of me always.*
>
> *Your Cousin,*
> *Rosamund*

From the signatures on the sketches, she made a fair copy of Rosamund's and hoped her printing was not too different. She folded the paper, wrote Adele's name on it in bold letters, and placed the note on the dressing table where Jenny would find it. If Jenny couldn't read, she would take it to someone who could and Adele would eventually read the warning.

No one was in any of the rooms on the ground floor so Roz wandered outside. Even in this world, it was an overcast day and rain threatened. She walked through the deserted gardens and found herself in the field where the fair was to have taken place.

Garlands of evergreen decorated the booths beneath the gay awnings, and cloths covered one or two tables. All drooped sadly, as if affected by Stephen Oldham's death. The grass between the booths was trodden flat, bare earth exposed in places, mute evidence of the activity that had taken place. The fair was as doomed as Scarbane House was, and if she couldn't speak to Adele history would— It would happen as written. It was arrogant of her to think otherwise.

But what about Rosamund's disappearance? That she, Roz, would disappear was obvious, but why hadn't they been able to find Rosamund? She hadn't run away with Madame Sauvé, because David would have known, but perhaps there had been a beau. Rosamund was barely seventeen. Adele and Jenny mentioned the nursery so it was unlikely Rosamund met anyone who could be a beau. Wild as they said she was, Rosamund didn't sound like anybody's fool. So where was she?

"Rosamund."

Roz whirled around. "David! You came back!"

He swept her up, covering her face with kisses. "Did you think I would ever leave you, sweet Rosamund?"

"They told me you had gone to London."

"Only until I thought no one would expect my return." He ran his fingers through her hair. "I have never seen you thus."

"Oh!" Roz put up a hand to her hair. In her rush to speak to Adele, she had forgotten it was still loose about her shoulders.

"They knew I would come back for you." He drew her between two stalls. "They could be watching even now."

Roz shook her head. "There has been a death. They are too busy or filled with grief to worry about me or you."

"Who has died?"

"Stephen Oldham."

"Poor Rosamund, first your mother and father and now your uncle." He held her tighter. "They won't have had time to appoint another guardian. No one has legal authority over you."

She drew away from him. "What does that mean?"

"It means you are free to go to London with me."

"To London?"

"We can be married there." He studied her face. "You will marry me, won't you?"

"Oh, David!" She threw her arms around his neck to hide the turmoil she felt. The feelings in her heart a few days earlier weren't as strong. When she thought he had deserted her, something changed. He had been all she looked for in a man, but now that David asked for her promise, she was no longer certain. "We hardly know each other."

"Do you deny me?"

Roz fought to ignore the petulant edge in his voice. "I love you, but will you love me when you know me better?" Would she love him?

"Let me prove to you that my love will last as long as we are together."

Unbidden, words from the marriage vows sprang into her mind—*until death do us part*. "We have to be sure."

"I am sure. Come to London with me."

"I will come with you, but I can't stay in London, not yet. There is something I have to do here first."

"Something more important than being with me?"

Adele's life, the family's survival; she had to make sure the note got to her, but she must get the brooch from Madame Sauvé for Minnie. "I can never rest unless I do this."

"Is it so important?"

Was it? She thought of Minnie and her kindness. "Yes."

"When will you to leave with me?"

"Perhaps later today, for now, I want you to take me to see Madame Sauvé."

He smiled, joy lighting his eyes. "I have a carriage in the lane. Are you ready to leave?"

"I am ready."

He caught her hand and together they ran across the field to a stile where he helped her over, kissing her at every step.

"I didn't dare take a coachman into my confidence," he explained when they reached the carriage. "I shall drive, but I want you to stay inside where you cannot be seen. Will you keep the curtains drawn until we reach Madame Sauvé's house?"

"I shall do as you ask." She entered the carriage and he raised the steps, folding them inside.

"Sweet Rosamund." With a smile, he closed the door.

Roz clutched the edge of the seat as the carriage rocked and moved forward. It was nothing like the sumptuous conveyance Imogen rode in. The leather seats were cracked and split, and enclosed within the leather curtains unpleasant odours permeated the gloom. As the carriage swayed over the ruts in the roadway, the curtains swung open now and again and she glimpsed trees and hedgerows passing in a blur. The carriage was moving fast, the wheels rumbling behind the galloping hooves, jostling her.

Why was David driving the horses so hard? The answer was obvious. He wanted to be away from Scarbane House before anyone knew she was missing.

She needed time to think, to sort out the change in her feelings towards David. She was being fickle. When David brought her back, she would tell him she couldn't marry him yet.

The carriage leapt over a series of deep ruts, throwing her to the floor. She grimaced as her knees and hands made contact with the grit and dirt. She hauled herself up, and grabbed the strap beside the door. Bruised, and with her hands and gown soiled, she barely regained her seat before the carriage slowed. Through the gaps in the curtains, she saw buildings. They had entered the outskirts of the city and now odours entered the gaps in the curtains—offal, human waste, horse droppings, rotting vegetables—and the gabble of voices was deafening.

They passed other carriages and a coachmen shouted abuse at David when their wheels nearly collided. A gig passed with a fashionably dressed driver who whipped his own horses and any others who came close. Once, the carriage veered sharply to one side and tossed Roz into a corner. "Road hog!" she shouted when she recovered and lifted the curtain to look out.

As they slowed for a corner, she saw a ragged child take a half-rotten apple from the gutter and rub it on his tattered sleeve before biting into the mess. On another street, two women screamed and tore at each other's hair and clothes while a crowd gathered around them. From a window above, someone threw a yellow liquid onto them and the crowd scattered. One woman ran so close to the carriage Roz could have reached out to touch as well as smell her. This was the London she thought she could live in with David.

Presently, they moved into a better part of the city where the houses stood back from iron railings. Even with the paintwork on their doors and windows peeling, compared to those in the slum they were palaces. Farther on, the houses were larger with small gardens behind the railings. At one of the gates, David drew the carriage to a halt and a scruffy man ran out to take the reins.

David appeared at the door and let the steps down. As he handed Roz out, he watched the street and appeared nervous. He put up the steps and slammed the carriage door before hustling Roz towards the house as the other man drove the carriage away. They were almost running when they reached the front door that opened as they approached.

Without a word, a heavyset man drew it wider for them to enter. Roz gasped when she crossed the threshold because an overpowering perfume filled the air.

"Is Madame Sauvé in the parlour, Rocko?" David asked, and the man nodded as he closed the door.

As they walked along the hallway, Rocko locked the front door. With growing unease, she clutched at David's arm. "Will she see me?"

"I informed her I would bring you."

"I would like to speak to her alone."

A wary look entered David's eyes. "I should introduce you to her."

"But. . . ." Roz ran her hands over her hair to smooth it as David opened the door.

The room was swathed in soft draperies. A froth of lace hung at French windows that allowed a glimpse of the garden. Here, too, the perfume was overpowering. In the centre of the room, Madame Sauvé reclined on a chaise. She was dressed in a silk wrap of rich red damask open to her waist to display a lacy corset, which barely contained her ample cleavage. Pinned to the corset, Minnie's brooch drew Roz's attention like a magnet.

Madame Sauvé pulled the wrap together and swung her feet off the chaise. "David! How nice of you to call. And you brought the girl."

"I am Rosamund." Roz took a step forward. "I played for you at my seventeenth birthday party at Scarbane House."

"Ah, yes. I remember you. And David's brought you to see me."

"Actually, a mutual friend asked me to visit you. Do you remember Minnie Wilton?"

Madame Sauvé paled, and the rouge applied to her cheeks shone livid against her pallor. "You come from—?"

"From Scarborough Lane." Roz didn't take her eyes off the other woman. "The message I have is private."

"I see." Her gaze shifted to David. "My dear, would you mind leaving us for a moment?"

"If I must. . . ." David gave Madame Sauvé a questioning look. "Do you think it wise?"

"It will only be for a moment." At David's hesitation, she added, "This is a matter for women."

Clearly puzzled, David nodded. "I will be outside the door."

Roz waited until he left before she spoke. In a low voice, she said, "We have little time, so I'll come straight to the point. I know who you are and where you came from."

"You came through the mirror?"

"I live in the flat now."

"But David thinks you are Rosamund Oldham."

"I must be her double. Everyone thinks I am she."

"Then the doorway through the mirror is open again."

A tremor of fear clutched Roz's stomach. "What do you mean?"

"The portal, or whatever you call it, closed. I had limited access to Rosamund's bedroom but when I tried to get back, I couldn't. The mirror was impassable, solid."

"I came through this morning. You can return with me."

The diva rose and crossed to a cabinet that held a variety of bottles and glasses. She poured herself a tot and drank it in one gulp. "I wouldn't go back now. I no longer want to. At first, I was terrified, and then David came to my rescue. He helped me adjust."

"Does David know you are from the future?"

"He believes I was stranded, penniless, by my theatrical agent." Madame Sauvé faced Roz. "I am a success here. In that other London, I was nothing. I couldn't find work. Here I am in demand."

"I understand your reason for staying. Your secret is safe with me." She couldn't tell anyone without revealing her own origin, but it worked both ways. "I have come for the brooch you borrowed from Minnie. Give me that and I shall leave."

"Where does Minnie think I am?"

"In another part of London. She is very upset at the loss of her mother's brooch. Will you give it to me so I may return it to her?"

"I cannot part with it. It is my good-luck charm."

Minnie's tear-stained face hovered before Roz and this woman's refusal to return the brooch made her angry. "Luck that will avail you nothing if I make known you are a thief. Will you be welcome in the houses of the gentry then? I hardly think so. They will probably force you to sing in taverns. Will you like that?"

An unpleasant smile played on the woman's face. "Are you threatening me?"

"Of course. I mean to have the brooch." Roz took a step closer. "Please hand it over."

"I can expose you as an impostor."

"And who will believe your word against mine. I am the daughter of gentry while you are nothing but a cheap entertainer. I mean to have the brooch."

"I will never part with it!"

"Very well, I shall take it." Roz rushed forward, wrenched the brooch from the woman's corset and shoved her with her other hand.

The diva lost her balance and fell heavily onto the chaise, the glass flying from her hand to smash against the wall. As she fell, she screamed, "David! Help!"

The door burst open and David ran in followed by Rocko. He glanced from the diva to Roz. "What have you done?" He rushed to the other woman. "Are you hurt?"

"David?" Roz expected him to show concern for her, not for Angeline Sauvé. Her cry of dismay was lost under the other woman's accusation.

"She—! She—!" Angeline pointed to Roz. "She attacked me."

David confronted Roz. "What is the meaning of this? Why did you attack her?"

"She stole something from a friend of mine and wouldn't give it back."

"She took it from me, David. Make her give it back."

David advanced on Roz. "Whatever it is, give it back to Angeline."

Roz backed away, afraid of the ice in his eyes.

"It's my brooch, David," Angeline whined.

"What's going on? What is there between you two?" Roz asked.

"You will find out soon enough." He held out his hand. "Give me the brooch."

"No." Roz stood her ground.

"Rosamund! I demand you give me the brooch."

"Never! She stole it and I'm taking it back to the owner."

"Oi'll get un." The other man moved closer.

"Do you want Rocko to get it, Rosamund?"

Cornered, Roz looked from David to Rocko. "Tell me what's going on."

"Yes, tell her, David." Angeline Sauvé echoed.

"You will not be returning to Scarbane House."

Roz stared at him in disbelief. Was this the same man who vowed he loved her? What was it he'd said—*as long as we are together*. "Where am I to go, David?"

"To a house near here and closer to the docks where you will stay for a few weeks, and then. . . ." He shrugged. "Who knows?"

Roz turned to Madame Sauvé. "Will you do nothing to stop this?"

"Why should she?" David asked.

"I suppose marriage is out of the question?" Roz couldn't resist the jibe.

His smile was evil. "Gentry do not marry whores, but I shall have the pleasure of the first few nights with you."

"A brothel?" Now the heavy perfume made sense, as did the bouncer at the door and Madame Sauvé in a wrap at noon.

"I see your tutor taught you all manner of things. Are you still a virgin?"

Defiant, she answered. "No."

His fist came up so fast she had no time to duck. It caught her squarely under the chin. She dropped the brooch but fell onto it and everything turned black.

**

CHAPTER TWENTY-THREE

Roz lost consciousness for no more than a minute. When she came to, Rocko was rolling her around as he searched for the brooch. She felt it dig into her hip and eased it into her hand.

"It ain't here," Rocko said.

"It has to be there."

David walked closer and then a foot nudged her.

"Check again."

Rocko fondled and pinched when he moved her. It took effort not to wince, and she kept her eyes closed. They didn't yet realise she had regained consciousness.

"You must find it, David." Angeline Sauvé sobbed.

"We will find it even if I have to tear her limb from limb."

"It ain't here. It must've rolled."

"Then look around."

She listened as they searched the floor and underneath the furniture. Slitting her eyes, she saw she was facing the wall. With as little movement as possible, she manoeuvred the brooch in her hand until she found the pin. It was bent, but intact. She closed her hand around the brooch but left the pin sticking out between two fingers. Not much of a weapon, but she had nothing else.

"It is not here," David said. "It must be caught in her clothing."

"Oi'll look," Rocko offered.

"Enough time for that when I've done with her. You can have her then."

She tightened her hand on the brooch as David dragged her away from the wall and turned her onto her back. Without time to aim or wonder at the consequences, Roz lunged at his face.

He caught her hand a fraction too late, and the pin scored his cheek. He leapt back with an oath, hand to his face as blood seeped between his fingers. "You bitch!"

He aimed a kick that caught Roz in the ribs. She cried out at the pain and rolled to fetch up against a chair. She grabbed it by one leg, swung it, and scrambled to her feet.

At that moment, the doors leading to the garden exploded in a shower of glass and a man burst into the room with a sword in his hand.

"Alex!" Roz gave a cry of joy.

Her attention taken from him, David grabbed her and held her before him as a shield. "You have no part of this, Mindon!" he shouted.

"Let her go." Alex spoke in a low voice. He held the sword pointed at Rocko and Angeline who slunk to behind the thug.

"You have no claim on her." David had one arm wrapped around Roz's waist, the other tight about her neck.

"On the contrary, I have every claim."

"I repeat—you have no claim. She has no guardian and you have yet to announce your betrothal to her."

"You are wrong, Ridley. I am her legal guardian. Oldham signed the paper before he died. She is under my protection."

"You have no proof of this!"

Alex took a parchment from his pocket and threw it to Rocko. "This is only a copy, I have the original. If your henchman can't read, your partner can. Let her read it to you."

Warily, and with one eye on the sword, Angeline Sauvé edged around Rocko and snatched the document. From behind the big man, she unfolded the paper and read.

"What he says is true, David."

Alex jabbed the sword towards Rocko and Angeline Sauvé. "Get out of here, both of you."

The diva needed no second invitation. In a flash, she was gone from the room. Rocko stayed where he was, looking from the sword to Alex to David.

"Try nothing foolish," Alex cautioned.

Roz realised they could attack Alex simultaneously from two directions, with David using her as a shield. Alex stood equidistant from the two men and she didn't like the way Rocko was eyeing David. Perhaps they'd been in a similar situation and all it took was for both of them to remember and act.

The soft slippers she wore were useless for stamping on David's instep, but she had the brooch in her hand. Before he knew what she was about, she hiked her hip sideways and stabbed backwards with the pin into David's groin. He screamed and released her.

Roz ran to the smashed window, shards of glass cutting through her satin slippers. She climbed out and then halted to look back. Rocko had taken advantage of her manoeuvre to jump Alex. He learned his error and cowered in a corner, nursing a slash that reddened his shirt from shoulder to waist.

She heard a movement behind her. Angeline Sauvé came around the side of the house and bore down on Roz with a knife in her hand.

As the woman rushed at her, Roz dropped into a dive and took Angeline down with the same flying rugby tackle that had taken Mike down. Then she was on her feet while the other woman, older and heavier, wallowed and tripped over her wrap as she tried to rise.

Alex stood in the doorway watching them. On his face was the amusement Roz despised. He bellowed with laughter and kicked away the knife the diva had dropped.

"I don't see anything to laugh at!"

"You weren't standing where I was."

"Where's David?"

The laughter fled from his face, replaced by a coldness that made her shiver. "Are you still concerned for him? Are you worried he may be hurt? Or dead?"

"Is he?"

Alex shook his head. "But he'll be quiet for a while." He looked across the garden. "At last, they've arrived."

Three men emerged at a run from horses reined in at the railings, and Roz pressed closer to Alex as he placed an arm around her shoulders.

"It's all right." Alex reassured her. "They're with me."

"Are they all in there?" one of the men asked.

"Ridley and Rockwell; the woman is here." He inclined his head towards Madame Sauvé.

"You should have waited for us," the man said as he motioned the other two into the house.

"Matters came to a head and I couldn't wait for you."

"Who are these men?" Roz asked.

"Friends of mine. One of them will drive you home. You must stay there until I come." He fastened the sword to his belt, put an arm around her waist, and drew her towards the gate.

Roz groaned when his fingers touched her ribs.

He withdrew his hand as if scalded. "Are you hurt?"

"Only a bruise."

"Are you sure?"

She nodded and tried not to limp. "Aren't you coming with me?"

"There are things I must attend to here."

Roz looked back to where the third man escorted a cursing Angeline Sauvé into the house none too gently. "They run a brothel."

"More than one and most of the inmates are women like you."

"What will happen to David?"

"He, Rockwell and the Madam will spend a short holiday in prison, and then they'll go to Tilbury."

"Why Tilbury?"

"To the docks. They will be among the first to be transported to Van Diemen's Land now Cook has claimed it for Britain."

Her knowledge of Australian history was shaky. "They transport people for running brothels?"

"Are you still concerned for Ridley?"

"I don't care what happens to him, but isn't transportation a bit harsh for running a brothel?"

"These are not brothels where women enter of their own free will; they are kidnapped and held prisoner. It is for kidnapping they will be transported."

Roz wondered if that was what happened to Rosamund. Ahead, a gig waited with a man at the head of the horse. "How did you know where I was?"

"Jenny brought me the letter you wrote to Adele and I gave it to Imogen. Then Jenny said she saw you with Ridley in the field set aside for the fair. I reached there in time to see the carriage racing out of sight."

"You took your time catching up to us," Roz grumbled.

"I had to elicit help from Robert Peel and his men. They have been watching Ridley for a while."

"Is that why you warned me against him?"

"His reputation is most unsavoury. Lord and Lady Ridley are not aware of his ventures in London so his arrest will come as a blow."

"Do my aunt and Adele know?"

"Only of the rumours, but in the society in which they move rumours go a long way in determining if a person is acceptable. As they had no proof of what they'd heard, for Lord and Lady Ridley's sake they allowed young Ridley access into society." He paused and looked into her face when they reached the gig. "Are you put out by the realisation Ridley is not what he pretended?"

Roz shook her head. David was not much worse than the men she'd dated in her own time. "He merely followed the pattern."

"What pattern?"

"It's a long story."

"Lord Mindon." The man beside the horse now moved to them. "Is this the lady I'm to take to Scarbane House?"

"This is Miss Oldham. Rosamund, this is Roger Morley. He will drive you home."

Something about Roger was familiar. "I am pleased to make your acquaintance, sir."

Roger grinned. "Not a *sir*. Not yet, any road."

"You can trust him. Roger is a Peeler."

"Before I go. . . . You knew about David but you didn't see fit to warn me."

"I tried."

"You sod! The hell you did!"

"We'll discuss this later."

"We'll discuss it now!"

"There are matters that need immediate attention here."

"All right, but don't think this is over between us."

"I didn't expect it would be." He glanced to where Roger was waiting. "Shall I help you up?"

"I don't need your help!" It hurt like hell, but she climbed onto the gig without help.

*

The gig was no more comfortable than the coach and travelled at a fast pace. Roz clung to the low side board, certain she would be thrown out at any moment, but Roger made no effort to slow down except at sharp corners where tree branches swept close above their heads. Occasionally, she glanced down to make sure Minnie's brooch decorated the neckline of her gown.

Every jostle increased the pain in her ribs and she remained upright with effort. Her gasps of pain were lost beneath the thundering hooves. She concentrated on holding the pain at bay; thankful Roger was not inclined to make conversation and knew the way to Scarbane House.

What had Alex called Roger? A *Peeler*? Vaguely, she remembered learning at school that somebody called Robert

Peel formed a group. Known as Peelers or Bow Street Runners, many considered them the forerunners of the Metropolitan Police. Roger was one of the first bobbies in Britain.

Roz shot him a sideways glance. He looked like the man she'd seen Jenny kissing.

How was Jenny involved? How did she know a Peeler? The gig made such a racket that it was impossible to question him and it wasn't her concern if he was Jenny's sweetheart, but it would explain how he knew how to get to Scarbane House.

For a while, her musings distracted her from the pain, but Roz was never more thankful than when she spied the chimneys of Scarbane House through the trees. From her seat on the gig, she could see over the hedge into the field where the fair was to have taken place. Most of the servants were there, dismantling the booths and removing the decorations, Jenny among them.

When they reached the driveway, Roger drew the horse to a walk and proceeded at a more decorous pace. Only then did he check the road behind them. He caught Roz's eye and smiled. "All clear."

"Did you expect to be followed?"

"One never knows. . . . But Lord Mindon must have had a reason for asking for the fastest horse in our stable so it's unlikely anyone would catch up to us."

Who could have followed, Roz wondered. David and Rocko were on their way to prison with Madame Sauvé, but they might be part of a larger gang.

As Roger drew the gig to a halt outside the steps to the front door, Roz scrambled down before he could come around to help her. The thought of Roger's hands about her waist and touching her ribs made her shudder.

"Will you be all right?" Roger stood in front of her. "Shall I come in with you?"

"I'll be fine," she answered. "Will you say a few words to Jenny before you leave?"

Surprise filled his eyes. "No, for they will be expecting me, and if I'm late they will think we were waylaid so I'd best be going."

"Thank you for bringing me back." Roz winced as the cuts on her feet took her weight. She gritted her teeth and smiled despite the ache in her jaw where David's fist connected.

"All part of the job." He leapt onto the gig and took up the reins. "You'll stay in the house until Lord Mindon comes, won't you?"

Roz nodded. "Have a safe journey."

She stood on the bottom step and watched him head down the driveway. With a groan, she bent double to nurse her side before taking a few cautious breaths and climbing a few steps. The effort to keep upright was almost more than she could bear. She wanted to lie in a hot bath with a couple of painkillers and a cup of tea. Holding her left elbow and forearm protectively against her ribs, she opened the front door.

The hall was deserted. She limped to the stairway and began to climb when she became aware of someone descending. She looked up. Bertie Briggs. "You!"

"So Miss Reid, we finally gets ta meet." His voice, nasal and reedy, was in keeping with his sharp features and sly look.

"What are you here to steal now?" As he drew closer, she backed down a step.

"Nufink," he answered. "But I wants ta show yer somefink."

"What do you have that would interest me?"

"Yer wants ta know where Rosamund is, don't yer?"

Though Roz was frightened because she was in no shape to fight him off if he should attack her, she had to meet Rosamund. "You know where she's hiding?"

"O' course. I helped her ta find the place."

Roz forgot her myriad of hurts. "Take me to her."

"This way, yer ladyship." He passed her and walked across the hall towards the library.

Roz limped at his heels even though she wasn't sure she should trust him. "How did you meet Rosamund?"

"See'd me stealin', didn't she. And she knew I weren't one o' the servants."

"Does she know about the portal?"

"O' course."

"Has she ever gone through to our time?"

"Nah."

Her uneasiness grew when they entered the library. "I've searched in here."

"She was hid here all the time. Same as she is now. Hid away."

Despite her mistrust of Briggs, she had to talk to Rosamund. "Where?"

"Over here." He took a firm grip on her arm and led her across the room to a panelled wall. "She's in there." He pointed to a panel.

"The secret passage?" Charlie had mentioned such a thing.

"More like a priest's hole. Put yer thumb on that corner up there."

"Here?" Roz reached up and pressed her right thumb where he indicated.

The panel flew open and light from the window slanted through the opening onto a metal trunk resting against the far wall. His grip on her arm tightened, and then a blow to her head and a shove sent Roz reeling into the hole. She fell against the trunk, fighting to stay conscious, and the panel closed.

*

Roz awoke to a frightening blackness and an unpleasant odour that had nothing to do with aged wood or dust.

With every move, the pain in her ribs flared. Roz stumbled across the small space and banged with her fists on the panelling. Head throbbing, and fighting nausea, she realised there was no one to hear her. Most of the servants were in the field dismantling the booths for the fair that wouldn't take place. If any remained in the house, they would be in the kitchen area at the other end of the building.

How long was she unconscious? Had Alex come back? Had he searched for her and believed her to be hiding again? Would he have stayed or would he have left for Scarborough to attend the funeral?

Although she was glad he had arrived before David could do her more harm, he was also the reason she'd been hurt. He knew all about David but he hadn't seen fit to tell her until it was too late. She'd have a thing or two to say to him when she saw him again—if she saw him again.

Roz renewed her pounding on the panel. Thinking someone might hear a sharp tap better; she unpinned the brooch and rapped it against the wood, careless of damaging the jewels. Next, she threw herself against the panel, hoping to break the catch that held it closed. Exhausted and in pain, she curled against the wood and tears of fear and frustration fell unhindered as she tried to gather her wits.

If they shut a priest in here, he would have a way to let himself out. She dragged to her feet, and examined the frame around the panel. She found nothing—no switch or button, no bolt or clasp—and earned a splinter. Defeated, she sat on the trunk and stared into the darkness.

Hunger and thirst added to her discomfort and gave her an idea of how much time had passed. It was the hunger of several hours, so it must be night. If she waited until daylight, she might see where light and air entered. With light, even a narrow shaft, she might see the trigger to open the panel. Perhaps it was not on the wood but fastened to the walls on either side. With a groan, she struggled to her feet again.

The stones were cold, dry, and warmer towards the bottom of the wall. She visualised the rooms on the ground floor and realised this was part of the ornate fireplace in the withdrawing room, cunningly built as part of the massive chimney. They kept fires damped down in this time period. In her time, they kept a fire lit to stave off the dampness that could damage the artefacts. She felt her way around the walls and her knee bumped the trunk.

There might be something inside she could use to break her way through the panelling. She knelt to undo the stout hasps. Her ribs protested as she strained to lift the heavy lid.

With a jerky movement, she got it partly open and a disgusting stench rose to wreathe her face. Trying not to breathe, she held the lid up with a shoulder and fumbled through the contents. Her fingers encountered—

Roz gagged and let the lid fall into place.

She had found Rosamund.

**

CHAPTER TWENTY-FOUR

Roz shuffled to the panel and pressed the hem of her gown to her face to stem the flow of tears and filter the vile and heart-breaking stench. Trapped on this side of the mirror, no one would know what happened to her. She would disappear just as Angeline Sauvé had. Even if Minnie told the police, and they came through the mirror, would she still be alive when they found her, if they found her. The thought brought a storm of despairing sobs.

Time passed before Roz grew calmer. She raised her head and stared into the darkness where Rosamund lay. Poor Rosamund, dead because she encountered a murderer.

For a moment, a light flickered on the wall behind the trunk. Roz struggled to her feet and studied the panel. At eye level, a pinpoint sparkled against the dark wood. She pressed her eye to it. Outside, a light beam flew around the room, as if someone searched for something. Not candlelight or a lantern, a torvh. Charlie! This was Thursday night and Charlie was doing his rounds.

"Charlie! Charlie Watts!" Roz screamed and pounded on the panel. "Help me, Charlie!"

The light hovered around the room again. Jim had been able to understand the words of those from the past; perhaps Charlie could.

"Over here! Behind the panelling! Let me out, Charlie!" Even as she shouted, the light faded from the room. She screamed again. "Don't go! Charlie!"

241

The light returned.

"Help me!"

The light moved deeper into the room.

"Charlie! Over here, to your left!"

The light hovered over the panelling.

"Yes! I'm here!"

The light stayed on the panelling, and then it drifted away only to come back, as though shining from side to side across the wall.

She pounded on the wood. "Here! I'm here! Help me!"

Outside the priest's hole, the room flooded with light. Charlie must have switched on the electric light. The corner of a glass case became visible and part of the cord that kept visitors away from the portraits on the wall. She was seeing the museum she toured with Charlie. How was it possible for her to be in one time and be able to see into another? How close to colliding were the two worlds?

"Here, Charlie! Over here!" She tried to push her finger through but the hole was too small. Even if she could have, would he be able to see her? She hadn't seen the maid run down the stairs the night she'd taken the tour with Charlie though the girl passed close enough to touch her. But the maid had been dead for two hundred years; Roz was still alive, still part of Charlie's time. Minnie's brooch! It had travelled through time and silver and jewels might be visible.

Charlie stood no more than two feet from the panel, looking from side to side as he studied the wall. Roz opened the brooch, thrust the pin through the hole, and wiggled it about.

"Here, Charlie! The pin. Look for the pin, Charlie!" She continued to wiggle it about, knowing only the tip would show on the other side of the panel. With her other hand, she ignored the protest from the ribs and pounded the wood.

Something pushed the pin back.

"Yes! You've found me!" She withdrew the pin and peered through the hole. Charlie was right on the other side of the panel. His lips were moving, but she couldn't hear what he was saying. She wondered if anyone would hear an echo of his words two hundred years in the future. He could hear her from the past, but she couldn't hear him because he was from the future and didn't exist yet She pushed the pin back into the hole and again she felt it thrust back.

"The panel, Charlie!" she shouted. "Top right-hand corner. Press it."

She withdrew the brooch and put her eye to the hole. Charlie had a perplexed look on his face.

"The panel! Top right!"

He tilted his head to look up.

"Yes! Up there! Push it!"

He studied the top of the panel.

He reached up.

The panel swung open and Roz tumbled out. She got to her feet as Charlie examined the priest's hole.

"Thank you, Charlie."

As she spoke, he turned to face the room with a puzzled look. She leaned forward and touched her lips to his cheek. He raised a hand to his face.

"You saved my life, Charlie."

He cocked his head as if listening to something and his hands came up to feel the air about him.

"Rosamund?"

The bright light faded to a mellow glow. Roz whirled around.

Alex stood in the doorway with a candle in his hand. Bookshelves, a desk, and chairs filled the room.

She glanced over her shoulder. Charlie was gone, the panel closed. It was as if both dimensions had merged for a few seconds but had now returned to their own time periods.

"Where in God's name have you been? And who were you talking to?"

"No one." She stood uncertainly.

"I've been searching for you." He put the candle down and walked forward, his gaze travelling over her.

Roz knew she looked a mess. Her gown was torn and filthy, and her slippers brown with dried blood.

"Where have you been? What happened to you?"

She couldn't tell him about Rosamund without revealing who she was and where she came from. She couldn't tell him about Bertie Briggs or could she?

"There was a man. . . ."

"What man?"

"A skinny, sly little man."

He looked around. "Is he here now?"

"I don't know."

"He's a thief, and although I cannot prove it yet, I know he's a murderer."

Detective Inspector Morgan was investigating a murder, and he was watching Bertie Briggs. Was it possible the nasty little man had killed in both worlds?

"Stay away from him, Rosamund. You failed to heed my warning about Ridley so hear me now. This man is a dangerous man."

"Your warning about David could have been more detailed. It's thanks to you, I got hurt."

"Is it more than the bruises I can see?"

"It's nothing sleep will not cure." And a long soak in a hot bath.

"Then you shall sleep." He placed an arm around her shoulders. "Come, I will take you to your room."

He picked up the candle to light their way.

Roz wondered if Briggs was hanging around outside the pool of light. She fumbled with the brooch so the pin stuck out between two fingers and shuddered at the thought of the last time she'd used it as a weapon.

The arm around her shoulders tightened as if to offer comfort. "I will instruct Jenny not to disturb you in the morning until you ring for her," he said when they reached her bedroom door. "Do you need her assistance now?"

"No." Roz eyed the door. Was Bertie Briggs waiting in there? Would he be waiting on the other side of the mirror?

"Then I will bid you goodnight." He touched his lips to her brow before handing her the candle. "Sleep well, my Rosamund."

At the open door, she paused. "Be careful, Bertie Briggs may still be around."

In the half-light, his eyes widened in surprise, and then he nodded and walked to the stairs.

What had she said to cause such surprise? *Good grief!* She'd mentioned Bertie Briggs by name, but Alex hadn't. She closed the door and stood with her back against it.

The bed looked inviting as she crossed the room. If she stayed, Briggs could come from either direction and she would be safer in her own flat. She doused the candle and walked to the mirror.

She went through quickly; hoping speed would allow her an edge of safety if Briggs should be waiting on the other side.

The flat was dark so Roz ran across the room and switched on the overhead light. The place was empty, and the alarm clock next to the bed showed her it was three o'clock in the morning. She placed the brooch beside it and went to the divider. She shoved it tight against the mirror and wedged it with a chair so Briggs couldn't topple it without a struggle. Next, she took a second chair and propped it under the doorknob. Satisfied no one could enter without her knowledge; she stripped off the gown and the bloodstained slippers and dropped them on the floor.

In the bathroom mirror, she saw a swollen jaw and the bruise on her temple had turned a vicious shade of purple with red streaks. Her rib area was the same colour as the bruise on her brow. She turned on the taps.

While water ran into the bathtub, she poured a glass of water and swallowed two painkillers. From the fridge, she shook ice into a tea towel, took a bread knife from the drawer, and carried everything into the bathroom. She sank into the warmth of the tub with the ice pack against her brow. With the bathroom door open, she could see most of the flat, including the divider, and she kept the knife within reach.

*

Either the rattle of the milk float or the chill of the bath water woke Roz. Stiff, aching everywhere, her ribs throbbed in time with her breathing. She pulled the plug to let the water out and turned on the shower. The hot water took away some of the stiffness and washed the blood from her hair.

She tried to remember if she was to be at the Nostalgie for the afternoon matinee or the evening show, then realised this was Friday.

Still in her dressing gown, for the thought of clothes made her wince, she made coffee.

Roz was slumped over her coffee when Minnie tapped on the door. "Just a minute!" she called out. The soles of her feet were tender and she gritted her teeth as she scurried to pick up the gown and slippers. She tossed them behind the shower curtain then glanced in the mirror. A fringe hid the bruise on her temple and her dressing gown covered the rest of the scrapes and bruises, except for her swollen jaw. Minnie tapped again, and Roz limped across to drag the chair away from under the knob.

Still in her cherry-red robe, Minnie entered and looked around. "I heard you up and about," she said by way of explanation for her visit. "You don't look well."

Roz ignored Minnie's comment. "Would you like a cup of coffee?"

"Please." Minnie took the chair Roz removed from under the doorknob and carried it to the table. Roz followed; glad she didn't have to hide her limp. Minnie sat down. "You went through last night, didn't you?"

"Yes." Roz took the two steps into the kitchenette. As she made the coffee, she had to concentrate hard to bring things into focus.

"You said you'd tell me when you did."

"I'm sorry, I didn't think of it." Although relieved to be able to talk to someone in her own time about that other world, there were things she could never tell Minnie.

"I came up in the afternoon, about four o'clock, because I heard you moving about."

"I wasn't here at four yesterday afternoon."

"Then it must have been the Briggs man."

"Or the woman." Roz brought Minnie's coffee to the table and sat opposite her.

"You don't sound too concerned, I must say." Minnie was looking at the swelling on Roz's jaw.

"He won't be bothering us much longer." Not if Alex found him, and not when she told Detective Inspector Morgan where to find Rosamund's bones. In a small way, she had changed history. Rosamund's whereabouts were no longer a mystery.

"Why do you say he won't be bothering us?" Minnie asked.

"They're searching for him on both sides of the mirror. He can't hide forever."

"What happened to you over there? The bruises I can see, however much you try to cover them with your hair."

"I fell and hit my head." Roz remembered the brooch. "I have something for you." She tried not to limp as she went to the bedside table. She glanced at the clock as she picked up the brooch. Six fifteen. She examined the brooch as she walked back to the table. Apart from the bent pin, it was intact. She handed it to Minnie. "I believe this is yours."

"My mother's brooch!" Tears filled Minnie's eyes. "My mother's brooch. . . ." She clutched it to her breast and looked at Roz through her tears. "Where did you find it?"

It would be easy to lie; to say she found it while sweeping the floor, but they'd torn the flat apart and Minnie wasn't likely to believe her. "Madame Sauvé gave it to me."

"You've seen her?"

Roz nodded.

"I hope you gave her a good ticking off for keeping it."

"Don't worry; she'll pay for what she did."

"Even though I'm glad to have it back, I can't help wondering how she'll get on without her good luck charm."

"We get the luck we deserve."

Somewhere in the house, a bell rang. A short while later, someone hurried up the stairs. They both stood with their attention on the door. Into her mind flashed a vision of

Bertie Briggs and Roz felt sure Minnie was thinking the same thing. Relieved she heard Marge's voice.

"Roz? Are you up?"

"I'll get it." Minnie went to open the door. "Good morning."

Out of breath after her rush up the stairs, Marge was also in her dressing gown. She nodded to Minnie, and then said to Roz, "There's a man downstairs with Archie. He said he pressed your buzzer, but it can't be working. Did either of you hear it?"

"No," Roz and Minnie said in unison.

"Anyway, he says he won't go away until he sees you. He says he'll ring the police if we don't let him. His name is Charles Watts. Do you know him?"

Roz smiled. "He works at the Nostalgie. Would you ask him to come up?"

"Okay. But I don't know why he has to visit so early in the morning." Marge walked across the landing and took a deep breath before starting down the stairs.

"I suppose I'd better let you see him alone." Minnie stood uncertainly beside the door. "Unless you want me to stay."

Roz shook her head. "Charlie's a friend." She didn't want Minnie to hear anything he had to say if it involved the night before in the museum. She put the kettle on when Minnie left and Charlie raced up the stairs. As she emerged from the kitchenette, he arrived breathless in the doorway.

"Thank God you're all right, love."

"Of course I'm all right." Roz watched him shut the door. "What brings you here so early?"

"Oh, God!" Charlie dropped into a chair beside the table, took out a chequered handkerchief and mopped his brow. "I been sick wiv worry all night, I have. I couldn't leave work 'til now, and I couldn't go home 'til I'd seen you was all right."

Roz made fresh coffee. When she brought the cups to the table, he looked up at her.

"You look like you been in a fight, love."

"I took a tumble." Roz dropped into a chair. "Now, tell me why you wanted to see me so urgently."

"It were last night. I were on my rounds, like, and I heard this voice calling me. Calling my name. *Charlie! Charlie!* Well, I don't mind telling you it fair gave me a turn."

"So you could make out the words, they weren't just muffled voices."

"Made them out clear as day, I did. *Help me*, the voice says. Well, I weren't sure I'd heard right, first off, but then the voice says *Charlie Watts*. Well, it ain't likely any o' them in the past would know my moniker, so I stops and listens. *Over here* the voice were saying, and I swear to you, love, I thought it were your voice. I couldn't rest 'til I'd seen you was all right, now could I?"

Roz patted his hand. "You are a good friend, Charlie."

"But that weren't all what happened. See, this voice were telling me to go to one o' they panels—it were in what used to be the library in the old days—and push on a corner o' one. So I did, and the whole blooming thing swings open like a door."

"The secret passage."

"Then I felt it." Charlie's face took on the appearance of a man who'd won the lottery. "See, I been working there all them years, and I never felt what you and Jim felt—you know—that air rush o' somebody walking past. I felt cheated, if you know what I mean, but I felt it last night. When that panel opened, I felt somebody rush past me out o' there, and you know what? I swear the girl I heard, the one what sounded like you, kissed me on the cheek. Any road, she said as I saved her life."

"Perhaps you did, Charlie."

"No." He shook his head, and the joy fled his face. "She were dead. In that hole in the wall. In a trunk, she was. There was nobbut bones. She died a long time ago. Mebbe all I did were let her spirit out."

"She would be grateful even for that."

"And bloody Detective Inspector Morgan. . . . I rings him. He'd give me his card, see, in case something happened.

So I rings him, right then and there, in the middle of the night."

"Was he upset?"

"Not him. Came right over; no more'n a quarter hour after I phoned." Charlie grinned. "I reckon as he had his jimjams on under his trahsers."

"Whose bones did he think they were?"

"Well, we had no idea, so he goes and rings Mr Coulter."

"A lot of people were disturbed last night, one way or another."

"Mr Coulter reckons as them bones belonged to some girl as went missing near two hundred years ago. Hey!" Charlie looked at Roz. "He said her name were Rosamund, too."

Roz shivered. It could be her bones they'd find years from now if Charlie hadn't rescued her.

"They gave me a rough old time them two did. Wanted to know how I knew how that bit of panelling opened. Were I searching for treasure. Well, I told them straight, I did. There were a voice telling me what to do, I said." Charlie took a gulp of coffee. "Morgan, he reckoned as I'd been drinking, but Mr Coulter, he stands up for me. Said I never drank when I were working."

"With the museum closing soon, I'm sure Mr Coulter is grateful to you for solving the mystery of the missing woman."

"You know about her?"

"He told me when I visited the museum. Has anything else been stolen?"

"Not that I've heard."

"Do you think it's Bertie Briggs stealing the things?"

A guarded look came into Charlie's eyes. "He done it before."

"You knew Bertie Briggs was friendly with Agatha's husband, didn't you."

Charlie nodded. "I didn't want to say nowt, what wiv you working wiv her, like. It were in prison Alfred and Bertie met." He got to his feet as if reluctant to say more. "Well, thanks for the coffee, love. I'd better get home or my missus will be wondering what happened to me."

The painkillers were wearing off but Roz pulled herself to her feet and walked Charlie to the door. When he had left, she swallowed two more painkillers with the dregs of her coffee and went to lie down while she waited for them to take effect.

If she met Briggs now, she was in no condition to fight him off. He got the better of her once because she turned her back to him, but how would Alex fare? Bertie Briggs could come up behind him and the sword would be of no use.

She had to know what was going on there. If only she could see Alex again, even for a short time, to make sure he was all right. Roz couldn't fool herself any more—the past she had thought so romantic was anything but. People lied, connived, stole and killed, and as for David. . . .

She had no friends there as she had here. Charlie proved to be a better friend than he realised and, nosy though they were, Minnie, Archie and Marge surrounded her with the feel of family. Even the people with whom she worked showed they cared for her wellbeing. John spoke highly of her work, and Derek— Derek took the time to bring her a cola after noticing she hadn't had anything to drink with her sandwich. It was a small kindness but, added to the kindness and caring surrounding her, it made the other world doubly unwelcoming.

If she returned there, they would force her to take on Rosamund's role because she knew Rosamund wasn't in hiding but murdered.

The painkillers, taken so soon after the earlier dose, dulled all the aches and pains except for the ache in her heart. Tears drenched her pillow, and she made no effort to stem them. Noises from the Lane filtered into the room. A car passed, its radio blaring; the road-sweeper's cart trundled by. A woman in high heels tapped her way along the pavement. Children squabbled on their way to school. A dog barked.

Then another sound . . . closer. A whisper. In the stillness of the room, it came again but the words came as if from a distance.

"Are yer hurt, Miss?"

Roz opened her eyes, expecting to see Minnie or Marge hovering in the doorway. There was no one. The flat was empty.

A shadow crossed the room.

Roz gasped and raised her head. It was no shadow but a shadowy form, the outline of a woman wearing a long dark dress and a white apron. "Jenny?"

"I'll send help, Miss." The whisper was indistinct; no more than a leaf rustling in a breeze, and then the ghostly shape flitted through the divider and mirror and was gone.

Jenny. The mystery woman, the ghost Amelia saw. Roz let her head fall back onto the pillow. She had always suspected Jenny knew Roz wasn't Rosamund; a maid knew her mistress better than anyone did. If Jenny had come through the mirror to make sure Roz was all right, whom could she possibly bring to help who would have more substance than a ghostly shadow?

Outside, two women walked by, their voices bringing an ordinary, this time period, feel into the flat as they discussed the Coronation Street episode aired the night before. At the end of the Lane, a car tooted a warning and then a motorbike grumbled past the house. Noises in the other attic flat told her Sandy Saunders must have come home. In a way, the sounds were comforting.

**

CHAPTER TWENTY-FIVE

Roz closed her eyes and tried to relax. A few minutes later, a wave of nausea threatened to soil her bedding and the carpet. In a stupor, she struggled to sit up. She concentrated on swinging her legs over the bed as a car raced up the road and screamed to a halt outside. The car door slammed two seconds before a doorbell rang.

Feet rushed up the stairs, a light tread, and then a heavier one. There was a tap at her door and Marge called out.

"Roz? Detective Inspector Morgan wants to talk to you."

Roz climbed off the bed.

"She's not very well. Must you disturb her?" Marge asked.

Roz opened the door. Minnie and Marge, both dressed now, crowded the doorway with the Detective Inspector behind them.

"Good morning, Miss Reid." He pushed past Minnie and Marge. "Just a few questions." He entered with the two women at his heels.

"Make it quick because I have to be at work." Roz moved away from the door and a wave of nausea hit her again. She thrust past Morgan and rushed to the bathroom. Without time to close the door, she knelt beside the toilet and vomited into the bowl. She broke into a sweat, placed her arm across the toilet seat and rested her head on it. She would stay here for the rest of her life. She would never move from here. If only everybody would go away and leave her here to die.

As if from a distance, Minnie said something, then a cool hand supported her brow.

"This is best." Marge's voice, heard above the running of water.

Someone placed a cold, wet cloth on the nape of her neck.

"Is there anything I can do?" Morgan's voice.

"Yes. Stay out of the way." Minnie's voice, harsh and threatening.

"Let's get her onto the bed." Marge said.

They hauled Roz to her feet, head lolling, then her arms were around their necks and they half carried her to the bed. They laid her on it and one of their hands touched her ribs. Roz groaned.

"Are you hurt?"

Roz opened her eyes. Marge hovered over her. "My ribs."

"You'd better turn your back, Inspector." Marge untied the knot and opened Roz' dressing gown. With cool fingers, she touched her ribs gently. "You've got one or two fractured ribs."

"No," Roz protested.

"I may be retired, but I was a nurse for many years and I know fractured ribs when I feel them."

"Would that make her vomit?" Minnie asked.

"Not on its own. Are you hurt anywhere else?" Marge pulled the robe closed.

"She has a bruise on her forehead." Minnie pointed out.

"That could do it, but there may be something else. Is there, Roz?"

"The back of my head," Roz mumbled.

With surprising strength, Marge placed a hand under Roz's shoulders and lifted her. She ran her hand over the back of Roz's head. "Oh, my, you'll have to get that seen too. You may have a concussion."

"That would make her vomit," Minnie said.

"I took—I took painkillers too soon after the first ones."

"And poisoned yourself." Marge said. "You are going to the hospital, my girl."

"But I have to be at work." They ignored her and Roz felt too weak to argue.

"I have the car outside," Morgan said. "We'll take her in that."

"And I'll go with her," Minnie said.

In a flash of lucidity, Roz protested. "But you have to visit your niece."

"I'll call her and go down later," Minnie said firmly. "Now, let me find you something to wear, and you, Inspector, had better wait on the landing. We may need your help to get her down the stairs."

From the wardrobe, Minnie unearthed a loose-fitting summer dress and both women helped Roz into it.

Marge knelt to put a pair of pumps on Roz's feet and let out a sharp cry. "Good heavens, Roz, your feet are covered in cuts. What have you been up to?"

Minnie shot a look at Roz and caught her frown. "Never mind that now, let's get her to hospital."

"I don't want to go." The protest sounded weak even to her ears.

"How long ago did you get the lump on the back of your head?" Marge asked.

What time was it? Had been daylight when Roger-the-Peeler dropped her at Scarbane House? "I don't know."

"Memory confusion," Marge said. "That's not good."

"But it was the pills, I tell you."

"Maybe, maybe not."

Between them, they hoisted Roz to her feet and walked with her to the door. On the landing, Morgan took over. He placed an arm around her waist.

"Careful, Inspector." Minnie warned. "She has broken ribs."

"Oh!" He took hold of Roz's right arm. "We could always call an ambulance."

"Just get her to the hospital," Marge said as she locked the door to Roz's flat. "I have your key, Roz. You ring our bell when you get back."

"Give it to me. I'll be with her," Minnie said. "I'll get my handbag and catch up with you."

They reached the ground floor and Marge opened the front door as Minnie rushed down the stairs to join them.

The driver of the unmarked police car was the man who accompanied Morgan on his earlier visits. He ran around to open the back door when he saw them emerge from the house.

"Been in the wars, have you, Miss?"

"Just get her into the car, Prescott." Morgan's voice was gruff. "You get in first, Mrs Wilton, and you can help Miss Reid from in there while Prescott helps from out here."

A couple of people stopped to watch. As they eased Roz into the car, she saw Morgan look at them before looking up and down the Lane. He didn't open his own door and get in until Prescott shut Roz's door.

Once they were all in and the car drew away from the house, Minnie pinned the brooch to Roz's shirt. "Just for good luck."

"But it's your mother's brooch," Roz protested.

"Which I wouldn't have if you hadn't got it back from that Sauvé woman."

Morgan eased around in the front seat to look at them. "Is there something special about the brooch?"

"It was—er—borrowed from me, Inspector. It was my mother's, and I never thought I'd see it again."

Roz squeezed Minnie's hand in an attempt to warn her to say no more.

Minnie returned the pressure. "It's all right, love; we'll be at the hospital any minute now." Then she went on, "As luck would have it, Inspector, Roz here met Angeline Sauvé, the woman who took the brooch, and got it back for me."

Morgan shot Roz a look she couldn't read before he faced front.

When they reached the hospital and Prescott got out to open the back door, Minnie commented, "We should have asked Marge to come. She would get us past the crowd in the waiting room."

"Don't you worry about that," Morgan said. "Miss Reid will go to the head of the queue." He grinned. "Sometimes it's not who you know but what you are. You leave it to me."

Prescott brought a wheelchair to the car and Roz sank into it with a sigh. It seemed every part of her body hurt. Her ribs throbbed, her head felt ready to explode, the cuts on her feet burned from the pressure of the pumps, and one shoulder and elbow seemed to grind with pain at every movement. Her jaw ached, her head weighed a ton, and she could barely see straight.

Morgan went in ahead of them. When Prescott entered with the wheelchair, with Minnie walking alongside, they were ushered into an examination room.

"Doctor will be with you in a couple of minutes," the nurse said then left.

Minnie helped Roz climb onto the examination table. She removed Roz's pumps and covered her with a light blanket. Then Morgan ordered her to leave. "You and Prescott wait outside. I have to talk to Miss Reid."

"You are not to upset her with a lot of questions, Inspector." Minnie drew herself to full height and stared down the man at least a foot taller.

"If you are not careful, Mrs Wilton, I'll charge you with obstructing a policeman in the course of his duty."

"Huh," said Minnie, but she left with Prescott.

"We have little time before the doctor gets here," Morgan said as the door closed. "Where did you get hurt?"

Somehow, lying on the hard bed, knowing she was safe and there was a doctor nearby, made Roz feel better. She relaxed. "I fell," she said in answer to his question.

"Where? In your flat?" He drew a stool up to the bed. "I saw nothing there that would cause such injuries. You tell me the truth, now. Where did you fall?"

"Does it matter?"

He studied her in silence for a moment, then, "This Angeline Sauvé who gave you Mrs Wilton's brooch, where did you meet her?"

"In another part of London, close to the docks."

"And Bertie Briggs, have you seen him recently?"

"Mrs Wilton thinks he was in my flat yesterday afternoon."

"But you weren't there."

Roz tried to shake her head and fought a wave of dizziness.

"Where did you go? And before you answer, let me tell you we saw Briggs enter the house, but you didn't leave all day."

Roz didn't know how to answer. If she told him the truth, he'd take her from this hospital to one with bars on the windows.

"Let me make this easier for you. Angeline Sauvé isn't in London, at least, not in the London we know."

Roz avoided looking at him. "What do you mean, Inspector?"

"We policemen aren't the clodhoppers some people make us out to be, but we failed in one thing. We know there is an entrance to the past in your flat."

Roz didn't speak. How was it possible for him to know about the portal, or even believe one existed?

When she didn't comment, he said, "Come on, we know you've been going through regularly."

"I found out by accident."

"And you've been going through at every opportunity. We have a man working on the other side with the police there. He told us."

"You have— Do you mean—" Wide eyed, she stared at him. How had their man gone back? Was he the one using the mirror in her flat? "Is he working with Robert Peel's men?

Morgan nodded as if going into the past was an everyday thing. "They've been on Briggs' trail since he was released from prison. A few weeks ago, a maid at Scarbane

House contacted Peel's men and told them she thought someone had murdered her mistress. The description of the man fitted Briggs."

Jenny. "She told the police but no one in the family?"

"She had no proof. We believed Briggs killed Rosamund Oldham, but we didn't find the body until last night."

"I know about that. Charlie, the night guard, called in to see me this morning."

"He was observed."

"Are you sure it's Rosamund?"

"Forensics will confirm the age of the bones, but from a cursory examination of the clothing there can be no doubt the fashion coincides with the time of Rosamund Oldham's disappearance."

"I see."

Unexpectedly, Morgan chuckled. "There's a lighter side to all of this, even though, at the time, it was so bloody frustrating I applied for permission to throw you in clink for a day or two."

"I take it permission was denied," Roz said dryly.

"We did our best, but the powers-that-be turned it down. We kept hoping you'd do something so we could nail you."

"Thank you very much."

"Our only intent was to keep you out of harm's way. Do you know what a problem you caused our man? The maid said someone murdered Rosamund and then you showed up posing as Rosamund. And you looked so much like her no one questioned it."

"I wondered about that myself. You said there was a lighter side. . . ."

"The maid who first contacted Peel's men knew you were an impostor and she let them know. And I may have the answer to why you are the double of the woman who was killed."

"Oh?" She should have talked about it to Jenny; should have trusted her instincts. The look Roz cast at Morgan held the doubt she felt.

"The idea you looked so like Rosamund Oldham and fooled everyone was so preposterous that we did a bit of research into your family genealogy. Do you know you are a direct descendant of Adele Scarbane?"

"That's impossible." Adele died of arsenic poisoning.

"Back in my office I have a copy of your family tree. I'm surprised Vincent Coulter didn't show you the Scarbane genealogy."

"You've talked to him about my visit to the museum?"

"We checked on everyone going to the museum and their reason for being there. He said Scarbane family history interested you."

"He told me of Adele's death."

"Influenza could be deadly in those days."

"She wasn't poisoned?"

"Not that we know."

Roz knew he was at a loss to explain the sudden joy in her face. Imogen and Adele followed her plea not to use the face powder. History was changed. The family survived. She tried to sit up but the pain in her ribs forced her back onto the pillow. "Who did Adele marry?" Roz held her breath as she waited for the answer. Had she married Alex? Would she feel happy for Adele?

"A man named Runston. Coulter says he managed the shipyards after Rosamund disappeared. The family were unhappy about the match. Runston had no title and no money, and no job after they fired him from the shipyards. They moved to Southend so he could find work. Adele bore him three children, two of whom died at birth. You are descended from their daughter, who was also called Rosamund."

Adele was her ancestor.

"It explains your remarkable likeness to Rosamund Oldham. And it explains how you fooled everyone except Briggs and our man."

"And the maid." Jenny had known all along. "Who is your man? What is his name?"

Morgan chuckled. "We call him Doctor Who. He kept well out of your way in both places."

"How did he go back in time? Is there another doorway to the past?"

Morgan looked away. "Your question breaches police confidentiality."

"So there is another doorway, maybe several. You are aware that frequent use might cause a catastrophe, aren't you?"

"Catastrophe?"

Roz studied him and the guarded look in his eyes. She might be adding two and two and getting five, but. . . . Morgan hadn't been very surprised when she admitted there was a gateway to the past. Why? Did the police have some sort of special branch where. . . . No, she was allowing her imagination to run away with her. "I suppose I'll get to meet your Doctor Who eventually, when all of this is over."

"It is over. Briggs got his just deserts earlier this morning."

"He's dead?"

"As a doornail. Our man got what you might call *peeved* when he realised Briggs was after you. He said he needed to protect you. *One of mine*, he called you, and it didn't take much to provoke him. He brought in Peel's men and they cornered Briggs. Justice was swift in those days so I won't question how Briggs met his end because we're too grateful for the warning you were back and might be hurt. That's why I was at your place so early this morning. I got the call less than an hour ago."

Jenny. . . . Thank you, Jenny. Roz felt regret mingled with relief. She'd like to thank Jenny in person. "So it's over."

"Not yet. We don't know who the woman is. The one you said was Briggs's accomplice."

"I was mistaken. The so-called ghost Amelia saw—and the one I thought could be Brigg's accomplice—was the maid who told the Peelers her mistress was murdered?"

At first, it didn't look as if he believed her, then he nodded. "Jenny. So it is over, or will be when we dismantle the mirror in your flat."

"But we could learn a lot from the past."

"As you said, there is a danger in allowing people to pass from one time frame into another. The experts we consulted are certain it will cause a catastrophe and the gateways, or whatever they're called, must be closed permanently."

He'd consulted experts. . . . Time travel must be viable for there to be experts to consult, and the police had a special unit with officers who travelled into the past.

Morgan stood as the door opened and a white-coated woman walked in. "You must be the doctor. I'll leave you in good hands, Miss Reid, and we'll talk again when you get out of hospital."

"Detective Inspector," Roz spoke with urgency and ignored the pain as she sat up. "Please don't dismantle the mirror before I get home."

He studied her for a moment and then nodded.

Her mind filled with what Morgan had just told her and her idea the police had some sort of special branch involving time travel, Roz suffered the poking and prodding in silence but Minnie did not. As soon as Detective Inspector Morgan left the examining room, Minnie walked in and stood at the side of the bed, watching the doctor's examination of Roz with a beady eye.

"Is this your grandmother?" the doctor asked.

"By proxy," Minnie said firmly. "Her own family isn't in London so I'm standing in for them. And I'm not leaving if that's what you're thinking."

Minnie said no more as the tight-lipped doctor finished the examination and a nurse came to take blood and urine samples for testing. While they waited for Roz to go for x-rays, Minnie asked, "So? Who hurt you?"

Careful to avoid any mention of the part Madame Sauvé played; Roz gave her the gist of what had happened.

"The monster," Minnie cried when she heard of David's duplicity. "So all he wanted was to kidnap you and put you in a whorehouse." Her anger fled when she looked at Roz. "I'm sorry. You were really taken with him, weren't you?"

"I was taken in by him."

"This other man you mentioned—Alex. He saved you?"

"I had met him before and he knew David Ridley's reputation. He tried to warn me but I wouldn't listen."

"Lucky he followed you."

"Yes." Roz closed her eyes.

"You are tired. You rest and I'll sit here and read this old magazine."

Grateful for the silence, Roz allowed her thoughts to drift. If Vincent Coulter hadn't told her Adele died of arsenic poisoning, Roz might never have made an issue of the face powder. Adele survived, and it was as much thanks to Alex as to her. He read the note and gave it to Imogen and Adele. Between them, they had changed the course of history, and—

Roz opened her eyes and stared at the ceiling. If Adele had died as the result of arsenic poisoning, Roz would never have been born. There was no way she could thank him or Jenny unless she went through the mirror one last time, despite the consequence if the time periods collided and she became trapped in the past.

She had to get out of the hospital. She had to get home before Morgan dismantled the mirror. She couldn't risk that he would keep his word to wait until she got there.

"Minnie?"

She looked up from the magazine. "Yes, love?"

"Will you do something for me?"

"Of course, I will."

"Go home. Go to my flat and don't let Detective Inspector Morgan in until I get there. Will you do that?"

"Right now?"

"Yes. It's important. He knows about the mirror. He wants to dismantle it and he said he'd wait until I got home, but I have to be sure. Will you go there and, if he tries to get in, stop him for me?"

"Why don't you let him just dismantle the mirror and we can have everything back to normal?"

"I have to see Alex one last time. Please, Minnie, help me?"

Minnie hesitated. "Will you be all right here on your own?"

"If I know the mirror is safe, I shall rest more easily."

**

CHAPTER TWENTY-SIX

After Minnie left, an orderly took Roz for x-rays. Trundled along with only the ceiling tiles to look at, she closed her eyes, but she was aware of everything taking place around her. She heard the nurses whispering and Detective Inspector Morgan's name came up more than once. They might think her a criminal because the police brought her in. Little did they know a man who kidnapped her to put her in a brothel caused her injuries more than a century earlier, and a murderer caused the other injuries.

All in all, she hadn't fared too well on the other side of the mirror. It should not have been that way. She had knowledge, which people in the past didn't have, but they had the skills necessary to survive in their world. She hadn't even known how to light a candle.

Roz decided to give the sugar bowl away when she got home. The woman depicted gave a false picture of what life was like then, just as the covers of Vogue falsely portrayed life as it was now. Two hundred years in the future, would another woman gaze at a cover of Vogue and sigh?

Roz was no martyr and not interested in impressing anyone by suffering in silence. She shrieked and groaned while the nurses took x-rays and a doctor strapped her ribs. When the procedures ended, she sank onto the pillow in exhaustion.

"We're moving you to a ward," the doctor informed her.

"I'm to stay in hospital!" Roz gave a cry of dismay. "For how long?"

"At least overnight. We'll see how you are tomorrow."

"Why can't I go home now?"

"That bump on the head was a bad one. I'd rather keep you in for observation. You are in for a rough time, Miss Reid. The nurses have instructions to wake you every two hours."

And they did. Beyond a curtained partition placed around the bed, Roz saw the shaft of sunlight in a different position each time they woke her. At noon, it disappeared; at two and four, it slanted at different angles. It was a way she could gauge the passage of time.

The elderly woman in the bed next to hers played a radio. It wasn't loud enough to disturb Roz, but a woman on the far side of the ward complained. The patient switched off the radio long enough to allow the nurse to leave and then switched it back on. The clinking of trays and cutlery signalled Roz they were serving a meal to the others in the ward, but all they brought her was a cup of juice.

A nurse arrived at her bedside. "Are you up to seeing a visitor?"

Roz nodded, tried to sit and gave up.

The nurse smoothed Roz's hair from her face. "You look good for someone who just got mugged. Shall I send your visitor in?"

"Please." So, that was the story—she'd been mugged.

Roz expected to see Archie or Marge, but the person who walked around the partition was the last man she wanted to see her in this state. "Derek? How did you know I was here?"

"Detective Inspector Morgan told me when he came to the Nostalgie." Derek placed a bouquet of red roses on the bed.

"He went to the theatre? Why?"

"They came to pick up Agatha for questioning. Did you know her husband is a criminal?"

"I heard this morning."

266

"Uncle John's sacked her, so when you get out you'll have to start interviewing replacements."

"Why would he sack her? She's never stolen anything, and she is a good seamstress."

Derek shrugged. "Take it up with him when you get back to work."

"I intend to."

He moved the flowers closer to her. "These are for you."

"Thanks." Roz sniffed one of the roses.

"They're my way of apologising. Our talk the other night made me realise how I was coming across to you. I'm sorry, Roz. Do you forgive me?"

"There's nothing to forgive. I could have been less blunt." She gave a wan smile.

"Can we call a truce?"

"Absolutely."

"Good, because there's something I want to ask you."

Roz held her breath.

"What do you think of Laura?"

"Laura?"

"Yes, our young actress. Do you like her?"

"I don't know too much about her, but I've always found her very sweet."

"She's quite shy when she isn't on stage."

"Are you going to ask her out?"

"I might."

"Oh." With surprise, Roz realised she was disappointed to hear Derek was going to ask another woman out.

"When I think of what you said that night—how you didn't want to be one of the fields where I sowed my wild oats— I wonder if she thinks the same thing."

"That's possible."

"Will you. . . . Would you talk to her? Tell her I'm not like that?"

"Why don't you tell her?"

"Do you think she would believe me?"

"Why not? I did."

Derek smiled. "Thanks, Roz. At the cast dinner, I'm going to arrange to sit next to her and perhaps I can convince her I have a serious side to me, one that isn't looking to sow wild oats."

Roz gave him a sideways glance. "Quoting a few lines of poetry couldn't hurt."

He laughed. "It surprised you, didn't it? Why?"

"I'd never pictured you as a reader, never mind a reader of poetry."

"How did you see me?" When she didn't answer, he went on, "I need to know, because that's probably how Laura sees me too."

"Okay, if you want me to be brutally honest. I saw you as a philanderer, into fast horses and fast women, and you drink too much."

"Me? But I hardly ever drink."

"You were drunk at the cast party."

"I had a sinus infection, and I made the mistake of taking medicine and then having a couple of drinks—just two. I've never felt so ill in my life." Derek took Roz's hand. "Thanks for the honesty."

"You are welcome."

"And when you come back to work, we'll go out for a slap-up lunch."

"I'll hold you to that."

He dropped a kiss on her cheek before leaving.

One way or another, the men in her life were gone. David was no loss and Derek. . . . He was turning out to be very different from her original picture of him. He'd been there all along, chivalrous and caring, but she'd ignored him and looked for love in a world that was long dead. He'd turned his sight from her and was going to ask Laura out, so Roz had lost again.

Suddenly, she was crying. She sobbed into her pillow to muffle the sound, but one of the other patients heard and sent for the nurse.

"Are you in pain?" The nurse held her fingers on Roz's wrist to take her pulse.

"No, not really, just uncomfortable."

"Is this the first cry you've had since it happened?"

Roz sniffed.

"I'm surprised you've held up this long." Satisfied with the pulse count, the nurse asked, "Is there anything I can get you?"

Roz began to speak, but the nurse uttered an oath.

"There she goes with that blasted radio again! I don't know why she can't use earphones like everyone else." She disappeared outside the partition to talk to the woman in the next bed.

"But I only wanted to listen to News at Six," the woman protested. "Have you heard about the fire?"

"What fire?" the nurse asked.

"Somewhere in St. John's Wood. There's a museum been on fire for hours. Three fire engines they've sent there."

Roz was up and sitting on the edge of the bed. "Was it the Scarborough Museum?" she called through the partition.

"I don't know. It's on Scarborough Lane."

"That's where I live."

Did the rift in time cause the fire? Roz ignored her discomfort, slipped off the edge off the bed, and opened the cupboard beside it to find her clothes as the nurse came back.

"You are not thinking of leaving."

"I have to. I live in the house that adjoins the museum. My flat could be going up in flames. I have to get there."

"But you can't leave."

"You just watch me." Roz threw off the hospital gown, struggled into her dress and gritted her teeth as she forced her feet into the trainers. "Where's my bag?"

"It'll be in the office," the nurse answered. "The other woman brought it by while you were asleep."

Had Minnie left the flat unprotected? "Did the woman leave a name?"

"Mrs Pym. An elderly man was with her. I didn't want them to disturb you."

Minnie was faithful to her promise, but what now. The time periods must have collided and caused this catastrophe. "I have to go."

"The doctor won't be happy about this. Isn't there anyone who could come to fetch you?"

"There's no one." Roz shouldered the bag. "I'll get a taxi."

Outside the hospital, Roz hailed a taxi, climbed in, and gave the address to the driver.

"Where the fire is, love?"

"Yes, I live there. Please hurry!"

It seemed to Roz the taxi crawled. When they got closer, police were guiding traffic away from the area. Roz paid the fare, got out and limped up the street until two policemen barred her way.

"I live down there," Roz protested "in the house next to the museum. You have to let me through." She peered down the smoke-filled street and saw Prescott, a head taller than most of the gathered crowd. "Ask Sergeant Prescott. He'll tell you."

As if he heard his name above the tumult, Prescott looked her way. Roz waved to him and he came to join her. "Miss Reid?"

"I have to get past and these officers won't let me. Tell them who I am."

"She lives in the house next to the museum. I think it's best if she gets down there." He took her arm and guided her into the crowd.

"Is the house on fire?"

"No. Luckily, the museum walls are thick and the fire is contained. There will be some smoke damage to the houses."

They drew closer and Roz saw several streams of water shooting at the museum. At the edge of the property, where water poured in the gutters and hoses lay coiled like snarled thread, Minnie and Marge huddled together.

"Will the firemen let me into the house?" she asked Sergeant Prescott.

"No, it's too dangerous. A fireman, one of our men and Mr Pym are inside checking the flats adjoining the museum wall. Earlier, they discovered a mirror cracked in your flat."

"No!" Roz gave a cry of anguish and tears scalded her eyes. The mirror hadn't survived the heat; it was cracked. What would she find on the other side even if she managed to go through? The fire hadn't taken place in that other time, only now. Everything blurred by tears, Roz edged closer to Minnie and Marge.

"Roz?" Minnie turned when she sensed someone beside her. "They let you out of hospital?"

"I let myself out. Does anyone know how the fire started?"

"The guard said it started in the room where they found those bones. He said the wood panelling went up like a flash. He was lucky to get out, and the curator too."

"Isn't that your friend, Charlie, over there?" Marge pointed to a place closer to the fire.

"He's with the curator of the museum." Roz limped towards them.

Charlie was the first to see her. "Roz, love, they told me you was in hospital."

"I just got out." Roz turned to Vincent Coulter. "I heard the fire started in the library. Is that true?"

He smiled at her. "I remember you. Unfortunately, what you heard is true. We lost a lot of the exhibits."

"How did it happen?"

"The fire chief thinks it has something to do with the priest's hole we found. You've heard about that, haven't you?"

Roz nodded. "Charlie told me."

"We usually kept a fire going in Exhibit Room Two and the fireplace was on the wall shared with the library. With the panel left open while the police investigated, they think a draught dragged the flames from the chimney into the wood braces of both rooms and the whole thing went up."

"Sorry, folks, have to ask you to move." A fireman hauled a length of hose across the road.

"I have to check the damage at the other side." Vincent Coulter started to walk away. "Come on, Charlie, I may need your help."

Roz went back to stand beside Minnie and Marge.

"There's goes one fire engine," Marge said. "They must be getting it under control."

"And there's Sandy Saunders with Archie." Minnie said. "I hope they locked up the flats after they checked them. Goodness knows who would take advantage of the situation, but with people like that Briggs man about, you can't be too careful."

"It looks as if Archie and Sandy are standing guard at the door," Marge said.

Roz looked towards the house. A mass of people stood between her and the front door, but then the crowd parted and she saw Archie talking to a man whose back was to her. Even so, she recognised him.

Her feet were giving her hell, she wanted to lie down to ease the pressure on her ribs, her jaw ached so much that she doubted she'd ever be able eat solid food again, but anger infused her whole body. Thanks to that sod, she was in the state she was in now.

He was the cop who travelled back in time as she had. He must have known who she was because Doris had seen him with Prescott in Scotland Yard.

Morgan made it clear they knew she was travelling back in time, so Alex–Sandy, whoever-he-was, had to have known who she was. Jenny knew she wasn't Rosamund and told her Peeler boyfriend. Morgan knew there had been a murder. They had to suspect someone murdered Rosamund—any dumb idiot would guess it was what happened to the missing girl—but Alex hadn't seen fit to warn her about David or Briggs.

Furious, Roz limped to where Alex stood with Archie. They saw her coming and Alex walked to meet her.

"Rosamund . . . ."

"Don't you Rosamund me, you sad excuse for a human being! You see the state I'm in? It's all thanks to you."

"I'm sorry about that, but I did try to warn you."

"The hell you did! You knew I wasn't the real Rosamund, and you knew Briggs had probably murdered her. Did you tell me? No, all you did was make coy remarks about David and Briggs! If I were in any state to do it, I'd punch your lights out! As it is, I will report you to the Police Commission or whatever it is where people make complaints about police behaviour."

The amusement she hated showed in his eyes. "Would they believe you?"

"Special Branch or not, they would have to investigate, and I would go the whole hog."

"What would you do? Take me down in a flying tackle?"

"Don't you mock me!"

"I wouldn't dare. You're one tough woman."

"Too damned tough to put up with a sod like you!"

"So I guess marriage is out?"

"What?"

"Rosamund. . . ."

"You . . . what are you talking about?"

"The contract still stands."

"Don't be silly!"

"I think two hundred years plus is over long for an engagement."

"You . . . ."

"I'm asking you to marry me." He opened his arms.

Roz laughed as she stepped toward him.

Arms around his neck, hurts forgotten, she kissed him in a way that made up for two-hundred-years.

***

Other novels by P. L. Crompton

Available in Paperback and Digital

http://plcrompton.wix.com/cromptonfiction

Land of My Fathers

A collection of interrelated stories set in a Welsh valley during the 1930s and 40s. Sometimes funny, sometimes sad, a glimpse of life as it may have been then.

The Last Druid

In Roman-occupied Cambria, a powerful druid does all he can to undermine Roman authority and influence the future.

He claims a young girl as novice because she has the Sight, but her sight opens into the past and she wonders how she can be of help to him. When the answer comes, it is not what she expected.

The Agency

In 2033, governments worldwide are bankrupt. There is no unemployment insurance, no social services or welfare, no pensions, and no health care subsidy. Unemployment sits at close to 60 percent, and those with jobs are the new elite.

Sheila Davenport owns a successful employment agency. When other agencies begin to go out of business, she attributes it to their inability to compete. Then she hears a hellish rumour: *Sign with Davenport; they'll find you a job even if they have to kill someone.*

Other agency owners are murdered and the Davenport Agency comes under police scrutiny. Sheila investigates and uncovers a sinister plot.

Witch Bay

In a coastal village in Wales, someone is committing the perfect crime: people are disappearing without a trace. An elderly woman is the most recent disappearance. A day later, police find her body washed up on the beach. Senior officers record it as death by misadventure, but Village Constable Gwyn Thomas is certain her death and the other disappearances are connected.

Police suspicion is inevitable, but as with many crimes, an unintended consequence follows. This time the consequence has a name—Bethan, the dead woman's niece. When she arrives from London to claim her inheritance, she refuses to accept her aunt's death was accidental. Bethan begins hunting down and questioning village residents who might have information. As the puzzle pieces begin to fall into place, suddenly the tables are turned. She discovers she is no longer the hunter—she is the prey.

www.ingramcontent.com/pod-product-compliance
Lightning Source LLC
Chambersburg PA
CBHW070843250626
47159CB00003B/907